Crowded Hours

Crowded Hours

Eric Roll

faber and faber

LONDON · BOSTON

First published in 1985
by Faber and Faber Limited
3 Queen Square London WC1N 3AU

Photoset by Wilmaset Birkenhead Merseyside
Printed in Great Britain by
Redwood Burn Ltd Trowbridge Wiltshire
All rights reserved

British Library Cataloguing in Publication Data

Roll, Eric, *Baron*
Crowded hours.
1. Roll, Eric, *Baron*   2. Bankers—Great
Britain—Biography
I. Title
332.6'6'0924   HG1552.R6

ISBN 0-571-13497-1

For our family and all those friends we have made in many places over the years without whose affection, companionship and encouragement our lives would indeed have been weary, stale, flat and unprofitable.

Such wind as scatters young men through the world
To seek their fortunes farther than at home,
Where small experience grows.

Shakespeare, *The Taming of the Shrew*, I, ii

Contents

Illustrations

Preface

I decided to write these reminiscences after persuasion by family, friends and publisher. I am not at all clear about my motives; nor am I sure that what many authors of memoirs have said about theirs can be accepted without question. I am, however, sure of one thing: an account of my own life could itself be of interest only to a very few people outside my family. Moreover, I never kept a diary and, though I have various papers, letters and appointment books, I would have to rely mainly on memory if I attempted to write a detailed account of my seventy-six years.

I resolved therefore that what I would be interested to write, and what I hope others may be interested to read, are reflections on some important events and aspects of the society in which I live as it has evolved this century. I did not, however, mean to write a series of essays, but rather put down some thoughts that arise directly out of experiences I have had myself. I have tried to distil from these experiences as an academic, as a public servant, as an international negotiator and as a businessman views on a number of themes – for example, on the processes of government, on some historic landmarks, such as European policy, of Britain's development in the last fifty years, and also on some of the personalities I have met.

I may have lived 'laborious days' but I have not had to 'scorn delights'; indeed, I have had more than my fair share of both of these and hope to have the good fortune to continue to do so.

Anyone leading a busy life needs much support of different kinds. Among the most important is that of able and devoted personal assistants and secretaries. I have been particularly fortunate in this regard and record here with gratitude my indebtedness to Peter Pooley and John Wiggins; and to Lura Pelton, Christine Lane,

Phyllis Dowse, Maureen Brown, Betty Atkinson, Anne Senanayake van Zeeland and Trudi Paulie.

Fludger's Wood   E.R.
Oxfordshire
31 August 1984

1

Early Days

In the midway of this our mortal life,
I found me in a gloomy wood, astray.
Gone from the path direct.
Dante, *Inferno*, Canto I, v. 1, trs. H. K. Cary

I was not conscious of it at the time but for me, too, midway
marked a sharp turn from what I had until then considered the path
direct, that is an academic career. The wood, however, turned out
not to be so gloomy.

Soon after I had turned 30 there was a significant change in my
life: from teaching economics for London external degrees in a
small, new university college in north-east England to the world of
Lend-Lease and wartime planning in Washington, DC, which was
to become the nerve centre of the Allied war effort; from there to
Paris for the Marshall Plan and post-war European reconstruction,
for NATO and for European integration; back home to British
economic policy as it evolved during the first twenty-five years after
the war; and finally to the City of London. Yet through these varied
post-academic experiences in governmental and in business affairs
there ran, I now think, a common theme: the need to negotiate
constructively not only with one party, but more often than not as
part of a group, the members of which had many diverse interests
but could – if all went well – be united in the pursuit of one
overriding common goal.

What may perhaps be of interest to others are my reflections on
men and events after I moved from university life. But, in 1939, I
had already come a long way from my starting point. As that earlier
journey may be relevant to later events and to the way I now recall
and assess them, I start with my beginnings in the small south-
eastern crownland of Austria, the Duchy of Bukowina (land of
the beeches) where I was born on Sunday, 1 December 1907, in
Nowosielitza near the provincial capital Czernowitz. The importance of Nowosielitza (there were two neighbouring villages of that
name, an Austrian and a Russian one) lay in its geographical
position. It was at the meeting point of Austria, Russia and
Romania, an important transport and trading point, particularly

for timber, grains and other food stuffs – an 'economic bridgehead'
as my father described it in one of his occasional articles in the
Vienna *Neue Freie Presse*.

The Bukowina, and with it Czernowitz, had old Romanian roots.
It had been part of the Moldavian principality which in the fifteenth
century had come under Turkish suzerainty and, until the later part
of the nineteenth century when it had a total population of about
70,000, it had remained extremely poor and backward. In 1775 the
country became part of Austria and within a relatively short time,
particularly after 1848 when it became a duchy, it had developed to
a remarkable degree. From 1875 it had an important university
with, from time to time, distinguished professors, such as J. A.
Schumpeter, the great economist, who had his first chair there. The
Duchy also had no less than five girls' secondary schools (against
two in Tyrol and one each in Upper Austria, Salzburg and Styria)
and ten grammar schools for boys. Economically the province had
developed. Apart from agriculture, there was a flourishing timber
industry and incipient manufacturing in textiles and leather. By
1910, the population had risen to 700,000, 41 per cent Ukrainian,
32 per cent Romanian, 20 per cent German and 7 per cent others.
About 10 per cent were classified as Jewish. This was a religious
classification, though it was not a rigorous one and included
practising and non-practising Jews alike. By language and culture
they were generally included in the German group, as in most other
parts of the Monarchy. Contrary to what is sometimes believed,
they were not only prominent in trade, finance and the liberal
professions, but provided substantial numbers of artisans and
craftsmen and played an important part in industrial development.

My father Mathias, who was 35 years old when I was born, had
studied at the Commercial Academy in Vienna, and having started
his career in the distinguished Bodenkreditanstalt (the bank of the
Emperor) was manager of the local branch of the Hypothekenbank,
an old-established agricultural mortgage bank which was also
active in financing trade. I learned much later that he had invented
some new negotiable instruments for financing goods in transit by
rail.

My father was one of seven children. After the death of his
mother in childbirth, his father, a toll-keeper in Czernowitz,
married again and had more children. I did not know my

grandparents on my father's side, but I just remember those on my mother's. She was the youngest of three, two girls and one boy. Her father was a grain trader in a fairly big way. I remember him only as a very tall man with an impressive long, blond beard. My mother's brother had, it seems, a brilliant career in the Law Faculty at the University of Vienna and won some coveted prize. He was a much-sought-after practising lawyer, but died young.

I have only fragmentary memories of my first seven years: occasional visits across the Russian border where the chocolate was especially attractive; an attack of diphtheria, cured by a serum injection administered by a Russian medical colonel hurriedly summoned in the absence of the local doctor; the tiny village school where the other children were nearly all Ukrainian peasants; and the wet-nurse, a sturdy village girl, Marie, whom we saw from time to time for many years afterwards.

I don't think I learned much from the feared, though kindly, peasant schoolmaster who taught us. But I learned a lot at home. My mother Fany was a trained teacher although, having married young, she had not had much practical experience. The village had an active intellectual group, of which my father was a leading member, together with the local doctor, lawyer and some of the younger grain importers. Our house was also full of visitors from Vienna, Prague and other parts of the Habsburg Empire, as well as from Russia. It was also full of books. I recognized later, hardly at the time, the liberal atmosphere, political and cultural, in which my brother Josef – five years older – and I grew up. The orientation was strongly towards Vienna: even in our small village there was that irrepressible tendency to create in every possible way a micro-Vienna in which the Austrian version of the German language and culture predominated, a characteristic of many parts of the Empire.

When the First World War broke out in August 1914 we were on holiday in a small mountain village in the Carpathians, Jacobeni, renowned for its sulphur springs. I have few memories of the holiday itself, mainly fog and rain and steaming sulphur baths in primitive wooden tubs, and astonishment at the number of books my parents carried with them. I do remember very clearly, however, the yellow volumes of the German translation of Romain Rolland's *Jean Christophe*, which had recently come out. But above all I remember the horror of my parents when they heard that our

village had been occupied by the Russians immediately after the
outbreak of war and had been almost totally burned down. They
both cried. We never went back, although Nowosielitza changed
hands several times thereafter. First we went briefly to Czernowitz,
but this too had become unsafe and my father's bank ordered him
to go to Vienna as soon as possible. My memory of the long trek
through the mountains, mostly in a horse-drawn cart, is very clear
though I cannot now say how long it lasted. After a brief stay in a
small Carpathian town where my father's eldest brother had a
sawmill, we crossed over the Mogura Pass going through what I
later learned in England was 'Dracula' country. We went through
Transylvania, with several brief stops, eventually boarded a train to
Budapest, where we spent only a day or two and, finally, with
hordes of other refugees from various parts of the Empire, arrived
in Vienna.

After a brief stay in the Ninth District in furnished rooms, we
graduated to the better-class Eighth District in a flat off the
Josefstaedterstrasse, very near the famous theatre and not far from
my father's younger brother Max, who had lived in Vienna for
many years. Here, my parents had to start refurnishing, a long and
costly process. My brother went to the Schottengymnasium in the
First District, founded—like the church of the same name—by Irish
monks but for some reason misnamed by the Viennese. I was kept
nearer home and went first to the Piaristenschule, then to the
Piaristengymnasium, both part of the complex round the local
church, the Maria-Treukirche, and its abbey. The basic curriculum
of the Austrian secondary schools, part of the great educational
reform of Maria Theresia, went back to 1776 and had been worked
out, as it happened, by a member of the Piarist order, Gratian Marx
(also known as à Sancta Barbara). Even in my day, although the
school had become 'the State *Gymnasium* in the Eighth District',
with a distinguished lay mathematician at its head, many of the
teachers were still members of the order. I particularly remember
my form master, Father Aschauer, a little bearded figure who
taught both Latin and German, and to whom I owe in large part my
abiding interest in the mysteries of language.

My memories of those four war years in Vienna are divided
between consciousness of the very severe food shortages; scepticism
about the war (almost from the beginning), particularly in the

intellectual, social-democratic circles in which my parents had
many friends; a precocious interest in the Burgtheater (where my
brother often worked with pride as an extra); the Opera, and
second-hand bookshops. One of my few clear recollections, when
the war was nearly over and I was recovering from the Spanish flu,
is of being taken by my mother to a black-market restaurant, the
only time either of my parents departed from their strict views in
these matters, part of their general attitude to life, in which
morality – though not based on religion and certainly not on any
particular religious observance – played a large part. Strictness in
matters of personal conduct not only did not contradict but went
hand-in-hand with their broadly liberal political and social ideas. In
the summer of 1918, my father, who had by then joined the
Merkurbank (or to give it its full name, Kaiser-Koenigliche
privilegierte Bank und Wechselstubenaktiengesellschaft, Merkur)
went to Czernowitz to open a branch there. The rest of the family
followed shortly afterwards and for the next seven years that is
where we lived.

My consciousness of what Austria and Vienna represented
started to develop only at this time. When I lived in Vienna I was
too young to have any serious perception, and the overriding
concern with wartime conditions, together with our status as
'refugees', combined to leave only a blurred picture. It was in later
years, during the twenties in Czernowitz where the Austro-German
culture had more incentive to assert itself against the new
Romanian influences, and when the family made its annual long
visits to Vienna and the Austrian (now Czechoslovakian) spas, that
I acquired enough of a basis of understanding to enable me to
appreciate what Vienna has contributed to European civilization.
This understanding was greatly amplified when, after the Second
World War, I was able, first as a British Government official, later
as a banker, to visit Austria frequently and to refresh my knowledge
of the language, the people and the country. (My father, though he
was generally rather sceptical about such things, would, I think,
have been pleased when I was given a high Austrian decoration in
1979.)

It is difficult to describe the character of 'Austrianism', although
having been subject to it for only a limited period of my early life I
could perhaps do so with reasonable objectivity. It is a tempting

subject, but I must resist the temptation to discuss it at any length, especially as an American scholar has fairly recently produced a brilliant and comprehensive study.* Whatever the reasons – the extraordinary mixture of peoples and languages held together more or less peacefully in one realm; the long (sixty-eight years) reign of one monarch, Franz Josef; the crucial role of its location (between East and West, North and South) – the dual Monarchy produced an astonishing amalgam of high intellectual achievement and low comedy, of administrative talent together with an inbred tendency to 'muddle through', examples of great heroism with at the same time a general readiness to bow before the storm. *Biegen nicht brechen* (to bend not break) was one of the apposite mottoes of its rulers, and *hoffnungslos aber nicht ernst* (hopeless, but not serious) a typical hyperbole by which the Austrians themselves often described their situation. That these characteristics often produced, to put it mildly, repugnant results – as in the Nazi period – is clear. (They also produced many examples of love-hate relationships with its own sons: Kraus and Freud, for example, or its adopted one, Beethoven.) On the other hand, they enabled the country to weather many convulsions in the last 150 years, including two world wars. Like the Abbé Sièyes, Austria may claim 'to have survived'; and its special talent of tenacity combined with an ability to compromise has rendered it outstanding service both politically and economically since World War II.

It was incidentally during one of these long summer holiday journeys I took with my parents – this time in 1923 to Bad Kissingen in Germany – that I first came face to face with hyper-inflation. Every price was multiplied at an ever accelerating rhythm by an index number: if you missed a haircut appointment before lunch, the chances were that the afternoon index was a multiple of the one in the morning. When we went on to Zurich, my father remembered that he had left a fair-sized balance in the bank in Bad Kissingen: by that time it would not have paid the cost of transfer.

In the autumn after our return to Czernowitz, the armistice and the collapse of the monarchy caused a good deal of economic and political chaos. A few vivid incidents remain in my mind: soldiers

*William M. Johnson: *The Austrian Mind – An Intellectual and Social History, 1848 – 1938*, Berkeley/Los Angeles/London, University of California Press, 1972.

streaming out of the barracks, one with binoculars round his neck, one riding his horse away and a third driving two cows before him. The severance from Vienna produced, before the province was assigned to Romania by the peace treaty, some monetary disturbances. But these were remarkably quickly dealt with by the branches of the three main Viennese banks, the Bankverein, the Anglo-Austrian Bank and the Merkurbank which issued overstamped banknotes and temporary deposit certificates (I remember my father spending hours adding his signature to these) which were accepted as currency. I also remember a most impressive Anglo-French military mission taking up offices in my father's bank and being particularly kind to us children.

After a few weeks, town (now renamed Cernauţi) and province settled down to the novelty of being part of Romania, with a local Romanian administration and a Romanian military garrison. We all, too, had to learn Romanian. I had resumed my secondary schooling in a private grammar school, shortly to be called the Liceul Emanoil-Grigoroviza after a distinguished Romanian man of letters. The German headmaster soon acquired a Romanian co-head and several additional Romanian staff members. Happily, these were men of considerable culture, with a traditional French inclination that blended well with the still flourishing Austrian cultural tradition. Since this included a solid measure of secondary education, this was particularly important for me from my eleventh to my seventeenth year. My school was a so-called *Realgymnasium*. Each pupil had to learn at least one classical and one foreign language (in my case, Latin and French) together with a good deal of mathematics and science. German was replaced by Romanian, and the maintenance and further development of my knowledge of German literature was left to the home influence. Quite apart from the new school's emphasis on French, my brother and I were given private lessons in which my mother joined, although she already knew some French. Our teacher was the daughter of a Russian general, a refugee from the Revolution. She had, as I later discovered, a slight Russian accent and I had some difficulty in getting rid of a rather liquid 't'. About this time (1919), I, though not my brother, started to learn English from a Miss Forster (how she got to Czernowitz I have no idea), who virtually lived in our house for a few years. She was what I then imagined to be typically

English-looking: very tall, thin, with a long, rather 'horsey' face, but extremely kind and with a deep feeling for literature which she passed on to me.

I remember the great excitement when, in the spring of 1925, just as I was beginning to prepare for my school-leaving examination, the Austrian *Matura* (equivalent to the German *Abitur*), the Romanian authorities introduced a new, much tougher, examination with many more compulsory subjects, modelled on the French *baccalauréat* as it then was. This I managed to pass in the summer. It had one advantage for me: when I came to apply for admission to an English university a few months later, the standard was recognized as being high enough to exempt me from the Higher School Certificate examination, which I would otherwise have had to take to qualify for entrance.

Romanian proved a relatively simple language, which I acquired quickly, though I remember little now. It was interesting in its mixture of words of Latin origin with a strong supplement of modern words taken from the French (which, in the Old Kingdom, was the language of the upper classes), Slavonic, Magyar and Turkish. There was a continuous debate in our house over which – if any – words could be identified as being of Dacian, i.e. pre-Roman origin. My mentor in these matters was an extremely amusing friend of my father's, Senator Hotinceanu (a local Romanian, not one who had come in from the Old Kingdom), who had a great gift for composing limerick-like verses in a mixture of all the local languages.

Generally, the social and cultural blending of the old and the new went on fairly smoothly in the town. At a later stage, there was some political friction when the emergence of various Fascist groups gave extreme nationalism in the new provinces an additional stimulus. In the countryside, the small villages maintained their separate identity. It was a constant source of surprise to foreigners (including, at a later stage, my wife on her first visit) to pass within a few miles from solid Romanian to equally solid Ukrainian and now and again to German (Saxon) villages. In Czernowitz, the 'blending' had a certain class character. The upper, middle and professional classes, in particular, seemed to have little difficulty in adjusting. One reason no doubt was that many of the Romanian newcomers, whether administrators, soldiers or business men (even from Bucharest, the relatively Westernized capital), were pleasantly surprised by the concern of their local equivalents with the latest Western books, plays and fashions. The Czernowitz theatre, though rechristened the Teatrul National, was a typical German or Austrian *Stadttheater* and for several years continued to present plays in German performed by competent repertory companies. The book-shops (a surprisingly large number) continued to be full of German books, but now also included French and English ones in addition to the new stocks of Romanian books. The two German-language dailies continued side by side with old and new Romanian ones.

I had by then given up my childhood ambition of being a sleeping-car conductor on one of the great international trains, though then as now I enjoyed travelling. But books had become one of my major interests and I was encouraged by my father. He entrusted me with the choice of books for his library, including bidding for rare books at auctions, and I would give him long lists of books to get on his visits to Vienna. I only have a handful of them now, although he often urged me to take some to England: they are (or at least were) all in the library of the University of Czernowitz – now further renamed Chernovtsy.

By 1925, the early honeymoon between the new Romanian masters and the old inhabitants was waning. This became particularly evident in the educational system and led to a strong urge among the members of the middle class to send their children to Western universities. Czernowitz was too far from Bucharest where a strongly French-inspired culture nourished the indigenous literary and artistic instincts, and, being cut off from Vienna, itself now the overgrown capital of a diminished rump, meant that the remains of Austrian culture were being steadily eroded. The exodus which then took place was essentially a cultural one – it was some years later, in the early thirties, with the growth of Fascism in the form of Cuza's party and the Iron Guard of Codreanu, that a second, racial and political one, took place. My contemporaries were thus largely moving to Western universities, Vienna, of course, but also Prague, Munich, Berlin, Trieste, Rome and Paris, but hardly anyone to England.

My parents, though not at all anxious to see me leave home, had made up their minds – particularly my mother who in these matters was the more determined of the two – that I, too, should study abroad, and they had long been anxious that this should be in England. The reasons were not very obvious. My father knew only a little English, my mother knew none at all, though they both had a considerable knowledge of English literature in translation. I think the main reason was – and in this respect my father's view was the more important – their enormous regard for Britain's social and political system and cultural climate. I remember conversations between them and an old friend, a deputy in Romania and formerly a deputy in Vienna, Grigorovici, at the time when the province's post-war fate seemed not finally settled, in which they all agreed that the ideal solution would be that it should become a British colony!

2

England 1925–39

By 1925, I had a fair, though largely theoretical, knowledge of English and, thanks to Miss Forster, knew large passages of poetry, particularly Shakespeare, by heart. Partly for this reason, partly because I shared my parents' views and partly perhaps because it was a rather unusual step, the idea of going to England was highly welcome. I wrote off to a number of universities and finally settled on Birmingham. In those days, if the applicant had the qualifications, he had a reasonable certainty of being accepted by the university of his choice as, indeed, was the case for me. The move was quite a formidable one: my first long voyage alone, involving an eighteen-hour train journey through Europe, a night crossing to Harwich and the arrival in Birmingham which presented a very different picture in 1925 from what it would today! But, somehow, at 17, I seemed to be able to take it in my stride, though my first impression was discouraging, even allowing for the circumstances: a Sunday, a temperance hotel (which provided a rather astonishing first acquaintance with ginger beer), and a bleak and dull-looking city. However, I soon learned that the reality was quite different, and that the city's motto, *Forward*, was not undeserved – even though it did not, I was told, lead the watch committee to allow Pavlova to dance without tights.

The social and intellectual life was extremely active. I began my studies in the autumn of 1925 in the School of Oil Engineering and the Faculty of Commerce but also had the advantage of taking some courses in the Arts Faculty which was situated downtown in the old Edmund Street building, where the original Mason College had started. The Medical Faculty was there, too, so in addition to meeting the 'hearties' of the Engineering and related departments on the main campus, I also mixed with the humanists and medicals and found this mixture both stimulating and refreshing. I also found the social as well as the intellectual life extremely active.

Birmingham had then the only School of Oil Engineering and Refining and the first Faculty of Commerce in any English university, which is why it had seemed to me a good combination, particularly as Romania was an important oil producer. However, my knowledge of – and interest in – chemistry turned out to be inadequate and my interest in economics, stimulated by excellent teachers, much greater than I had expected, so at the end of my first year I devoted myself completely to economics.

The faculty was a remarkably effective group. I only just knew Sir William Ashley, the great economic historian. He had the reputation of being kind but stern with the young. He usually invited a group of his students to tea on Sunday. At five fifteen he would take them on a tour round his house that ended twenty minutes later at the front door where he bade them goodbye. One young woman who did not wish to be subjected to this indignity got up to go at five ten. 'Do sit down,' said Ashley. 'All my guests will be leaving in twenty-five minutes.'

His successor, J. F. Rees, later Principal at Cardiff, brought an interest in the political and social aspects of economic development to bear on the traditional Ashleian emphasis on technological change. John George Smith, Dean of the Faculty, who taught economic theory, a kindly Irishman who, through a slight speech defect, had failed to obtain the appointment he wanted after a brilliant passing of the Civil Service examination, had a healthy scepticism of 'schools'. His economics, though broadly in the Marshallian tradition, was illuminated by strong elements of practical wisdom and a deep knowledge of the world of business, not surprising in the author of a standard work on *Organised Produce Markets*. He was particularly scathing about the great controversies that started towards the end of my time in Birmingham between Cambridge and the newly imported Austrian school which had found a foster home at the London School of Economics, but he was a gentle person and the worst he could say about the more doctrinaire members of the latter was that they were 'failed priests'. It was characteristic of the climate in the faculty that I was told to read Marshall's *Industry and Trade* long before his *Principles*.

Hilary Marquand, later to become a Labour cabinet minister, then just returned from a Rockefeller Fellowship in the United States, taught Money and Banking, a course that began, significantly, not with the standard textbooks, but with a daily reading of the City columns, later to be followed by our having to write our own money-market reports. To Hilary Marquand I also owe my first extended motor tour through much of the English and Welsh countryside. This included a stay in Cambridge, where among other economists we met Austin and Joan Robinson, and my first acquaintance with Ludlow, which became of interest much later when my wife started to write on Tudor history. Marquand had just acquired a car and asked me to join him during the Easter vacation of 1928. We ended our trip at the house of his mother in Cardiff, where I also met Ray Rees whom he later married.

Accounting was included in the curriculum and was taught by Professor Martineau, a distinguished practising accountant. I learned a good deal of agricultural economics, taught by Paul Barrett Whale, and the course on industrial organization, first taught by Philip Sargant Florence, later (after I had graduated) by G. C. Allen, was supplemented by a heavy diet of industrial visits. But there were plenty of opportunities to get to know students and teachers in other faculties. I particularly recall Sergey Konovalov, son of the Trade Minister in the Kerensky Government, an economist by training, then Professor of Russian (later at Oxford) with whom I shared an interest in the theatre. He tried to teach me Russian; but I had no time to persevere and remember little of it now.

Nothing that I have seen in subsequent decades in many universities on both sides of the Atlantic and the Channel has diminished my admiration for the skill with which the Birmingham curriculum was devised and implemented in lectures and seminars. It certainly helped me to acquire and maintain a balanced view between economic theory and its application both to public policy and to business. Nor have I regretted – despite what I learned later were considered to be the advantages in British society of an Oxbridge education – having gone to a redbrick university placed in the middle of a bustling industrial community and with each of its faculties in the closest propinquity to the others.

But my life was not all study and my friends not all from the academic world. Apart from the usual lighter side of being at a university, which included indulgence in my then passion for dancing (the Palais when hard up, the Westend Ballroom when feeling less so, and the elegant Tony's when really flush), and the pride of winning a ballroom-dancing competition, I also had the opportunity of mixing in theatrical circles. One friend, Clifford Bladon Peake, worked in the City Treasurer's Department, but was also a highly talented amateur producer (later a professional one in Norwich and Dublin) as well as a drama critic for the *Manchester Guardian*, covering performances at the Birmingham Repertory Theatre as well as the many pre-West End shows that came to Birmingham. Through him, I got to know several producers at the 'Rep': Barry Jackson, H. K. Ayliff (responsible for the first modern-dress *Hamlet* of recent times), and actors: Cedric Hardwicke, Phyllis and Eileen Shand, daughters of a famous music-hall comedian, and many others. On our occasional excursions to Stratford (for example for the 'timeless' Theodore Komisarjevsky *Macbeth*) I also met some of the old giants among the critics: Ivor Brown, Hannen Swaffer of the *Daily Express*, Chance Newton of *Reynolds News* and Crompton Rhodes of the *Birmingham Post*. I lived for a time in theatrical digs. My landlord and landlady and ballet-dancing young daughter knew, and gave lodgings to, many well-known music-hall artists and this provided an interesting contrast to my friends in the legitimate theatre.

In my last undergraduate year, I received a Romanian government scholarship, which was very welcome as my father's fortunes had taken a turn for the worse. The scholarship went on for three years and, when after my first degree I was encouraged by Professor Smith to stay on to read for a Ph.D., it was supplemented by a University Research Scholarship. For my thesis I worked on the abundant material (and up to then not much examined, except from a technical point of view) of the Boulton–Watt partnership in the manufacture and marketing of steam engines during a crucial period, 1775 to 1800, of British economic history. Thanks to the encouragement of my teachers, this was published in 1930 soon after I had received my doctorate.

By the time I received this I had decided I wanted to stay in England. Every long vacation I had gone home to Czernowitz, sometimes stopping in Vienna to see uncles and aunts, but my real interests and friends were no longer there. The family life was a happy one, but the economic situation and social conditions had deteriorated. My father's bank was going through a very difficult time, but he derived much additional income as an adviser and arbitrator: he was considered a more reliable and honest adjudicator than the law could provide. Occasionally he sold a picture. But he never stopped the habit of giving to the poor: one day each week there was a queue at his door, and no one was turned away empty-handed.

Five years after arriving in England (the allotted time) and encouraged by my teachers and parents, I applied for naturalization. In the spring of 1931, within a few months of my arrival at Hull as an assistant lecturer at the University College, the papers came through and I had become a British subject.

My first few weeks in Hull were a difficult period of adaptation, though my chief, G. C. Allen, and his wife Nell could not have been more helpful. The thought of earning my own living, of teaching students virtually of my own age, the move to a strange, new environment and rather forbidding 'digs' – all this caused considerable misery. My gloom was soon dispelled when I moved into a house with two other bachelors, T. H. (Sammy) Searls, Professor of Adult Education, and Louis de Chazal, just down from Cambridge and working in Reckitts. Soon also I met Freda Taylor, then in her third year in the English Department and President of the Students' Union. For the next four years we spent most of our spare time together, and in September 1934 we were married. By this time, she had got her degree, done her teacher's training and started to teach – very briefly, however, since she caught diphtheria, very prevalent at that time in Hull and still a killer disease, from which she recovered completely thanks to the speedy and skilful treatment by Dr Leete at the local fever hospital.

I had finished my first three years' probation in 1933 and become Lecturer and Head of the Department, following G. C. Allen's departure to Liverpool. His chair had been left vacant as I, at the age of 25, was considered too young. However, I became Professor two years later. Both John Maynard Keynes and Josiah Stamp, neither of whom I then knew personally, supported my appointment.

At Hull, where I was busily engaged in learning to teach undergraduates – mainly Economic Theory and applied subjects, such as British Industry and Agriculture – the smallness of the college presented exceptional opportunities for keeping in touch

with members of other departments and for making friends.
Among these were such stimulating colleagues as Sherard Vines,
poet, novelist and former tutor to Prince Chichibu of Japan; Jacob
Bronowski, at that time professionally a geometer, but already
well-known as a poet and with interests in all fields of knowledge;
Norman Poole, alas to die in Malta in the early days of the war; A.
J. Jenkinson, lecturer in the Education Department; Alister Hardy,
zoologist; his pupil the oceanographer Cyril Lucas, and T. E.
Jessop, philosopher and expert on Bishop Berkeley. The Principal,
Arthur Eustace Morgan, was an exceptionally kind and fatherly
adviser; his daughter Diana and her husband Maurice Barley (later
Professor of Archaeology at Nottingham) lived next door and the
friendship then formed has continued to this day. There were also
others not directly connected with the University: our doctor Eric
Halliwell and his wife Mouse; Leslie and Sadie Martin, architects
then teaching at the Hull College of Art, whose love of modern
architecture and design we shared and through whom we met many
of the Bauhaus artists who had had to leave Germany; and the
various members of the Scarborough Rowntree family who were
particularly kind to me when I met them through my extensive
extra-mural lecturing (which provided a useful addition to a
modest academic income).

I was also able to get to know and keep in touch with teachers
and scholars elsewhere: Henry Hardman at Leeds, Robert Hall and
Hugh Gaitskell at Oxford, Lionel Robbins and Lance Beales at the
LSE and Austin and Joan Robinson at Cambridge. Through Beales
I met Leslie Rowse, a fellow of All Souls who had just published a
book with Fabers' that created quite a stir, *Politics and the Younger
Generation*. He read the manuscript of my *Spotlight on Germany*
and showed it to Geoffrey Faber who published that, as well as my
next two books, *About Money* and *A History of Economic
Thought*. (With only three later exceptions Faber and Faber have
published everything I have written since.) Beales, at the time of
writing this, is 96. He was one of those remarkable teachers whose
greatest achievements are to be found in the works of pupils and
friends. He has written relatively little himself but he was
responsible for inspiring probably more doctoral theses and books,
particularly on the nineteenth century, than any other social
scientist of his generation.

I should add a word here about my book *A History of Economic Thought*, not only because it has lasted longer than any of my other writings (several editions and many translations) and been used in universities in many countries of the world, but because the writing of it was a particularly exhilarating experience. It was a subject that I had never taught, but had been very interested in during my student days and I remain so to this day. So, when Fabers' encouraged me to write another book for them it was the subject I chose. Another one, on international trade, never got written and my interest in that subject had to be satisfied in practical terms in my later career. In the summer of 1937, we rented a cottage with Bronowski (always known to us as Bruno) and Eirlys Roberts at Wendens Ambo, not far from Cambridge where I was able to get access to the great Marshall Library and to see and read many of the oldest economic classics in their first editions. Bruno was then working on his first major book, *The Poet's Defence*, and I had started on the *History*. We sat at opposite ends of the garden, he typing his texts directly, I writing mine in longhand (as I have always done), my wife typing as the pages were written. In this way I finished the first draft in six weeks and it was not much altered afterwards.

This was the first summer vacation I had spent in England. In 1935 and 1936 I had taken Freda to visit my family in Czernowitz and Vienna, but we no longer looked forward to the journey when we were only too aware of the unrest in Europe. My mother had died in 1934 shortly before our marriage and we knew that my father did not expect us to continue the habit of visiting him every summer. He visited us in 1939 and managed to get back on virtually the last international train before the outbreak of war. We did not see him again until 1947 when he came to live with us in England and then in France. Nor did I see my brother again before he died in Vienna in his early fifties, a year after my father had died in 1954.

T. S. Eliot was then a director of Faber and Faber. Although I failed to persuade him to publish in the *Criterion* an article that I had written on the Austrian writer Karl Kraus (at that time almost unknown in the Anglo-Saxon world) he did take a kindly interest in my work and I still have the typescript of my book *About Money* with numerous marginal comments by him. I had met Eliot a

number of times at the Russell Square offices of Fabers', but an
opportunity for a more extended talk came when he gave a lecture
in Hull at the invitation of Sherard Vines who had known him well
in the twenties. (The theme, as I recall was much the same as his
After Strange Gods.) My wife and I lived opposite the Vineses in
Cottingham and were asked to dine with Eliot. The conversation
was not confined to literature, poetry or politics: indeed the greater
part was devoted to the merits of different cheeses of which both
Vines and Eliot were connoisseurs and we at least amateurs.

But it was also impossible for us in the thirties not to be
concerned with what was going on in the larger world: the
development of Fascism in Italy, the rise of Nazism in Germany and
the Spanish Civil War. The abandonment of Czechoslovakia by the
Western countries moved us to write a detailed chronological
account of the course of events accompanied by statements by
ministers that, though devoid of all comment, gave a devastating
portrayal of the appeasement policy of Britain and France. We
circulated this among our friends. Bronowski wrote a number of
poems on the Spanish Civil War which were privately printed and
circulated, and all of us under the leadership of my wife took part in
organizing the 'Humber Food Ship' for Spanish relief. What stirred
us above all was the deepening depression with its appalling
paradoxes of destruction of commodities (farmers hanging themselves 'on the expectation of plenty'), unemployment, and misery
and poverty in the world which no one who was not alive then can
perhaps fully appreciate now. This naturally led most of us to what
today would be called a left-wing view of public affairs, and,
although the simple categories in which we, together with most of
our generation, were then wont to define the issues have long since
ceased to be regarded as adequate by me, the imprint left by the
events of that period has not disappeared.

When about to leave Birmingham in 1930 after five years of
undergraduate and graduate study I had been nominated by Hilary
Marquand to a Rockefeller Fellowship in the United States. But this
was a time of heavy unemployment so, when I was offered the post
of Assistant Lecturer at the University College of Hull, I had
reluctantly refused the fellowship. Noel Hall, who was at that time
Head of the Department of Economics of University College,
London, and Secretary of the British Advisory Committee of the

Rockefeller Foundation, had not only fully understood my decision but had kept a benevolent eye on me. He was responsible for reviving the offer in the spring of 1939. This time I accepted. Noel Hall was thus responsible for the second major move in my life. It was at least as decisive as the one that brought me to England, and my subsequent career stemmed from it.

3
The War: USA 1939–46

I obtained leave from the college, which appointed a temporary successor, and we made arrangements to go to the United States in the autumn of 1939 on the *Nieuw Amsterdam*, having read all the travel brochures and decided that the food and accommodation were just what we wanted. On the outbreak of war, however, all new fellowships were temporarily suspended and boats from Europe cancelled. For a while I was left stranded without a job and without money. Bruno lent us £100, which we were able to pay back when Norman Poole left Freda £100 in his will. During the 'phoney war' period my fellowship was reinstated. The authorities indicated to me that the presence of young British scholars at American universities could be useful, so, about the middle of November, we set off for New York on the *Hushimi Maru*. This was a ship of about 11,000 tons of the NYK line that had been taken in prize in the Mediterranean with a cargo of chalk for Hamburg, brought to Tilbury and was being sent back to Tokyo via New York and Panama. Most of the passengers were Japanese diplomatists being evacuated from Europe. It was the first transatlantic crossing for the ship and its captain – as well as for most of the passengers – and the journey had its adventures: a sister ship, the *Terukumi Maru*, anchored near us off the Goodwin Sands, was blown up by a magnetic mine just after we had left – one of the first victims of this new weapon; we experienced a typhoon in mid-Atlantic and drifted with the wind as we had no authorized sea-lane; after nearly ten days at sea, the captain had some difficulty finding the Nantucket lightship. The Statue of Liberty was invisible in the fog and our first view of the New York skyline was of the tops of skyscrapers rising ethereally out of the mist. However, in the end we landed safely in Brooklyn, the day after my thirty-second birthday, which we had celebrated with the captain whose birthday it also was, toasting Winston Churchill – the day after his.

For the next seventeen months while the war was developing in earnest we, with a few British and other foreign fellows of different foundations (including David Glass, the distinguished demographer, shortly to be drawn into the British team in Washington as a member of the Petroleum Mission) were wandering scholars as so many before us, including most recently the eminent statistician Roy Allen and his wife Kathleen who were soon to return to Washington to work in the British Missions. We travelled widely, staying at Harvard and Princeton with short visits to Chicago, Berkeley and other universities. We attended meetings of the Cowles Commission in Colorado Springs and of the American Economic Association in Philadelphia, New Orleans and New York, which gave us further opportunities for meeting fellow students, teachers and researchers – American, Canadian, European – many of whom we still know. Above all we had many opportunities to experience the extraordinary friendliness and hospitality of Americans. People we met in one city introduced us to their friends in another, and our pleasure during our progress through the forty or so states we visited during that period was immensely enhanced in this way. In Princeton I worked at the Institute for Advanced Study, with Walter Stewart (who had constructed the first American Index of Production and had been economic adviser of the Bank of England), Win Riefler and Bob Warren, on Britain's balance of payments problems during the inter-war years (originally planned as 'during the post-war period' until the outbreak of the Second World War necessitated a change of title).

This was a time of acute soul-searching in American public opinion when pro-European, particularly pro-British, sentiment was battling for predominance against isolationism and 'America First'-ism, not in the Administration but in public support for the policy that the Administration was in any case anxious to follow. Among our introductions to academics, bankers and Supreme Court judges from people who knew the United States well – people as diverse as Josiah Stamp and Harold Laski – there was also one from Lord Middleton, the President of the College at Hull, to Lord Lothian, the British Ambassador. I visited him and met members of his staff on the economic side and he urged me to continue my fellowship activities and also to keep in touch with the Embassy.

But, given the very difficult state of the American neutrality posture, I and others in my position were enjoined to conduct ourselves meticulously as 'normal' scholars.

Our slightly nomadic existence – we possessed only such luggage and books as could be stowed in our 1934 Ford bought for $120 from Francis Rundall, then British Vice-Consul in Boston – was climaxed by a semester's teaching at the University of Texas in Austin, which required a memorable visit to Mexico (in company with Ken and Kitty Galbraith) in order to change our visas to the 'preacher and teacher' variety since on my existing visa I would not have been able to occupy a teaching post. One of the professors, Clarence Ayres, had gone for a semester to the University of Washington and I was asked to replace him and give two postgraduate courses. Ayres had lent us his house in Austin. We had never met and he had already gone when we were due to arrive. So when we got there in the middle of the night, after a day-long drive from El Paso, we found the house key under the mat and a well-stocked larder and refrigerator. The next day Texan hospitality was further demonstrated by a stream of visitors, students, faculty colleagues, tradesmen, all offering to help us settle in. As we left before Ayres could return, we never actually met.

Those few months in the vigorous and hospitable atmosphere of Texas were so stimulating that an invitation to stay on a permanent professorship was tempting. However, we decided to return to Princeton. Many years later, when President Lyndon Johnson heard about this from David Bruce who was at that time United States Ambassador in London, he said to me, 'You should have stayed, we might have made something of you.' Our stay in Princeton was brief. In May 1941, a visit from Maurice Hutton, a merchant banker turned temporary official of the Ministry of Food, led to my recruitment as a temporary civil servant and brought the academic phase of my life to an end. Indeed it was not until six years later, at the time of the Marshall Plan and the European Recovery Programme, that I was able to resume a real interest in wider economic problems.

When we went to the United States, it was not only the remarkable flowering of economic theory (with Paul Samuelson, then a junior fellow at Harvard, as the exemplar) but also the concern with public policy in the wake of the New Deal shared by so many brilliant economists old and young (Ken Galbraith in Princeton, Dick Gilbert in Washington, at Harvard Ed Mason, Wassily Leontief, Paul Sweezy, Svend Laursen, a brilliant Danish Rockefeller fellow, David Lusher, a Canadian, Robert Triffin from Belgium, and Shigeto Tsuru now a distinguished elder statesman of Japanese economics, and many others) that provided an extraordinary stimulus. Keynes's theories had by then been fully naturalized in America. (The good and bad results of that process have been brilliantly analysed, sympathetically by Galbraith and, somewhat idiosyncratically, by Schumpeter – whom I had the pleasure of getting to know at Harvard.)

Looking back now at the thirties and early forties as far as the evolution of economic thinking is concerned, it was undoubtedly dominated by the figure of Keynes. I did not meet him until he came to Washington during the war, although I had had reason to be grateful to him before, as I have mentioned, when the Hull chair was to be filled. I shall have more to say about his role during the war and in its immediate aftermath, when he was mainly concerned with practical problems of international economic policy, and about his continuing influence – and that of his opponents – in supplying inspiration for practical politicians. Here I shall add only a few words about his achievement as an economist in the main stream of economic thought.

This seems to me to lie primarily in two related propositions, each not in itself novel. The first, already to be found in Malthus and others who had written about the possibility of 'general gluts', is that the economy does not necessarily always, except in a 'long run' which may in practice never be reached, tend towards an equilibrium position at full employment. It is incidentally worthwhile dwelling for a moment on Keynes's famous phase, 'in the long run we are all dead' (which appears in his *Tract on Monetary Reform*, 1923). His detractors, most recently F. A. Hayek, have taken this almost as a sign of some moral deficiency – presumably indicating an indifference to provision for the future. This interpretation not only ignores Keynes's own practical work as Bursar of King's and chairman of an insurance company, but the context in which Keynes uses this phrase shows the interpretation to be a complete perversion of his real intent: to show the inadequacy for certain practical purposes of long-run equilibrium theory. Among the more specific conclusions that he drew was the proposition that Adam Smith's famous dictum that what was wisdom in the conduct of a family could 'scarce be folly in that of a great Kingdom', did not necessarily hold in all circumstances: the macro-economic universe is not always the micro-economic universe writ large; prices at which 'markets clear' do not always emerge; the state's budget can have a decisive influence on the level at which the economy operates, as can monetary policy.

I mention these points, which seem to me fundamental, simply because these propositions, indissolubly linked with the name of Keynes, have profoundly influenced – mainly for good as I believe, wholly for bad as some think – the course of the world economy in the last four decades, and in particular many of the events with which I have had some connection. Their main consequence has been to make legitimate an active role of the state in economic matters, something that had been the practice ever since the emergence of the modern economy but that had (except by Socialists who derived their policies from quite different doctrines) somehow come to be regarded as an aberration. What Keynes made possible – and what puts him firmly in the tradition of English Utilitarianism – was practical enquiry, case by case and with due regard to actual circumstances, whether this or that action by the state was likely to lead to more advantageous results than would its avoidance.

But, as I have said, until 1946–7 I had had neither inclination nor time to reflect on these matters. The imminent passing of the Lend-Lease Act and the proliferation of British Missions in 1941 was the cause of my direct involvement in the war effort. Maurice Hutton, himself a postgraduate fellow in the United States, had enquired about me from Riefler at Princeton, and invited me to join the British Food Mission. Within a very short time we had moved to Washington, taken temporary lodging in a furnished room in the house of Walter Stewart's sister, Stella (a senior official in the Department of Labour), and my civil-service life had begun. At the same time Freda also started to work, first, briefly, in the New Zealand Supply Mission, then (until our first child was born in 1944) in the War Trade Department of the British Embassy with Noel Hall, who had come to the Washington Embassy as Minister in charge of war trade matters.

The Lend-Lease Act was signed on 11 March 1941. Like the Marshall Plan, the statutory foundation of which came into operation seven years later, it was an outstanding example of the ability of the United States to undertake extremely large, quite unprecedented actions in which generosity of spirit and self-interest conceived in the largest sense play a balanced part. In the days of Britain's direst need, when food and other supplies, domestic and foreign, were physically disrupted and financially unprocurable, the Act made possible a stream of supplies – on deferred terms, as it were – from the United States and other dollar sources. Our work in the Mission was first and foremost the procurement under Lend-Lease of food supplies, but we were also concerned with a number of other commodities such as tobacco, resins and cotton, which, though within the purview of the British Raw Materials Department and its Washington Mission, was on the American side under the control of the Department of Agriculture with which the Food Mission had the closest ties. From rudimentary beginnings, the Mission and its counterpart on the Washington scene – in the first place, the US Department of Agriculture, but also the office of Lend-Lease Administration and, more peripherally though sometimes of crucial importance, State, Treasury and the staff at the White House – developed into a remarkably smooth-running mechanism, particularly after the creation of the Combined Food Board in June 1942.

I have elsewhere* given a detailed history of that extremely successful part of the inter-Allied war effort and, in so far as it has a bearing on post-war international machinery and provides more general lessons for the conduct of international relations, I will refer to it again later. I should, however, say here that, as far as my own development is concerned, I could not have had a more effective introduction into international diplomacy than in my five years in the British element of the Washington wartime machine. Here were all the ingredients necessary for perfect tuition: the consciousness of working in a powerful and just cause and working with and alongside people – Americans and Canadians primarily, but also other members of the Commonwealth for whom the British Food Mission acted, and later the European Allies in exile – who were all similarly inspired.

---

*The Combined Food Board, Stanford, Stanford University Press, 1956.

A special word should be said here about Canada. The British Food Mission 'to North America' had an almost autonomous Ottawa office, but when the Combined Food Board was formed on a tripartite basis, our contacts with Canadian ministers and officials became much more frequent and close. I was thus able to see at first hand the remarkable quality of so many Canadians in the public service – by any kind of 'proportional representation' far more numerous at that time than those of any other country. Hume Wrong, Mike Pearson (at the time Minister at the Embassy in Washington), Ed Ritchie, Alexander Skelton, Bob Bryce, and Wynne Plumptre are very much in my mind, and they were to be followed by many others after the war. I should also mention the many charming and highly efficient Canadian girls, mostly graduates of McGill, who cheerfully helped in the various British Missions in Washington. Many of them have remained good friends. Though not directly through the Food Mission, I also got to know Louis Rasminsky, later to be a distinguished Governor of the Bank of Canada, who with Keynes and Harry White played a most important part in the Bretton Woods negotiations.

Organizationally, too, I could not have had better schooling. We were, of course, a part of a Whitehall ministry *in partibus* and also a part of the whole Whitehall inter-departmental microcosm, which with that remarkable mixture of orderliness and improvisation (one must hope that this will never cease to be part of the British genius!) was quickly created and instantly and deeply admired by our American colleagues. Indeed, one of our main achievements in the early days after America's entry into the war, and before the balance of the Allied war effort shifted decisively in favour of the United States, was, by precept and example, to help organize the Washington departments more effectively for their wartime tasks. In this work, I am bound to record, the 'temporaries' were almost to a man wholly successful in the sense of avoiding the impression of superiority that so many of the diplomatic regulars (though by no means all) sometimes tended to give.

Another aspect of this work, which, as I have said before, stood me in good stead in many of my later activities, was to learn how to conduct negotiations at the same time with a number of opposite numbers who, while sharing the same basic objectives, had often quite different subsidiary but important objectives to pursue or had to take account of very different political or other constraints. It taught me what are the elements out of which success in what was later called 'alliance politics' are fashioned. These are to recognize the constraints under which you are working and never to lose sight of the interests you are defending but, at the same time, not to jeopardize the greater, common objective and, by the practice of the art of persuasion, to make your negotiating partners conduct themselves in the same way.

Of course, the human element was extremely important. The Food Mission was almost completely staffed at the professional level by 'temporaries'. R. H. Brand and Maurice Hutton were both merchant bankers, though Brand had had a good deal of political experience as a member of 'Milner's Kindergarten' – as the collection of young men from Oxford whom Lord Milner had recruited to help him in his task of administering the Transvaal, were known. From Maurice Hutton, in particular, I learned a great deal in this, my first experience of 'business' in the public domain. Among the others were Guy Chilver, an Oxford classics don, Frank van Zwanenberg and Joe Hopkins, prominent members of the food trades, and so on, with only a sprinkling of regular civil servants. This mixture provided a high degree of adaptability, particularly vis-à-vis our American partners and also made for easy relations with the other British Missions, which were similarly staffed, and with the British Embassy, which had at least a strong element of temporary recruits.

The members of the Mission paid frequent visits to London. One of the ones I paid is particularly memorable to me because it gave me the occasion to meet Alan and Babette Sainsbury who have been close friends of ours ever since. The Mission, in turn, was supported by visits of ministry officials from London including Herbert Broadley, the Deputy Secretary in charge of the General Department. Of special significance was a prolonged visit by E. M. H. Lloyd (supported by George Dunnett) who had an unrivalled experience of rationing in the First World War as well as, particularly in the institution of points rationing, in the Second. He was of great assistance to the Americans in setting up their control machinery and formed a valuable link between the Mission and a number of central US departments.

While securing scarce food supplies for the British civilian population and the armed forces and, with the Ministry of War Transport, scheduling their dispatch to where they were needed were our main tasks, we were naturally involved in a large number of related problems. These included domestic American ones, such as price control, allocation and rationing (it was in this context that I met again in Washington Ken Galbraith) and, jointly with the representatives of the British Treasury, financial problems, particularly those related to Lend-Lease. One of my first experiences in this regard, when I was in charge of the Mission while Hutton was in London, was to negotiate with the Lend-Lease Administration the financing, under Lend-Lease, of the whole Dominican and Haitian sugar crops, which the British Sugar Controller, Sir William (Jimmy) Rook, with his outstanding trading instinct and experience, had already bought even when he knew that it could not be paid for through lack of foreign exchange. This became an important precedent for so-called 'off-shore' Lend-Lease.

I also had some contact with the Lend-Lease and, later, loan negotiations conducted by special British missions led by Keynes, as also, though more peripherally, with the negotiations that led to the setting up of the United Nations Relief and Rehabilitation Agency, the Food and Agriculture Organisation and the Bretton Woods 'system' – the International Monetary Fund and the International Bank for Reconstruction and Development. Needless to say, these proved much more difficult and generally less harmonious than the normal operations of the established British missions, since they were concerned not with winning the war, but with the economic arrangements of the post-war world. In this regard the clash of interests was inevitably deeper and more acute. Much has been written about these matters by others who were more centrally concerned; and we now have Keynes's own writings and letters as the main source.

The British teams that were assembled for these tasks were the now familiar mixture of officials from the Treasury, the Bank of England, the Board of Trade and other departments, academics either already working in Whitehall and the Washington missions, or specially recruited for the purpose, City people and a sprinkling of men from other areas of business as well as professional diplomatists. The galaxy is very numerous and since most of them have already been commemorated in other writings, including

Keynes's, there is no need to identify them here, except for Frank Lee (who combined tough negotiation with great popularity with the Americans and of whom more will be said later) and the central figure of Keynes. His role cannot be overestimated, particularly when one remembers the extraordinarily complex character of the negotiations, which raised problems not only of real intellectual difficulty, but also of technical financial intricacy and of conflicts of national interest as perceived for an unknown future. Ideas of what a future trading and financial world (after an Allied victory) should look like had to be reconciled in the light of estimates of the economic structure and strength of individual countries, particularly the USA and the UK. The position of the different Commonwealth countries was one factor that the British negotiations had constantly to take into account. (One distinguished member of the British team could be relied on at every meeting to ask at least ten times, 'Has the Commonwealth been consulted?') On this, as on relations with the Allies after liberation, the positions of the two countries were more often than not wide apart.

It is impossible to imagine how the Lend-Lease settlement or the loan negotiations or the arrangements for the post-war institution would have come out if the guidance of Keynes in the preparation of policy and in actual negotiation had not been available.

I had some opportunity, though not as much as many others, to see Keynes in action during those Washington visits, having met him through Bob Brand and Maurice Hutton (who had known him in the City and who invited him to join us for meals with members of the US Administration other than the Treasury) and through Lucius Thompson-McCausland who accompanied him on his earlier visits. The extraordinary – and extraordinarily fascinating – power of his intellect, his analytical, expository and debating brilliance became evident to anyone who met him within a very short time. But not all Americans were ready to accept it, let alone fall for it. Superiority in argument was often a drawback, and when it was consciously displayed, as on occasion it was, it aroused resistance, which persisted even against cogency in debate.

Unfortunately, Keynes could not always resist the temptation to indulge in biting sarcasm. I remember him describing one – very mediocre, but at the time unfortunately powerful – member of the Administration as 'having his ear so close to the ground that he could not hear an upright man'. Whether this got back to the man in question, as such witticisms have a habit of doing, I do not know, but there was never much friendliness shown by the victim. Keynes apparently said of this same man that his face reminded him of the 'buttocks of a baboon' – and 'baboon' was then chosen as the code word for telegrams in one direction for the particular negotiations. (Many years later the story went round Whitehall that a snide remark by Harold Macmillan about a highly placed American was said to have got back to him and soured a particular negotiation for a while.) But Keynes could also be extremely funny without that wounding effect. His account of visiting Mr Henry Morgenthau and attempting to give an exposé to him, which was constantly being interrupted by telephone calls, then taking his leave, going back to his hotel, telephoning the Secretary of the Treasury and 'getting his undivided attention for half an hour' was a telling example.

For my part, the change of atmosphere from that of total co-operation to one of more direct opposition of national interests appeared most strikingly in the sudden abandonment of Lend-Lease on 21 August 1945 after the end of the Japanese war. I may well have been the first to inform London of this since I heard in the middle of one night from the Ministry of War Transport representatives in New York that one of our cargoes had been stopped by order of the Lend-Lease Administration and at once telephoned Maurice Hutton who was in London. It was only the next day that formal notification of the end of Lend-Lease was received by the British authorities.

The formal food machinery had a more lingering end. The Combined Food Board was replaced by an International Emergency Food Council with an enlarged membership but this neither lasted long nor was it particularly effective while it did. I had myself by then become much more interested in general problems, particularly those arising out of the loan agreement negotiated by Keynes. When it was suggested to me that I might return to London to the Ministry of Food before making up my mind what I wanted to do eventually, I readily agreed. Neither the offer of a chair at a Canadian university nor that of an important (and lucrative!) post with an American food company tempted me to stay in North America. To part from so many friends was, however, a great wrench. Happily our lives later on gave us the opportunity to maintain these friendships: to this day many of our closest friends are on that continent. In July 1946 we (with two baby daughters, Joanna and Elizabeth) sailed on the *Queen Mary* (still equipped as a GI brides carrier) for England where we landed on 15 July just after the British Parliament had ratified the loan agreement.

4

Whitehall I

My wife and children went to our house in the then East Riding village of Cottingham were we had lived before the war. I stayed with friends in London, trying to make up my mind whether to return to academic life or to remain in the Civil Service where I had been offered establishment and the prospect of eventually being employed on more central economic work. I had applied for the chair at Liverpool about to be vacated by G. C. Allen (who was going to University College, London) but one of my old Birmingham teachers, P. B. Whale, was appointed. I sought and received a good deal of advice. Geoffrey Faber warned me against the lure of an active career in worldly affairs, one to which 'one was always subject in middle life'. My old principal at Hull, Arthur Eustace Morgan, thought I would miss the intellectual freedom of an academic environment. Keynes on one of his visits to Washington had already urged me to stay in the Civil Service after the war and had initiated the necessary processes through Edward Bridges, Permanent Secretary of the Treasury and Head of the Civil Service. Both he and Bridges, as well as Henry French, the Permanent Secretary of the Ministry of Food, many colleagues in the Ministry and John Strachey, soon to be Minister of Food, pressed me to stay in the public service. After much heart-searching, we decided on this course. Perhaps Henry French's last telegram to me while I was still in Washington had helped persuade me: 'Will you now authorize me to go straight ahead with view your joining much harassed, much maligned but on the whole useful and necessary body of permanent civil servants?' (It is interesting to note that already then a senior civil servant spoke of his profession as 'much harassed, much maligned'. What would he have said now?) We moved to Beaconsfield and I started on a typical Whitehall commuting life.

It was at quite an early stage during my new role in the Ministry

that a fresh opportunity to get back directly into the international
arena arose. One day I received a telephone call from David Owen,
Deputy Secretary General of the United Nations, asking me if I
would accept the post of Secretary General of the newly formed
General Agreement on Tariffs and Trade (GATT). Any temptation
I might have had for another proconsular post was quickly
dispelled when Percivale Liesching, Permanent Secretary of the
Ministry of Food, made it quite clear that such a move would not
be welcomed by the Ministry.

In common with the rest of Whitehall, the Ministry of Food was
under pressure to revert to pre-war patterns, but the pace was
necessarily much slower than in other departments, although one of
my earliest experiences of the more rigorous technical aspects of
administration (though at a somewhat later stage) was to be
involved in the 'run-down' of a number of divisions from their
war-time strength. Allocation and rationing to the trade and the
consumer were still the order of the day due to supply, shipping
and, above all, foreign-exchange shortages, and so were bulk
contracts with foreign suppliers as well as with the farmers.
Moreover, many temporaries from the trade were still active in the
department and continued for some time to give it a somewhat
special flavour.

I worked in what was called the Supply Secretariat, a central
staff, where I was primarily, though not exclusively, concerned
with international matters. As the balance of payments was still the
major economic constraint and since food imports were still the
biggest charge on our foreign-exchange resources, I was at once
involved in the central economic policy problems and represented
the department on a number of committees. The most important
was the Treasury committee, concerned with the balance of
payments and the determination of our import programme,
presided over by Otto Clarke. I first knew him during his brief stay
in wartime Washington where he worked in the Combined
Production and Resources Board. We quickly became close friends,
both professionally and privately, and remained so until his
untimely death in 1975. Through this committee, I was able to
follow at close quarters the rapid disappearance of our foreign-
exchange reserves and the protracted and complicated discussions
on domestic and international economic policy that this caused and

to have this invaluable background and stimulus in the many more
specific negotiations – for example for the renewal of our Canadian
bacon contract – in which I was engaged.

It was through this particular committee that I was able to
persuade the Treasury to be directly represented at such negotiations – normally they kept in the background, issuing their
thunderbolts to the hapless Whitehall department concerned. I
remember on one occasion Otto Clarke, who represented the
Treasury, asking me who the 'very clever Canadian' was who was
arguing on the other side. When I told him that he was the Ministry
of Food's representative in Canada, Otto decided that he himself
would have been better advised to stay away.

While I was able in those early months in the Ministry to learn
something of the conventional ways of Whitehall, the tasks that
faced us and the variety of people and mechanisms involved in them
were still of a sufficiently special kind to make the whole
experience, as far as I was concerned, something very different from
what was – and is still considered – the traditional life of the Civil
Service. No doubt my own conduct did not always conform to the
traditions. I remember one specific occasion that must have caused
my superiors some concern. As an Assistant Secretary, a modest,
though at that time perhaps a more weighty grade than it would be
today, I had to represent the Ministry at a high-level meeting in the
Foreign Office concerned with allocation of bread grains to the
occupied zones in Germany. The meeting was presided over by
Frank Pakenham, Chancellor of the Duchy of Lancaster, who
argued with great vigour the plight of the Germans while I had to
plead for the need to meet the British bread ration. When in the
heat of the debate he attacked Maurice Hutton, the Ministry's
representative in Washington who had the difficult task of looking
after the claims of the British civilians as well as those of the
military authorities responsible for feeding German civilians, I
protested and started to walk out. It was the Commander-in-Chief
in Germany, Air Chief Marshall Sholto Douglas who strongly
sympathized with me and persuaded me to stay!

I did not have much time to acquire the proper ways of an
established Civil Servant. There were still many 'special assignments', for example a trip in February 1947 to Canada and the
United States with the Minister, John Strachey, and his Private

Secretary, George Bishop, in the PM's aircraft. John Strachey, whom I had met before the war when he came to lecture in Hull, had greatly moderated his left-wing views and had become an effective Minister. Though not in the Cabinet, he was a 'constant attender'. He had maintained a wide interest in affairs, literature and arts and was a delightful travelling companion.

Our journey was memorable for three reasons. Instead of our going via the Azores, the weather caused us to stop over in Iceland. Just at the time an Icelandic delegation was in London negotiating about fish oil. Strachey, having congratulated himself on escaping this ordeal, found that during the twelve hours enforced stay in Reykjavik he had to face heavy Icelandic fire on the problem. The second, even less agreeable, incident occurred when on landing in Ottawa the aircraft skidded into a snowdrift at the end of the runway and had to be left behind — I think a total write-off. I remember the captain coming into the cabin, saluting and saying quietly and slowly, 'I think it would be as well if you left now. We may have a fire.' We went on to the States by train and returned to England on the *Queen Mary*, which we almost failed to board. Ken Galbraith in his autobiography recounts how he managed to get us through a police line, which, owing to a fire on a neighbouring ship, had cordoned off all access. George Bishop and I spent most of our time on board reading, John Strachey, much to our chagrin, having refused to introduce us to the film star Paulette Goddard, at whose table he managed to get himself placed.

5

Europe I: The Marshall Plan

By the spring of 1947, our foreign-exchange resources were rapidly running out. We were fast 'going down the drain' as one Minister put it to his colleagues. On the Continent, too, the post-war reconstruction and the alleviation of shortages were not keeping pace with the expectations of liberated populations and the stability, indeed survival, of the first democratic post-war regimes was threatened, notably in France and Italy. This was the situation when, almost at the eleventh hour, General Marshall made, on 5 June 1947, his famous Harvard speech in which he invited Europe to 'draw up a plan of reconstruction' and offered 'friendly aid' from the United States in its preparation and the prospect of 'later support for such a programme'. I became very quickly involved in the sequelae of this unprecedented initiative, and for several months the 'Marshall Plan' became my sole activity.

There were three phases in my involvement, which coincided with the development of the programme based on the Marshall speech, the first being the Committee of European Economic Co-operation, which prepared the European reply to General Marshall. During this period, as a member of the British delegation led by Oliver Franks, I represented the food and agricultural interests. I was in charge of the writing of the report on these matters and had the distinguished Dutch agricultural economist, later Director General of the Food and Agriculture Organisation (FAO), Aed Boerma, as my deputy. Later in the summer of 1947, I was transferred from the Ministry of Food to the Central Economic Planning Staff under Edwin Plowden, which was at first part of the Cabinet Office, responsible to Herbert Morrison as Lord President, later in the Treasury under Stafford Cripps as Chancellor. I was not able to take up this post until after the Franks Committee had reported and a group of us had been to Washington to discuss the report with the American authorities.

My next phase with the Marshall Plan came in the spring of 1948 after the setting up of the Organization for European Economic Co-operation (OEEC) as the continuing body for implementing the European recovery programme. By that time I was mainly concerned, within the planning staff, with balance-of-payments problems. Through Otto Clarke's initiative with Edward Bridges, I was asked to represent the UK on the OEEC's Programmes Committee, of which I was made Chairman. In this capacity, too, I was later to take part, as one of the 'four wise men', in the first Division of Marshall Aid in 1948. Finally, in January 1949, having travelled innumerable times between London and Paris, I moved to Paris as a permanent member of our delegation, with the rank of Minister and the third phase, both for me and the programme, began.

I shall have something to say later about the significance of the Marshall Plan and the OEEC for the European, and particularly the British, economies, for the ensuing efforts at European integration, and for international economic diplomacy generally. At this point I should like to say something more about the organization and personnel of this extraordinary enterprise, which left a profound and lasting mark on the conduct of affairs between the Western countries (and, incidentally, on me).

I represented the Ministry of Food from the second meeting onwards. That meeting between the French, British and Soviet Governments took place in Paris between 27 June and 3 July 1947, the British delegation being led by the Foreign Secretary, Ernest Bevin, the French by Bidault, and the Soviet by Molotov. The events of those few days and the two weeks that followed are all now part of history: the refusal of the Russians to participate, the withdrawal by the Czechs of their earlier acceptance of the invitation by France and Britain, the yielding by Poland and Yugoslavia to Soviet pressure to stay away. So also is the fact that on 15 July representatives of sixteen European countries met in Paris under British chairmanship (the venue and chairmanship were an Anglo-French deal) and with a secretariat for which the French had provided the nucleus with Robert Marjolin effectively at its head.*

---

*Hierarchic and bureaucratic considerations were responsible for his not being formally the Secretary General, but that is what he really was.

I have a few particularly vivid recollections from this initial period. The first is of Bevin's return to the Embassy after the last tripartite meeting on 2 July when he immediately telephoned the Prime Minister, Clement Attlee, and in the hearing of several of us from his delegation reported that "'e walked out, uttering threats', which is the way we first learned that the Russians, despite their presence with a delegation of eighty-eight, had never budged from an initial position that made their participation impossible and, almost certainly, never really intended. Bevin's phrase was a slight dramatization in that Molotov did not actually walk out, although the meeting ended shortly after his uncompromising statement and a few closing remarks by Bevin and Bidault.

An anecdote may illustrate the depth of feeling created by the decision of the Soviet Union, and some other Eastern European countries, not to participate in the Marshall Plan—though this was only one feature of the widening East–West split. One evening during the early days in 1949 we were in a night club in Paris with some friends. It was one of the 'intellectual' ones on the Left Bank, which during the occasional acts was plunged in complete darkness except for the spotlight that fell on the performer. During one of the pauses with the light on I found that I was sitting next to Oscar Lange, the distinguished Polish Marxist economist, whom I had known before the war in England and during the war in the USA, where he was Professor at Chicago and later the first Polish Ambassador to the USA. He asked me what I was doing but before I had time to answer his female companion said pointedly, 'Don't you know, he is working with the Marshall Plan.' When next the lights went on and I looked Lange and his friend had disappeared.

Another impression is of the first meeting of the Committee, which was chaired by Oliver Franks. I was sitting next to Edmund Hall-Patch, then Deputy Secretary at the Foreign Office in charge of economic matters, as members of the other delegations walked in. Nearly all were unknown to us then, though this changed very quickly. We amused ourselves by trying to guess their nationalities. We got every single one of them wrong.

The first meeting of the Committee was on 15 July; on 22 September the ministerial representatives signed the report, an 86-page first, general, volume and a 355-page second volume containing the reports of four technical committees: Food and Agriculture, Fuel and Power, Iron and Steel, and Transport.

The production of the first volume, for some reason that I cannot recall always referred to in the delegation as the 'torso', gave us a great deal of anxiety. It was clear that it was most important that it should have the maximum impact in the United States: on the Administration, the Congress and public opinion. Several 'scribes' were successively produced from London without the desired result. An attempt was made to persuade Isaiah Berlin, passing through Paris on his way to his first post-war holiday, to take on the task. After reading what had been produced so far, he said that he had the strong impression that the cart of European economic recovery might, with some pushing and pulling by Europeans and Americans, be got out of the mud in which it was stuck, only to get stuck again soon after! He declined the task and it was Otto Clarke who was largely responsible for the final version.

It is, I believe, impossible for anyone who was not associated in one way or another (I include in this association the newspapermen and -women) to appreciate how formidable was the achievement—in just over two months—of this complex, technical, intellectual and diplomatic task. The speed and hothouse atmosphere in which it was accomplished helped to weld together those who participated, at least at the official level, into a remarkably integrated team. At the same time, had they not become such a team, spending, more often than not, some sixteen hours of every day together, the report and all that it led to could not have been produced.

The British delegation certainly quickly became a well-knit team. This is not to say that all of us were always of the same mind: we had quite strong disagreements within the delegation, usually on detailed points of tactics, but sometimes on major points of strategy, on the one hand *vis-à-vis* our European colleagues, on the other in regard to the 'friendly aid' we were receiving from a large number of Americans. In particular, those of us who were concerned with specific areas of planning for the future European recovery (in the early stages when I was responsible for food and agriculture, this included me) tended to be suspicious of the diplomatic members, from the Foreign Office or elsewhere, whom we regarded, unjustly I am sure, as more concerned with pleasing political masters at home. Our group was soon known in the delegation as the 'resistance movement', and one of our members developed a particular talent for warning the rest of us at delegation meetings when he thought that some particular bit of trickery was afoot. He would draw a corkscrew on a piece of paper which he managed to display to us without those who were under suspicion being aware of it.

These differences were not however serious or lasting and when it came to the major questions we could not have been a more united team. A great deal of the credit must go to the extremely close links – in terms of speed and efficiency of reciprocal responses – between the Paris delegation and Whitehall. I remember sending a telegram to Whitehall on one occasion with a *cri de coeur* on a statistical problem asking how we could be expected 'to make bricks without straw'. The immediate reply was, 'Goldman expert strawless brickmaker is on the way.' This was one example of what usually happens when the Whitehall machine is put into top gear for a particular task. No effort was spared to make the British delegation as effective as possible. The cream of the various departments involved was made available. In the case of Food and Agriculture I had a number of extremely valuable assistants, particularly George Dunnett from the Commonwealth Economic Secretariat, an old friend from his wartime service in the Ministry, whom I managed to extract for the Paris operation. For a brief period we also had the help of Stuart Hampshire, the noted philosopher.

What is more, so close were the bonds, professional and personal, that were formed during this period between the participants, that for decades afterwards the people concerned formed a sort of stage army, wandering on and off in many of the subsequent dramatic events that marked Western co-operation. It is my firm belief that the existence of this body of people – some of whom had already been active in the wartime inter-Allied machinery – has played a major part in producing a strong cohesive element, a sort of all-purpose instrument, for so many other enterprises, such as the civilian side of NATO, the zig-zagging, but still progressive, march of European union and the variety of multilateral trade negotiations. Even in the larger international bodies, such as the International Monetary Fund and the World

Bank, at least some members of this same group also reappeared to play valuable and honourable roles.

It is not altogether easy to form a just view of the contributions made by the different countries that collaborated in the Marshall Plan. The British and French were naturally in the lead as the inviting powers and as the prime respondents to the Marshall challenge to Europe. On the French side much help, apart from the official delegation, came from Jean Monnet, not only as the head of the Commissariat au Plan (which had a major responsibility for the French input) but also as an indefatigable – at that stage, in the official British view a far too insistent – advocate of closer European union. Through his earlier links, as well as through his advocacy of integration, Monnet had a special line to Washington. But far and away the most important French contribution was to have supplied Robert Marjolin as Secretary of the Committee, later to become the first Secretary General of the OEEC. I had met that brilliant young economist during the war in Washington when he was on a mission for the French Government in exile and during the Marshall Plan operation. A friendship developed between his family and mine, which still continues. He had been Monnet's chief lieutenant on the Commissariat au Plan and brought to his new task not only all the expert knowledge needed but also a talent for distilling a consensus from the disparate interests of the participants, which made him the obvious choice for Secretary General when the OEEC was created in the spring of 1948.

The preparation of the report, arduous though it was, also gave rise to many amusing incidents. At the first ministerial meeting Bevin suggested that some minor problem could be referred to an *ad hoc* committee. One delegate, not surprisingly, having heard 'haddock' committee, insisted that his country, as an important fish producer, should become a member. On another occasion, a late-night meeting, one Minister who was missing was traced by an aide who knew his gastronomic habits to a well-known restaurant and brought to the meeting where he promptly went to sleep. When called upon by the Chairman to express his point of view, he woke with a start and said in a loud voice, 'l'addition, s'il vous plaît.'

The initial task had been to prepare questionnaires of require-ments for reconstruction to be sent to capitals with a very close deadline for return. Late one night when Marjolin and I were leaving the Grand Palais where our meetings were held, just after the questionnaires had been handed to the delegates, we found one of them by himself busily filling out the questionnaire. When we pointed out to him that this was intended to be sent to his capital, he replied, 'I know that, but I think I know better what to put in than they do back home.' He was clearly following the view of another delegate who, when confronted with the highly elaborate questionnaire, exclaimed, 'On fera de la poésie.'

After the presentation of the report in Washington, there was a pause while the American Administration proceeded with the preparation of its foreign-aid legislation. This was passed in April 1948 and at the same time the continuing organization, the OEEC, was set up. I had in the meantime taken up my duties in the Central Economic Planning Staff (CEPS), and this too provided another opportunity for making new friends: Edwin Plowden himself, Hugh Weeks who was the number two, a few 'temporaries' from the universities, Kenneth Berrill, Robin Marris and Austin Robinson among them. Robert Hall, then Head of the Economic Section at the Cabinet Office, whom I had known for many years when we were both teaching, worked extremely closely with us in the CEPS and so did the Treasury, thanks to very close and cordial relations between Plowden and Bridges. Another friendship I formed then was with Douglas Allen, who had come from the Board of Trade to be Plowden's personal assistant, but who was soon transferred to my division to work on the balance of payments.

These were the days of 'planning', the domestic efforts to this end, first under Morrison, then under Hugh Dalton, then under Cripps, fortifying and being in turn fortified by the need to provide the UK segment of the European Recovery Programme. In between, Otto Clarke and his Balance of Payments Working Party and later his so-called 'London', i.e. European Recovery Programme, Committee, played a vital part. He was substantially the author of the Economic Survey, 1947, which was the first major effort at an analysis, forecast and plan combined and, thus, the first British equivalent of French indicative planning. The reason for the close connection between the domestic and the Marshall Plan aspects of these Whitehall exercises lay in the fact that the balance-of-payments deficits and the rapidly dwindling foreign-exchange reserves were the major constraints on economic activity, and the prospect of substantial dollar aid was the major factor determining outlook and policy.

From my new seat in CEPS, but with my recent activity in the Paris Committee and the more distant one of my work on the import programme in the Ministry of Food, I was very much involved in the Whitehall work on these matters. One of my particular responsibilities was to chair the Sterling Area Working Party which dealt with export promotion and import substitution possibilities as between the dollar and the sterling areas. I was not sure at the time, and I am even less sure in retrospect, whether the heavy emphasis on this distinction between the dollar and the overall balance of payments was justified. There was much argument in Whitehall about it. Keynes had died more than a year before the Marshall speech and his posthumously published article on the dollar balance of payments had taken an optimistic – in my opinion and that of some others, including Otto Clarke, a grossly over-optimistic – view of the continuing threat of dollar scarcity. There were subsequently to be many conflicting assessments and they all were inaccurate at least as far as their time-scale was concerned. With hindsight, it would seem that not only had the apparatus of macro-economic analysis, linking domestic policy with general external equilibrium, not yet been adequately developed, but Whitehall thinking was totally absorbed by the US loan and the Marshall Plan with a consequent exclusive focus on the dollar reserves.

Be that as it may, when in the spring of 1948, after the passage of the Foreign Aid Bill, the new European organization was set up, it turned its efforts towards the development of a comprehensive European Recovery Programme. The requirement for dollar aid to be appropriated by the American Congress under the new legislation became the essential 'missing component' of European economic recovery. On the pattern of its predecessor's technical committees, the OEEC set up a number of 'vertical' committees concerned with particular commodities or sectors of industry, together with a number of 'horizontal' committees: on the balance of payments, on intra-European payments, on manpower and so on, as well as a Programmes Committee, of which I was Chairman. Its task was to draw up an import programme that could be translated into a dollar requirement programme as a basis, or at least as one of the documents, with which the US Administration would construct its own presentation to Congress.

It is perhaps worthwhile at this point to say something more about the main features of the organization, which was so quickly created, and about the main attitudes of the different national delegations. Once again the British and the French were in the lead. The French, as Monnet has rightly pointed out in his memoirs,* were the only ones who already had a fully-fledged planning machinery and a domestic plan for economic renewal and investment. Much of the thinking of the OEEC, and perhaps even more of the individual members in their domestic economic policy, was influenced by the knowledge they acquired of the French planning methods. However, given the overriding importance of the impending flow of dollars from the USA, the British insistence on the dollar shortage in relation to import programmes became the decisive determinant, not only of the programming effort of the OEEC but of the manner in which the organization dealt with all other, at that time less central, problems. These included the treatment of quantitative restrictions on trade, the way in which liberalization in respect of tariffs should be dealt with, the study of the possibility of a European Customs Union (on which, as indeed on all wider measures of economic integration, the Americans were very keen) and on the possibility of creating a European payments system, i.e. with transferability, if not complete convertibility, of currencies.

I shall have more to say later about some of these points and particularly about the already very evident difference between the British approach and that of a number of other Western European countries, as well as that of many of the Americans to many larger matters, such as general trading and financial problems, as well as the unification of Europe. At any rate, the need for dollar aid was so great everywhere that the British had little difficulty in making programming for the purpose of obtaining it far and away the central preoccupation of the OEEC during its early months.

As far as the technical organization of the programming operation – and indeed of much other work of the organization – was concerned, the British were very much in the lead, and, whatever their wider political differences with the Americans, the operation was very much an Anglo-American one, inspired

---

*Jean Monnet, *Memoirs*, London, Collins, 1978, p. 268

to some degree by the wartime collaboration of the two countries in combined planning in and outside the combined boards. With his background of a two-year postgraduate fellowship in the United States and his experience of the wartime combined machinery in Washington, Marjolin had no difficulty with this 'Anglo-Saxon' approach.

It is not necessary, in retrospect, to go through all the minutiae of the changing scene in those spring and summer months of 1948 that resulted in the final flow of nearly $5 billion of American aid during the next twelve months to the sixteen participating European countries, including the French and Anglo-American occupation zones of Germany, and thus to a fundamental change in the economic, social and, above all, political orientation of Western Europe. At the time it led to an immense amount of activity in Paris, in Washington and in the other capitals. Every change in the forecast of action by Congress both as regards the amount of aid it would allocate as well as of the conditions it might attach, every new idea on matters of technique of programming, of the implications of changing perspectives in the immediate economic outlook of countries, every fresh realization of the implications of this or that amount or condition of dollar aid on intra-European payments or on trade flows, became the subject of prolonged discussion in the committees of the OEEC and in the national administrations. Innumerable visits and telegrams were involved.

6

Sharing American Aid –
European Co-operation

In the end, it became certain that Congress would act and that the aid would be forthcoming. But this was accompanied by a bombshell, for in June 1948 the American Mission in Paris informed the OEEC that it would be up to the European recipients themselves to propose to the Economic Co-operation Administration of the USA how the total amount appropriated by Congress should be divided. As far as the Americans were concerned, this was, as so often, a brilliant combination of political realism and far-sighted idealism. To put this most sensitive and potentially divisive task on the Europeans meant at one and the same time that the Americans would be free from what might well have been insistent lobbying by individual European countries and by American interest groups, free also from any political odium that might attach to their response, and that, if the Europeans could muster the necessary degree of co-operation to do this job themselves, it would give an enormous boost to the cohesion of the new organization.

Needless to say, the reception of this American proposal was mixed. Happily, the British view very quickly crystallized in favour of accepting the American challenge, and so did the French, with the other countries following their lead. Machinery had to be set up and the Programmes Committee was given the task of formulating 'realistic' dollar requirements programmes, keeping in close touch with the Americans with a view to arriving at a total that was reasonably in line with what was expected to be the amount appropriated by Congress. This involved the Committee in a detailed scrutiny of the import programmes of each of the participants. A series of cross-examinations was organized at which every country had to defend each item in its programme in the face of questions designed to test the reality of each import requirement against consumption standards, investment and production programmes, domestic availabilities, current and prospective foreign exchange resources, and above all the justification for relying on a dollar source as against possible other, particularly European, sources.

I was in the chair during the first year's screening of aid and I cannot think of many operations I have been involved in, before or since, that equalled it in complexity. First there was the application of more or less objective tests in which a whole series of macro- and micro-economic data were brought to bear on countries' stated requirements, including often quite wide-ranging enquiries into historical data, expected trends and so forth. Then there were the more political glosses to be applied: first, as I have already mentioned, the likely gap between the requirements as originally stated, and then as they were likely to emerge from the Committee's screening process, as compared with what Congress was likely to appropriate – both terms of the calculation, and particularly the latter, being unknown and estimates of them fluctuating.

Obviously the rigour of the screening process was related to the estimate of this gap in the minds of those of us responsible for conducting the exercise, as was our conception of the degree of 'padding' in the figures submitted, either as deliberate policy or merely arising from inadequate statistics or planning machinery in the various capitals. The fluctuation of congressional expectations as transmitted to us by Averell Harriman who was the American Ambassador in charge of the Paris office of the European Co-operation Administration (ECA) and his officials gave rise to particularly troublesome and irritating, but also amusing, incidents.

On one occasion, some time after midnight, while in the middle of a particularly severe cross-examination of one delegate, I was called to the Secretary General's office in the Hôtel Royal Monceau. There I found Marjolin with Dick Bissell of the ECA (a distinguished economist whom I had known at Yale during my Rockefeller Fellowship years) who had brought the latest and rather more optimistic forecast of the likely amount of total aid. It was clear that the degree of severity with which our screening had been conducted could well result in the embarrassment of a lower European requirement total than Congress appeared at that moment ready to appropriate. To the utter astonishment of my (Dutch) Vice-Chairman of the Programmes Committee and my own colleagues from the British Treasury and the Central Statistical Office, I returned to the Committee's meeting with a very different attitude to the examinee's claims. When I suggested that perhaps we had taken too optimistic a view of the progress of productivity in the country concerned and, therefore, of its dollar requirements, one of my colleagues, after working on his slide-rule, whispered that this might mean another $200 million on the total requirement. It was only after the meeting, somewhere around five in the morning over a sandwich and a beer, that I was able to explain this sudden volte-face.

Personality, inevitably, also played a part in the screening process. This was one of the many occasions when I was able to observe what a difference the varying attitudes of the negotiators can make to the outcome of what they are battling for. Patience, quiet persuasion, meticulous knowledge of one's brief with the consequent ability to answer the most unexpected questions, but also sarcasm, indignation, even carefully calculated loss of temper, all these were brought to bear by one side or the other – with varying success.

By the time the Programmes Committee had finished, the amount of aid was virtually known and the question arose how the division of this amount was to be handled. There was much debate and diplomatic manoeuvring but, as in the earlier phase, the pressure of the timetable concentrated minds wonderfully. It was decided to set up a 'Committee of Four' – soon dubbed 'the four wise men' – composed of the chairmen or vice-chairmen of four horizontal committees.

This committee consisted of Guillaume Guindey (Chairman of the Balance of Payments Committee, head of Finances Extérieures of the French Finance Ministry and at the time the most important man responsible for French economic policy), Dick Spierenburg from the Netherlands (Chairman of the Trade Committee), Professor Stoppani from Italy (Vice Chairman of the Intra-European Payments Committee)* and me. After a further series of

---

*While, because of his position on the horizontal committee, Professor Stoppani was formally a member of the Committee of Four, the effective member was Giovanni Malagodi, a distinguished banker, later to become an important politician in Italy as leader of the Liberal Party. Malagodi was a highly skilful and combative negotiator and we had many sharp encounters which did nothing, at the time or since, to spoil a close friendship.

cross-examinations of each country, the members of the committee with one assistant each and with Marjolin and a few members of his staff retired for a week to an isolated hotel and there produced their recommendation for the division of the $4,875 million available aid. Those days at the Hôstellerie du Lys in the forest of Chantilly must by any reckoning be regarded as a most extraordinary, not to say bizarre, yet extremely important episode in post-war history. The discussions went on during as many hours of each day as we could keep awake. Formal plenary sessions consisted of at most twelve people; they alternated with sessions at which only the four members and Marjolin were present, and there were also long walks in the gardens when two or at most three of us continued the discussion and negotiation. There were two major underlying clashes of interest: the main one being the treatment of each of the 'big four' countries, which were in fact represented by the members of the committee; the other, the treatment of the rest and, within that, the aid to be recommended for the occupied zones of Germany, particularly the 'Bizone', i.e. the jointly represented British and American zones. At a slightly later stage another complication arose, namely the amount of 'drawing rights' within the intra-European Payments System, and this for some countries became an essential element in deciding whether or not to accept the Four's recommendation on dollar aid.

We returned from Chantilly with our report and then, after discussion with the Americans, proceeded to communicate the figures to the individual countries together with as much explanation of the bases on which these had been arrived at as we could reasonably muster. Our total was $4,835 million (allowing for a reserve of $40 million) but this was later increased to the full ECA total $4,875 million. The reactions were mixed and sometimes fairly violent. France and the UK, which had received the lion's share, $989 million and $1,263 million respectively, quickly accepted the report. (I had been under instruction to try to get, if at all possible, $1,200 million as against a stated requirement of $1,271 million, so the result was considered satisfactory from our point of view.) The Dutch also accepted, but the Italians fought very hard for a larger allocation. Even more difficulty arose with some of the smaller countries, particularly over the reasons that the committee – with some difficulty – was able to produce to justify their having reduced a particular country's dollar requirement. The main reason was the 'switching' to non-dollar sources, which provoked mixed feelings. For example, Greece and Turkey greatly welcomed countries being told to substitute their tobacco for Virginia, while Ireland fought particularly hard against this on the ground that its people had never smoked anything but cigarettes made exclusively of Virginia tobacco. Yet another country, France, insisted on wanting to import Californian prune juice as this was a traditional means of 'softening' their cognac which, in turn, was an important dollar earner. The British had to argue vigorously that to accept French 'soft' cheeses in place of the customary 'hard' ones, which had to come substantially from dollar sources, was not only contrary to traditional taste but would present an insuperable problem as far as rationing was concerned. So while countries welcomed potential new customers for their products, none of them liked having its own requirements for imported goods redirected away from dollar sources. On coming out of a meeting with the Four, one delegate was heard to complain in loud and doleful tones: 'On m'a switché.' Fortunately, the word did not become naturalized into the French language!

There were also various minor technical complications. The American aid had been appropriated for fifteen months and in tabulating the recommendations for each country, the figures had to be recalculated on a twelve-month basis. This led to a formula where A was the original demand, B the amount by which it was reduced and the recommendation was then:

$$\frac{A-B \times 12}{15}$$

My Irish colleague, a splendid character, Tim O'Connell, said mournfully that if in reply to 'What are we going to get, Tim?' he presented this formula in Dublin he would certainly be greeted with 'Ah, the British have again pulled the wool over your eyes!'

The Committee of Four completed its report on 13 August. It was nearly a month later before the various technical and diplomatic complications had been resolved, agreement reached on net European drawing rights to be granted by the European creditor countries and the whole package approved by the Council of the OEEC and submitted to the US Administration.

There were several problems that remained to be cleared up, some of them continuing for a long time, such as the settlement of the intra-European payments system with its drawing rights, which served at one and the same time as a subsidiary form of (non-dollar) aid and as an embryonic form of transferability of European currencies among themselves. The question of the use and accountability of counterpart funds – that is to say the receipts in local currency generated by the sale of American goods received under Marshall Aid – was another. The Americans were extremely interested in both these problems: in the first, because it was to them both a proof that the Europeans were helping each other and not merely relying on the flow of funds from across the Atlantic as well as a step towards the ultimate creation of a system of convertible currencies. This was an objective to which all were pledged under the agreements reached at Bretton Woods. Few Europeans, however, particularly the British after their experience of the premature and short-lived attempt at convertibility in 1947, thought that it could be achieved quickly.

The second problem was of concern to the Americans for a mixture of motives. There was a fear that there could be political problems arising from a feeling, irrational though it might be, that the European governments were getting their aid twice over – benefiting improperly in some way from the sale of gifts. More real was the fear that unless these local currency funds were frozen or sterilized, strong inflationary tendencies would be generated. Each country negotiated with the Americans its own method for dealing with this matter. The French under Monnet's shrewd guidance were particularly successful in convincing the Americans that the use of these funds for the implementation of the plan to develop and modernize the basic industries of France would not be inflationary, and the success of the Plan in creating a modern infrastructure for France was certainly greatly helped in this way.

We ourselves had counterpart funds in France and I tried to convince Whitehall that a part of these should be used to acquire flats and houses for British personnel. (Both the Minister at the Embassy and later I, as well as many others, lived in rented accommodation in Paris.) I persuaded Cripps that this would be sensible, but the resistance in the Whitehall machine to acquisition of property, for reasons that I never understood, could not be overcome.

Before the flow of funds could begin, each country had to sign a co-operation agreement with the United States. As far as the United Kingdom was concerned the terms of the agreement and, even more, its implications for future policy – a foretaste of the problems of the next two or three years – gave rise to fresh hesitations and considerable division of opinion among Ministers that could roughly be described as being between the more ideological Left and the more pragmatic Right. Officials were as usual asked for a report and I chaired a working party under the Economic Steering Committee on 'The consequences of not receiving Marshall Aid'. The conclusions, which were almost entirely confined to the economic sphere, were obvious, although some of the political, national and international implications were also apparent. They may have contributed something to the Government's decision to go ahead, although I believe that that decision was never seriously in doubt. With the signing of the Co-operation Agreement, the first phase of the Marshall Plan was at an end.

For me also it was an important landmark, for after all the commuting that I had been doing in the spring and summer of 1948 I was asked to join the UK delegation in Paris on a permanent basis and had to make up my mind whether to accept the post as one of the Ministers under Edmund Hall-Patch and move my family to Paris. With the encouragement of Edwin Plowden and Stafford Cripps (and of my wife) and in the knowledge that I would continue to be responsible to the 'Planners' in the Treasury, I agreed. In January 1949 we took up residence in Garches, a near suburb of Paris where we found a delightful house with a very large garden and orchard. The rent was enormous in French francs but reasonable in sterling. It was paid by my taking every month a large suitcase full of banknotes to our landlord. We were extremely lucky in inheriting the Italian staff of our American friends and neighbours, Jean and Alfred Friendly who were about to return to the United States: Luigi Rizzo, not only a wonderful cook, but a second paterfamilias and Anne-Marie Rosa-Sentinella, *femme de chambre* and companion to our children, who were happily placed in the local school, the Institution Blanche de Castille.

The head of our delegation had the title of Ambassador and was elected Chairman of the Executive Committee of the OEEC. (The French had the location and the Secretary General, and the Belgians the Chairman of the Council, Baron Snoy.) Edmund Hall-Patch was an exceptional member of the diplomatic service. A varied career after he came out of the army at the end of World War I included a spell in Siam, as it was then called. Hall-Patch's account of the process by which the Governor of the Bank of England, the legendary Montagu Norman, persuaded him to take this post provided one of the finest examples of that man's hypnotic quality. After a lengthy interview, the great Montagu Norman put his arm around this young man's shoulders and accompanied him right to the Bank's front door in Threadneedle Street. Hall-Patch said that he was half-way down Cheapside before he realized that he had committed himself to going to Siam for some years. He also spent some time in China and, somewhat peripherally, in the Treasury. I always understood that Bevin, anxious to make the Foreign Office more aware of the economic and financial realities of the world, had brought Hall-Patch into the office where he eventually attained the level of Deputy Under-Secretary.

He had known Paris well before he came to the OEEC – among the many real or contrived mysteries of his life, or at least those invented by others, was that he had played in a band in a night club and had acted as chauffeur to Yvonne Printemps, when she was on her way to a rendezvous with Sacha Guitry – as he discovered to his sorrow. He spoke French well, with a slight accent, which was more Scottish than that of the *Français d'Ambassadeur* and he had a particularly large vocabulary of idiom and argot, to which he constantly added by an assiduous reading of Simenon. But he was always essentially *le milord anglais* with his impeccably cut but slightly old-fashioned clothes and a splendid array of Ascot ties. He had an enormous fund of anecdotes – many, no doubt *ben trovato*: Bevin trying to persuade the Foreign Office members to pay more attention to economic matters, for example by getting to know Jouhaux (the leader of the French trade unions). For a long time they could not understand why the Sultan of Johore was being recommended to them as a source of economic wisdom. Another anecdote concerned Hall-Patch's arrival at the Foreign Office. He was taken to see the Permanent Under-Secretary by the latter's private secretary who went into the room first but left the door open, thus enabling Hall-Patch to hear: 'I suppose I shall have to call the blighter Edmund.'

My wife and I became very close friends of this able, erudite and very reserved man, a friendship that continued after we were all back in England and he had become Chairman of the Standard Bank (of South Africa as it then was). In Paris, the maintenance of the prestige, influence, indeed power, of Britain in European councils owed a very great deal to Hall-Patch who managed to combine all the outward appearance and manner of the Establishment with an essentially open and experimental mind. He had a love-hate relationship with France and the French, and often quoted to me, surprisingly for a Scot, with approval Philippe de Commynes's report of the English view of the French.

Jamais ne se mena traité entre les François et Anglois, que le sens de François et leur habileté ne se montrast par dessus celle des Anglois: et ont lesdits Anglois un mot commun, qu'autrefois m'ont dit, traitant avec eux: c'est que, aux batailles qu'ils ont eues avec les François, tousjours, ou le plus souvent, ont eu gain; mais en tous traités qu'ils ont eu à conduire avec eux, ils y ont eu perte et dommage.

It is interesting that this view of the superior skill of the French in negotiation, so widely held by the English, was already common in the fifteenth century. My own experience in governmental as well as in business affairs does not bear it out. Many Frenchmen are, indeed, superb negotiators; the training in the *grandes écoles*, the Ecole Nationale d'Administration and the subsequent experience in the *corps d'élite* fitting them splendidly as analysts and rhetoricians for negotiation. But the almost magic quality that so many Englishmen attribute to them is not justified. Two of the most persuasive Frenchmen in their different ways I have ever come across, Jean Monnet and Robert Marjolin, were not particularly skilled negotiators in the ordinary sense of the word. At any rate, in my own experience with them, I have met at least as many Frenchmen as any other nationality with whom it was possible despite a tough negotiation to reach an amicable and mutually satisfactory result. When I was recently made an Officer of the Légion d'Honneur, the French Ambassador, M. de Margerie, added to my pleasure by referring to these experiences in the past negotiations.

One consideration that made the move to Paris particularly

attractive was the number of people I now knew well, who had by this time assembled in Paris, or were soon to come there, either permanently or, as in the case particularly of some Americans, on a continually commuting basis: Robert Marjolin and his two deputies at the OEEC, Guido Colonna and Harry Lintott as well as many others on his staff; Erling Kristiansen (whom I had met in Washington during the war, with whom I later negotiated on Danish bacon imports into the UK and who subsequently was for many years his country's Ambassador in London) who came to head the Danish delegation; Arne Skaug (a former Rockefeller Fellowship colleague in the USA and later Ambassador in London) who headed the Norwegian delegation; and Dag Hammerskjöld who for a time headed the Swedish.

There were many others, particularly in my own Programmes Committee, who were destined to play important parts later in their own countries, such as Alberto Capanna (later Chief Executive of the Italian state steel company Finsider), Guido Carli (for fifteen years Governor of the Bank of Italy), Otmar Emminger (who finished his public career as President of the Bundesbank) and Ernst van der Beugel (Deputy Foreign Minister of Holland and involved in numerous international organizations). In the French Administration there were from the Ministry of Finance, Guillaume Guindey, Pierre-Paul Schweitzer, Thierry de Clermont-Tonnerre; from the Plan, Etienne Hirsch (who had succeeded Marjolin as Monnet's deputy, but whom I had already met in 1946 when he was still known under his Resistance name of Capitaine Bernard) and Pierre Uri; and several from the Quai d'Orsay, including that remarkable polymath, Olivier Wormser, then the number two on the economic side, with whom I was to have many further encounters, particularly during the Brussels negotiations in 1961–3. Among the Americans, apart from Harriman himself, there was his deputy, later his successor, Milton Katz, who had been the American Joint Secretary of the Combined Production and Resources Board during the war, a distinguished Harvard law professor, and Lincoln Gordon, an eminent economist, also of the wartime Board, who had been responsible for the Controlled Materials Plan, a major factor in breaking the impasse that the original system of priorities had created. And there were the many American visitors, not only officials like Dick Bissell, but also unofficial ones like George Ball with whom I had worked when he was Assistant General Counsel of the Lend-Lease Administration, then 'just' a lawyer, but through his past connections in Washington, but above all through his long-standing close friendship with Jean Monnet, a most important source of information and inspiration.

The phase of European co-operation that opened as I came to live in Paris (though continuing to commute almost as much from Paris to London as I had done the other way) was, at least until the second division of aid, a very different one from that which had lasted during the first nine months of the OEEC's existence. Not that the preoccupation with the dollar problem had disappeared – indeed it was to assert itself before long as powerfully as before. Other problems, however, came to occupy the centre of the stage once the almost intolerable financial, economic and political pressure of the 1947–8 period had abated. Foremost among them, though perhaps not everywhere and immediately so perceived, was a powerful new impetus towards closer European economic co-operation. The pressure had several sources, of which the idea of integration – never even slightly relaxed by Jean Monnet and by some Americans – was not the only one, though it was soon to become the most important. One regional piece of integration was already in existence, Benelux, and a number of people, including some Americans, particularly Bill Tomlinson (of whom more later), were beginning to toy with the idea of associating France and Italy with the economic union of the Low Countries. A customs union agreement was signed in March 1949 between France and Italy, the *soeurs latines*, and attempts were made to create a wider union with the rather comic title of 'Fritalux', but nothing came of these. Nevertheless, they showed that the idea of wider and deeper economic co-operation in Europe was gaining ground, a fact that was noted in London, though it is certain that its full significance was not then appreciated.

The tendency received great support from the Americans who from the very beginning of the Marshall Plan had been hoping to use the powerful lever of dollar aid to encourage closer economic co-operation in Europe. This was not merely due to a naïve belief in the virtue of creating a new United States of Europe in America's own image: it was inspired by the memory of two fratricidal wars, brought to an end only by America's intervention, as well as by the belief that the creation of a larger and freer market was the essential condition for ensuring Europe's lasting economic well-being. That a desire to remove obstacles such as quotas, tariffs and exchange restrictions for the benefit of America's trade was also present may be taken for granted.

America's pressure for the liberalization of trade was paralleled by most, if not all, the European countries, other than the United Kingdom. Pressure to abandon quotas came from many quarters and was by no means confined to the import of such luxuries, still anathema to austerity Britain, as Belgian grapes and azaleas. ('Toujours les azalées!' complained one British Minister to Paul-Henri Spaak.) This caused much heart-searching in London, where there was some readiness to make concessions for the sake of intra-European trade, but this was tempered by the fear that continued or indeed aggravated discrimination against the United States and the rest of the dollar area could not be sustained and was, in any event, less in the interest of a country with far wider trading links (a powerful doctrine even if it proved less than far-sighted). Moreover, it was already evident that pressure would not be confined to the removal of quantitative restrictions but would quickly extend to tariffs, a tendency that once again came up against the 'universalist' attitude of the British. On this point, however, a more effective defence was available, namely the existence of a special organization, the GATT, designed to negotiate disarmament in the matter of tariffs on a wider basis, i.e. principally including the Americans. Transferability, and eventually convertibility, of currencies was naturally the most extreme form of liberalization and here too American and at least some Continental (particularly Belgian) pressures tended to coincide.

Alfred Friendly, the well-known journalist (who was then in charge of public relations in the Harriman Mission) and his wife produced, for private consumption, a splendid record 'La Sterlina Dollarosa' (or 'Stop Pounding My Pound') in which each of the principal characters, Cripps, John Snyder (the American Secretary of the Treasury), the Belgian bankers, the French Minister without Portfolio and without Finances, etc., argued his case on convertibility, gold, imports of wine, the sterling area and so on to the tunes of popular songs.

Other problems also arose during the first few months of 1949. Manpower was one of these and was particularly strenuously pursued by the Italians with their grave and intractable (at least then) problem of the *Mezzogiorno*, the underdeveloped, poor South, which suffered from considerable unemployment. A multiplicity of other detailed issues came before the vertical committees, and although I was no longer involved with one of them, Food and Agriculture, I had, through the Programmes Committee, to keep myself closely informed of how the work of all of them was developing.

At this time much larger events began to impinge on the work of the OEEC. The year 1948 had been not only the first year of European co-operation, American–European joint peacetime economic planning, and European recovery; it had also been the year in which the rift between East and West had widened decisively. Germany, put on the path to its 'economic miracle' by the currency reform, was suddenly threatened by the Soviet blockade of Berlin. This, coming after the Czechoslovak coup of February 1948 and a number of other events, demonstrated the extent to which Europe was divided and convinced the leaders of Britain, France and, above all, the United States that their mutual defence needed to be strengthened. Thus, 1949 became, after much diplomatic activity and congressional debate, the year that saw the passing of the American Mutual Defence Assistance Act and the setting up of the North Atlantic Treaty Organization. Although the full impact of this development on the work of economic co-operation was still some way off, there was at once some shift of emphasis and attention, particularly in London where the economic consequences, in particular of enlarged requirements for defence, became quickly apparent. What it meant was that the dollar problem suddenly reappeared in as grave a form as ever. Already in the early part of the year the storm clouds had gathered and thoughts in Whitehall were beginning to turn to the problem of maintaining the exchange rate against a worsening balance of payments, which the impending increase in the defence programme, burdening particularly what were then called the metal-using industries, the very ones particularly needed to increase our exports, was going to make more precarious still.

As far as the machinery of the OEEC was concerned, the

organization had begun to work out its so-called long-term programme, which had to portray the achievement by 1952 of the accepted goal of European viability. It was also thinking of embarking on its second annual report, which would show the stage reached at the half-way mark of the four-year recovery programme. And it had also now to turn its thoughts to the division of the second year's aid, that for 1949–50, which it was clear from the beginning would be less than that made available for the preceding year. Of these, the division of aid inevitably engaged most of our energies and called for more debating and negotiating skill. Between May and August the Programmes Committee again went through the process of examining the programmes of the member countries, cross-examining their representatives, all in the knowledge that the Congressional appropriation would be at least 15 per cent less than in 1948. (It was in fact established at $3,776 million for actual programme expenditure against a comparable figure of nearly $4,500 million.)

This time, however, the Programmes Committee quickly arrived at the end of its own ability to reach agreement by negotiation. The Committee of Four procedure could not be applied again as it would have smacked too much of the 'big boys' once more being put in a privileged position as far as their own claims were concerned. The decision was, therefore, reached to adopt something more like an arbitration procedure, by entrusting the task of making a recommendation to the Chairman of the Council, Baron Snoy, the representative of Belgium (i.e. of a country that because of its strong reserve portion was not a recipient of dollar aid) and to the Secretary General, Robert Marjolin, universally accepted as objective and fair. By the end of August the two reported. The UK was allocated $962 million, in all the circumstances a favourable result. There was little difficulty in getting the recommendations accepted, and from that moment the division of Marshall Aid ceased to be the one overriding preoccupation of the OEEC.

So much has been written about the economic significance of the Marshall Plan that I do not need to add a great deal to what I have already said about its contribution to the creation of institutions (not only organizationally but through the development of practices and attitudes) that had a most important influence in strengthening the cohesion of the West. In economic terms its value cannot be exaggerated. There was a good deal of debate in the early stages about this. I remember myself taking part in one in the United States at Williams College when I had to argue against the thesis that the Plan was simply a device for getting rid of American surpluses and staving off depression in the United States. That elements of sheer commercial pushing and pulling were present – not only as between the United States and Europe, but also as between the European countries themselves – cannot be denied. But many of the products wanted for European reconstruction and recovery were equally needed in the United States for reconversion.

As Hall-Patch said in his valedictory despatch in July 1952, it contributed 'to the flow at a critical juncture of roughly £1,000 million of American money to a sore-pressed national exchequer'. There can be little doubt that without this great flow of dollars to finance the flow of goods, our own and European recovery generally would not only have been much delayed, but it must be doubtful whether the shock to European living standards and employment possibilities could have been borne without the gravest social and political consequences. Directly, as well as through the provision of the financial means, the Marshall Plan made a major contribution to the achievement of a more liberal trading pattern. The European Payments Union, apart from mobilizing further funds to finance recovery through the granting of drawing rights, including the release of a sizeable proportion of sterling balances, was the first means for loosening restrictions on financial flows, marking a real breakthrough in the transferability of currencies and thus a major step towards their ultimate convertibility.

7

NATO I

After 1949 some of the wider themes which I have already mentioned became increasingly important. Of these, the two that were to have a particularly strong impact on the Western economies and on their relations with one another were the movement for European integration and the setting up of NATO. I deal with these developments side by side not only because they happened at roughly the same time but also because both were to be of special significance in the evolution of British policy and in the relations of Britain both with the USA and also with her European partners. I propose to take first the early history of NATO as far as it affected the activities of the OEEC and my own part in them. The development of the general structure of NATO, including the command structure, the Military Committee and the Council of Ministers, is not directly germane to my theme, nor was I specially involved in these aspects. It was, however, clear from the very beginning of NATO that it was going to have important repercussions on Western economies and almost at once the question arose whether it was itself going to be concerned with these or whether all the already existing Western economic organizations were to be looked to for the continuing discussion of the economic effects of combined, and presumably enlarged, defence programmes.

For some specific purposes, certain NATO infrastructure programmes and combined military production and research activities, for example, no suitable multilateral organization was as yet in existence, and it was, therefore, accepted that these would have to be dealt with directly within NATO. As for the way to deal with the wider economic issues that were bound to arise opinion was sharply divided. Although it took a little while for the central economic issue – the impact of the defence programmes on European viability or in another, later, formulation the ability of the various NATO countries to bear the economic burden of defence programmes – to appear in its simplest and starkest form, it was clear from the very beginning of NATO that the recovery programmes would be profoundly affected.

For Britain, the organizational implications were clear. Having committed herself to a substantial defence programme, on any reckoning the largest after the United States, Britain was determined to regard NATO as the proper focal point for dealing with the wider economic implications. Even Gaitskell, first acting as Chancellor during Cripps's illness, later himself Chancellor, though fighting some defence expenditures, was basically in favour of the rearmament programme – much to the chagrin of one of his officials who told me at the time, 'A Chancellor has no business to be in favour of *any* expenditure programme.' It was thought in London that the British position – Britain still being far and away *primus inter pares* of the Europeans and cherishing the 'special relationship' with the United States – could be best maintained in NATO, and a series of economic policies commensurate with that position secured. So, from the beginning, the British were doing all they could to have the economic work of NATO developed even though, as the suspicious Europeans with support from some Americans argued, this would be at the expense of the OEEC.

The NATO civilian headquarters were at first in London (the 'Deputies' of the Foreign Ministers) and an Economic and Financial Committee was set up under the Deputies. Partly to quieten the European fears and to provide some link with the OEEC, I was made Chairman of that 'Committee of Twelve'. (I was at the time Chairman of the Economic Committee – the new guise of the Programmes Committee of the OEEC.) As the military establishment was near Paris, the Deputies were also soon transferred to Paris, the British delegation being headed, as Ambassador, by a distinguished diplomatist, Derrick Hoyer-Millar, with whom I had worked in Washington. I was made a Minister in the delegation and continued as Chairman of the Committee of Twelve, now also in Paris. At this point, the differences between Britain and her European partners about the respective roles of NATO and OEEC became particularly acute, the British being suspected of wanting to empty OEEC of all substance. These suspicions were strengthened when, after the American intervention in Korea, Clement Attlee went to Washington to discuss among many other matters the impact of the Korean War on commodity prices. Whether my presence among the large number of officials who accompanied the Prime Minister, designed to reassure the Europeans that the role of the OEEC would be duly safeguarded, actually had this effect, rather than the opposite, I am not sure. At any rate, the Washington discussions resulted in the setting up of the International Materials Conference (IMC); but this body was as short-lived as the rise in raw-material prices. However, the British attitude was not universally appreciated by the Americans either, and those among their officials who were particularly attached to the idea of European integration were specially critical. 'You will end up', said Dick Bissell (who from being a Professor of Economics at Yale had passed through a number of wartime governmental posts and was now deputy head of the Economic Co-operation Administration), speaking particularly of OEEC, 'by leaving the landscape littered with derelict international organizations.' (I think he felt that the British were particularly inclined to an 'off with the old love on with the new' attitude – even if the old love could not be removed from the scene altogether.)

Within the NATO organization other problems also appeared. On the transfer of the Economic and Financial Board of NATO (as it was named) to Paris, it was agreed that a Frenchman should take the chair. However, the nominee, a distinguished French economist, a member of the Institut and Inspecteur Général des Finances, Jacques Rueff, was not *persona grata* with Hugh Gaitskell. Rueff had in the twenties written an analysis of the relation between unemployment, wages and unemployment benefit (a sort of anticipation of the Philips Curve), which through Josiah Stamp had been published in articles in *The Times* and was regarded in certain Labour circles as extremely reactionary. I had, therefore, (on the strict personal instructions of the Chancellor) to oppose the election of Jacques Rueff (with whom, many years later, I became better acquainted and on friendly terms) – something that caused a good deal of friction between the French and British delegations as well as personal embarrassment to several of us on both sides. In the end, a compromise was reached, and Paul Leroy-Beaulieu, whom I had known in wartime Washington days and who later was Financial Minister at the London Embassy, was nominated and elected with strong British support.

However, our problems were not yet over. This was the time of French pressure for much closer integration of defence budgets within NATO. France was also pressing for the creation of a European Defence Community in the wake of the successful launching of the Schuman Plan for integrating the European coal and steel industries. The European Coal and Steel Community had been set up by the Treaty of Paris; at this point, therefore, the powerful impetus for European integration came to trouble existing relationships and organizational patterns on top of the uncertainty created by differences of view about the role of NATO in matters that were not directly military.

8

Europe II: Integration

I must go back here to describe briefly the earlier stages of the European movement. This is most appropriately linked with the name of Jean Monnet, even though future historians may take a somewhat different view of his role from that which so many of his contemporaries held and which appears in his own memoirs. I had met Monnet first in Washington in 1941 when he was a member of the British Supply Council (after starting with the Anglo-French Purchasing Mission) and had had some opportunity to experience the extraordinary force of his personality, to be aware of his almost legendary influence on the thinking of the Roosevelt Administration, particularly in the construction of the decisive 'Victory Programme', and, in my own more specific discussions with him and Christian Pineau (who later became French Food Minister) to see his powers of persuasion in action. Later, during the Marshall Plan, my contacts with him in the Commissariat au Plan, during the NATO 'burden-sharing' exercise, and then during the later stages of the long process that led to British entry into the European Community, I had also had ample occasion to see his magnetism at work. In my view, Monnet was not an intellectual. For example, I am not sure how well read he was or whether he read much at all, except current memoranda and the like. His great strength lay in his tenacious and single-minded pursuit of whatever objective he had before him at any particular time, his uncanny talent to focus on those most influential for his purposes – by no means always, or only, those best known and in the most obviously important positions – and his eagerness to seek ideas and suggestions, provided they were sympathetic to his main purpose, from many junior and often quite obscure people.

He was convinced of two things: first, that the experience of two world wars that had originated in Europe required ultimately federal institutions – France and Germany at the core, but Britain

also a member, and the whole supported by the United States – and
that this could best be advanced by the removal of economic
conflicts. This process was to begin with the major sectors of the
European economies. In the second place, while prepared to
support co-operative efforts on an intergovernmental basis as in the
Marshall Plan, i.e. without some partial fusion of sovereignty, his
experience in the old League of Nations had made him certain that
there were very narrow limits to what could be achieved by
'conferences in permanent session' serviced by a secretariat. From
this view flowed the concept of supra-national institutions, and he
believed that these could best be established on a sector by sector
basis; hence the Schuman Plan for putting together the coal and
steel industries of the member countries (with its semi-sovereign
High Authority); Euratom, to combine their atomic energy
industries, and the much more ambitious and abortive European
Defence Community, which was designed to create virtually
communal armed forces.

While this approach has not proved to be as productive as
Monnet thought – even the much more far-reaching economic
community became in the main a customs union with a common
agricultural policy – it had its interesting consequences. Siegmund
Warburg, who, from his position with Kuhn Loeb, the American
investment bank, did the first bond issue of the European Coal and
Steel Community in the New York market, told of the difficulty he
had in explaining the nature of this new animal to the institutional
investors in New York. He finally succeeded with a large insurance
company by comparing it to the New York Port Authority and
stressing its ability to impose levies and thus have an income of its
own.

Monnet, as I have already said, was particularly adept at
enlisting help from sources most likely to be effective. He had many
helpers, high and low, notably David Bruce, one of those
remarkable Americans (John J. McCloy is another) who are apt to
turn up whenever a particularly important and difficult task is at
hand. Much less known, though at least as important, was Bill
('Tommy') Tomlinson. Apart from Monnet's own memoirs and
some more esoteric studies of the period, his name will not be found
in the more widely read annals. A young man from Idaho, a
graduate of Brown University, a minor official in the US Treasury,

he had spent a year in London immediately after the war (not the most comfortable place then for a young man with a wife and baby) before coming to Paris as Treasury Representative at the Embassy. In the next six years, before his death in his early thirties, he played a vital part not only in fashioning American policy and transmitting it to the French (and other Europeans) but also in fashioning French policy in economic and financial matters domestic and international. The tribute to him paid by Monnet is only just adequate. Although by the criteria of British economic foreign policy – as then conceived – he was a thorn in our side, he was undoubtedly of the younger generation the most active and, I would say, most far-sighted influence on European and American-European policy at the time.

The British reaction to the launching of the Schuman Plan and its subsequent development has been exhaustively treated, not only in the memoirs of some of the politicians involved and by Monnet himself, but by many historians and commentators. While, being in Paris, I was not directly involved in the formation of Whitehall policy, I could through my frequent visits to London (where I was still regarded as a member of the Central Economic Planning Staff) as well as by what I learned in Paris, form a fairly clear idea of the considerations that went to form that policy. Curiously, my one direct involvement did not provide a great deal of illumination. After it had been decided in London that we would not actually participate in the attempt to create a coal and steel community, it was agreed with the French Government that Britain would appoint two 'observers' and that William Hayter, then Minister at the Paris Embassy, and I, as Minister with the OEEC delegation, would act in this capacity. However, our role was confined to daily meetings with Hervé Alphand, the head of the economic section of the Quai d'Orsay, at which he gave us an account of the previous day's negotiations among the 'Six'. This was noteworthy mainly because of the gift for comic, often sardonic, narration and the extraordinary talent for mimicry for which Alphand was famous. In so far as Whitehall needed to know how the attitudes of each of the six negotiating partners were evolving in order to formulate their own, there was a good deal more information to be got both in Paris and in the other capitals through the more normal channels.

While the policy of the French Government appeared to be totally committed to going ahead with the Schuman Plan and that of the British to be equally firmly opposed to participation, there were, in fact, some doubts on both sides. It is reasonably clear that, for example, Maurice Petsche, the French Finance Minister, was not committed to the idea, and I became almost by accident privy to his attempt to find a different solution on an Anglo-French basis. The British Government was at the time in some disarray because three of its principal members, Attlee, Bevin and Cripps were all, within more or less the same period, ill and absent from duty. Cripps's job was exercised by Hugh Gaitskell who, among other things, was very much involved in the final negotiations in Paris for setting up the European Payments Union.

I was only marginally concerned as this was very much a matter for the Overseas Finance Division of the Treasury and the Treasury member of our delegation. However, at one stage, almost the last, some difficult problems arose and Gaitskell did not want to take a decision without consulting Cripps, who was at the time convalescing in Briançon, in a house lent to him by Petsche. Having been asked to see Cripps at once, I travelled overnight by train from Paris and arrived very early in the morning at Briançon where, to my surprise, Cripps met me at the station. We breakfasted together in the garden and very quickly settled the point at issue. As I had to wait to get back by the evening train, I spent the rest of the day with Cripps and his family walking in the beautiful countryside and I still have a walking stick with which he presented me at the time.

Contrary to the image so often depicted, Cripps was not a cold, monklike figure. Though he had been a lover of the good life in his youth, it is true he had become a vegetarian and total abstainer by the time I knew him. He was nevertheless a very warm character with a very wide range of interests and was always ready to show great kindness. It is not without significance that his favourite poet – a volume always on his bedside table – was Robert Browning.

Cripps told me about his plans for returning to England, which involved a few hours' stay at the Embassy in Paris, and he asked me to arrange for him to call on Petsche on that day, ostensibly to thank him for the loan of the house. When the day came I went with Cripps to call on Petsche. Both Jean Fillippi (Petsche's

Directeur de Cabinet) and I were asked to wait while the two
Ministers had a private conversation. When we were called in we
were told that they had agreed to try and explore the possibility of
joint production programmes in specific industries, civil and
military; that this was to be an alternative to the Coal and Steel
Community; that it was to be kept out of the 'machine', and that
Fillippi and I were to be the exclusive channel of communication
between the two Ministers. It is hard to say now what might have
been the result. I feared then that some incautious words of mine to
the Ambassador had caused him to alert the Foreign Office to this
escapade into foreign affairs by the Chancellor of the Exchequer
and had led to some evasive action, but in any case a number of
events, including Cripps's continuing and worsening illness, intervened to frustrate it. I suspect that the Foreign Office, though
opposed to our participation in the Schuman Plan, was very
anxious to avoid any suspicion that we, the British, were taking
sides in any dispute between different members of the French
Government, particularly Petsche and Schuman.

In my view at the time (and today), the British refusal to join was
the result of a complicated amalgam of a number of factors.
Scepticism about the success of the enterprise itself played an
important part; so did uncertainty about the balance of direct
economic advantage from a national point of view. Fear of loss of
sovereignty was powerful in both the major parties – in the Labour
Party and the Government not so much perhaps in constitutional
terms as in the fear of losing the ability to 'plan', particularly in two
such basic industries as coal and steel. As in the case of the trade
liberalization moves within the OEEC, the hesitation was also
strengthened by a desire to preserve world-wide links and, in
particular, to maintain a special position *vis-à-vis* the United States,
despite the clear evidence of the existence of a very strong American
trend to encourage European integration with (and indeed in some
American minds only with) the inclusion of Britain.

A deeper political fear was also present: the latent neutralism on
the Continent and the illusion, as it seemed in Whitehall eyes, that
an effective 'third force' could be created, a Europe with a virtually
even-handed attitude towards both the United States and the Soviet
Union. There was also the fear that despite the attitude of some
important Americans who favoured European Union, progress

towards that goal could well promote the revival of American isolationism, thus repeating the pattern of the American attitude to the League of Nations after the First World War. The American failure to ratify the International Trade Organisation was a powerful warning of a possible American withdrawal from the 'Consolidation of the West' that was the keystone of British foreign policy and that could not be achieved without the total co-operation of the United States. When to all this is added the fact that memory of the way victory had finally been achieved was still very fresh and with it a sense of wanting to preserve a certain distance from the Continent, the outcome is not surprising.

Probably the most expressive way in which this amalgam was rationalized into something that could pretend to be a coherent policy was in the famous doctrine of the three circles. I am not sure who was the author of the concept, or of the phrase, though I believe that it was Churchill who first enunciated it. It said that Great Britain stood, and had to continue to stand, at the intersection of three circles: the Commonwealth, Europe and the United States. As a description of the varying, and so often conflicting, interests that Britain had to take into account at that time this description was accurate enough. The trouble was that it became a statement of, and implicit belief in, the ability of Britain in the post-war world to go on balancing these interests successfully. Worse still, it often carried an implication of power to influence the designs, purposes and actions of each of these rings far beyond our real capacity to do so. We still had enormous material and, above all, moral and intellectual resources and enjoyed a status that perhaps reflected more the past than the present, but these moral resources were most potent when least paraded to the public gaze. This was particularly true of the 'special relationship' with the United States, something undoubtedly very real but tending to be eroded every time it was explicitly referred to or relied on publicly.

The difficulty of choosing between the different interests as they appeared from time to time when specific decisions had to be taken showed up in a certain paralysis of action, covered up by a prolonged search for an ideal solution, which in the nature of the situation it was impossible to find or at least to be confident about in advance. This was a particular instance of what I have found to be a general attitude the Whitehall system tends to promote, namely, the search for the perfect answer. Since this often leads to inaction or dangerously delayed action it is usually a recipe for running the greatest risks. At any rate, as I later discovered, it is not the attitude one can afford in business. It was particularly apparent in our relations with Europe and affected the whole course of our policy from the beginning of the Schuman Plan to our entry into the European Economic Community – and, indeed, beyond.

9

NATO II: Burden-Sharing

In the early fifties matters were further complicated (as I have already indicated) by the economic aspects of rearmament under NATO. Here again Monnet made a brief appearance apart from his support for the European Defence Community (EDC) or the European Army, as it was usually called. During the discussions on the NATO Economic and Financial Board, the French delegation consistently tried to insert references to the EDC proposal, which I, as the British delegate, had as consistently, on instructions from London, to oppose. We were saved from a continuation of the bickering when the French Parliament killed the EDC proposal. NATO also realized by the time of the Ottawa Council meeting in the autumn of 1951 that the proposed enlarged defence programmes were meeting with strong resistance in virtually all the member countries, other than the USA, because of their effects on the countries' economies.

That Nato Council meeting at which Morrison, Shinwell and Gaitskell represented Britain is, among other things, memorable to me because of the astonishment and resentment that all three Ministers could barely conceal when they received a telegram from the Prime Minister to say that he was calling an election. However, before the meeting ended, it had been agreed between Dean Acheson and his colleagues, René Mayer and his, as well as the British Ministers, that a special procedure should be adopted to deal with the question of the burden-sharing of the economic effect of rearmament, a concept that had been launched by Paul Nitze, then head of the State Department's Policy Planning Staff (and now still very active as the American negotiator in the Geneva negotiations on intermediate nuclear weapons).

This time, three 'wise men', Averell Harriman, Jean Monnet and Edwin Plowden, and three deputies, Lincoln Gordon, Etienne Hirsch and I, were to cross-examine countries and arrive at a programme to be recommended to NATO. As it would have been very difficult to persuade NATO to leave the matter entirely in the hands of representatives of the 'big three', a Temporary Council Committee on which all members were represented was set up, to which the smaller group was to report, and the NATO Council meeting scheduled for February 1952 in Lisbon was to take the final decisions. The seat of the work of the Group of Six was Paris and a small contingent of the OEEC secretariat (particularly Marjolin and Bryan Reddaway, then economic adviser to the OEEC) was brought in, together with a few military people, particularly Colonel (as he then was) Andrew Goodpaster (later Commander-in-Chief of NATO).

The burden-sharing exercise was one of the most fascinating experiences I had during my work in the public domain. Like the construction of the Requirements Programme for Marshall Aid, the subsequent division of that aid among the recipients (or that much earlier wartime Consumption Levels Enquiry of the Combined Food Board – in my experience the earliest diplomatic document that appeared in the guise of an economic analysis), it was a combination of respectable economic analysis, hard bargaining, and diplomacy, which had to take account of political realities, both international and domestic, and which it is virtually impossible to describe in the terms of a political-science textbook. We had barely three months, including the Christmas and New Year holidays, to complete the task. This involved night sessions, trips to our respective capitals for instructions, numerous telegrams and telephone calls, and all the usual paraphernalia of an operation of this kind. The solid foundation was the endeavour to find some valid factor or factors against which the ability of countries to sustain and enlarge their defence programmes could be assessed. National accounts analysis, with its Gross National Product (GNP) and related concepts were the basis, but this was far from straightforward. Not only was the theoretical framework incomplete, but the NATO countries, ranging from Portugal, Turkey and Greece on the one side, to the USA, UK and France on the other, had very different statistical resources.

Even when approximate quantitative comparisons could be made, the true significance of the figures from the point of view of their inward social and political significance – with the varying stresses and strains of this or that policy change that might be proposed – differed a great deal from one country to another. This was most vividly expressed by my colleague from the Treasury, Gerald van Loo, when we had finished our report and were arriving in Lisbon for the Council meeting (Portugal having, on any measure, been at or near the bottom of the 'ability to sustain' table). We had left London, where there were still many shortages and some rationing, in miserable February weather and were driving along the coast road to Estoril in beautiful sunshine with every sign of abundance of food, when he said, 'I wonder if these people need any GNP!'

After much labour and searching cross-examinations of individual Foreign, Defence and Finance Ministers, always delicate and sometimes stormy, we finally produced a report. Even though this was not, and could hardly be expected to be, precisely implemented by each country, it nevertheless gave a considerable impetus both to defence programmes and to the cohesion of NATO.

While we were in Lisbon, the new British Government, elected at the end of 1951, a Conservative one (first under Winston Churchill), which was to remain in office for over twelve years, was faced with mounting economic problems and with the old question of how to manage the domestic economy in the fact of severe balance of payments constraints with their constant threat to the exchange rate and/or the reserves. The effect of the 1949 devaluation had spent itself and once again the question was how much of the external strain to 'take on the reserves' and how much the exchange rate could be allowed to remain exposed or defended by other means. The debate came to a head, at least temporarily, with the so-called 'Robot' proposal, an ingenious name, not only expressive of what the plan was designed to achieve but combining parts of the names of its authors, Leslie Rowan and Otto Clarke, both of the Treasury, and George Bolton of the Bank of England. The plan, briefly, was for full convertibility of sterling for non-residents; a blocking of the sterling balances (the over-generous settlement of these at the end of the war and the premature convertibility of sterling due to American pressure in 1947 were surely two of the gravest errors of Britain's post-war economic policy), and a domestic monetary policy, i.e. in regard to interest rates fully responsive to fluctuations in the exchange rate, which was to be freely floating.

I was not involved in the discussions around this proposal nor is this the place to discuss what might have been. I mention it for two reasons, first because it illustrates the strong pressure the new Government and particularly the new Chancellor, Rab Butler, were under, which was inevitably reflected in the NATO discussions. The second reason is that on the periphery of the Lisbon meeting, given the presence of Ministers and important advisers, such as Edwin Plowden, there was much coming and going of mysterious emissaries from London and a good deal of the discussion that finally resulted in the abandonment of the plan took place in Lisbon.

The rest of 1952 and the early months of 1953, as far as I was concerned, were largely occupied with the completion of the OEEC's long-term report as well as with the discussion of a large number of more general, macro-economic problems with which the Economic Committee of the organization was increasingly concerned. In NATO, too, the study of a number of more general problems, particularly in connection with the planning and execution of infrastructure and joint research and production programmes, continued. There were also a number of very agreeable semi-social occasions such as those connected with exercise 'Mainbrace' in Norwegian waters. While the Ambassador dined on the American flagship and had to put up with the dry tradition of the US Navy, as the 'number two', I had the pleasure of a sumptuous dinner on the aircraft-carrier *Eagle*.

On the whole, however, the period was, if not an anticlimax, certainly one of relative calm after the exciting events of the previous two or three years. This, combined with the increasing importance of the development of Britain's economic problems – and also the approaching need of settling our children's educational future – made me ready and anxious to return to London. In the summer of 1953 this was finally agreed and I returned to my old department, the Ministry of Food, the 'Planners' having meanwhile been virtually absorbed within the Treasury and Edwin Plowden having left to run the UK Atomic Energy Authority.

10
Whitehall II

I have already commented on the factors, real and artificial, that had a debilitating effect on British external economic policy, particularly in relation to Europe, and a series of vacillations that persisted for some years afterwards. As I left Paris, I could not help reflecting on the change that had taken place in the five years or so since I had first become involved in the Marshall Plan. This change affected in a quite perceptible degree the role that we were able to play not only in policy-making itself, but also in the more specific questions of position and influence in the organizations to which we belonged. Whereas at the beginning the leading role of Britain and, therefore, the almost automatic allocation of the most important positions to British officials (shared only by the French) was unquestioned, by the end of the period this was no longer so: a certain decline in automatically accorded authority was clearly visible. Today, for a British personality to be appointed to a major international post is rare and occurs only when exceptionally powerful reasons are present—for example, Lord Carrington as Secretary General of NATO—and is then regarded as a great feather in our cap.

It would be tempting to ascribe this to our undoubted weakened economic (to say nothing of military) strength. I doubt, however, whether this is a sufficient explanation. It is clearly not easy to make moral and intellectual authority take the place of the ability to send 'a gunboat up the Yangtze', or 'a cruiser to the River Plate',* or of settling many countries' domestic economic policies by actions in the City of London in terms of the exercise of that ill-defined and elusive concept of international power. But I do not think it is impossible, and where we had a clear idea of our

*This was written before the Falklands War, but I do not think my general argument is affected.

objective and of our strengths and weaknesses in regard to it, we were successful in maintaining and increasing our influence. And it is not altogether fanciful to suppose that had we had an earlier and clearer view both of the strength of the integrating tendencies within Europe, as well as of our own changed position in the world, we might have taken the leadership, which was indisputably ours in 1945–7, into the next phase of European history. It is an interesting sidelight on the situation as it existed at that time that almost immediately on coming again into power at the end of 1951, Churchill commissioned General Sir Ian Jacob to write a report on existing 'inter-Allied machinery' with some comparison with what existed during the war and how it had worked. That report may well now be available under the thirty-year rule. I am not aware that it had any significant impact on policy at the time.

My return to a normal Whitehall existence was not the easiest of transitions, quite apart from the domestic problems of finding a house, arranging for schools and all the other accompaniments of a return after nearly five years abroad combined with the sharp reduction in the living standard on relinquishing a foreign post. The pace in Whitehall was very different from that of what a colleague described as the 'proconsular' activities in Paris. Moreover, almost from the time I rejoined it, the Ministry of Food was one of the main departments in Whitehall to have a rather uncertain future. Rationing and allocation had disappeared or were on the way out, and so were the various domestic controls and 'sponsorships' of the food trades for which the department was responsible. Bulk contracts with foreign suppliers continued for some time – I was within two years to pay my first visit to Australia and New Zealand to renegotiate our meat contracts – but the improved supply situation in the world, the general desire of the Conservative Government to remove controls, and the greater attention now being paid to macro-economic management of the economy all contributed to changing the environment in which our work was carried on.

There were, nevertheless, many challenging practical problems of policy with a strong intellectual ingredient to make the work interesting. The most important and, to me, the most interesting part was that which related to the implementation of the guarantees to British farmers laid down in the remarkable Agriculture Act of

1947, one of the outstanding achievements of the first Labour Government. As far as the Ministry of Food was concerned, it had an important role to play even though the conduct of the negotiations with the farmers was in the hands of the Ministry of Agriculture. The Ministry of Food was the guardian of the consumer's interest and, in this connection, had to try to bring to bear on the negotiations the need to balance the farmer's return against both the price paid by the consumer and the interest of the Treasury in keeping the taxpayer's burden down. At the same time, we had to have regard to the need to keep the British market as open as possible in the interests of consumers, foreign suppliers, notably from the Commonwealth, and the food trades alike. This gave rise to many a tussle, curiously enough more with the Ministry of Agriculture than with the farmers themselves. Indeed, I often found myself working particularly closely with Jim Turner, the President of the National Farmers' Union.

I have often wondered why this should have been so. The Ministry of Agriculture had at that time perhaps not recovered from its somewhat more strictly defined and technical/regulatory role during the war. The new analytical and negotiating techniques that the implementation of the Agriculture Act required, and their close integration with the bulk-purchase and other import-regulating operations for which the Ministry of Food was still responsible may have suited the experience and personnel of the latter somewhat better. The problem became, however, an academic one when the two departments were combined, first in October 1954 by a 'personal union' with Derry Heathcoat Amory becoming Minister of both, and then by an actual fusion in April 1955 when the Ministry of Agriculture, Fisheries and Food was set up. There was much argument at the time about the wisdom of this change – apart from the hoped-for economies of staff. Some of my colleagues were convinced that the consumer would suffer by no longer having an independent Minister to argue his case in Cabinet – the taxpayer had, of course, the powerful Treasury to defend his interest – but I was not sure that the same Minister, having himself to reconcile the different interests, would not produce a better result.

In the two years that followed the amalgamation, I had more opportunity to learn the ways of Whitehall than I had had during the short period from my establishment to my involvement in the Marshall Plan or during the eighteen months or so in the old

Ministry of Food after my return from Paris. I had a number of commodity divisions to administer, particularly all those concerned with meat and fatstock, a task that included a considerable reduction both in wartime machinery and numbers employed. The replacement, or renegotiation, of our overseas purchase contracts, in some of which, such as Australian and New Zealand meat and Danish bacon, I was directly involved, was itself a major and highly interesting task and sufficiently close to what I had been doing before to give me a good deal of satisfaction. For example, a tour lasting several weeks of Australia and New Zealand and negotiations with 'Black Jack' McEwen, the Trade Minister, in the one and with Keith Holyoake, then Agriculture Minister, in the other were among my most valuable experiences. I was also able to get to know Denmark, its economy and many of its politicians, officials and business men well, including meeting again some of the old Paris hands. This is a relationship that I have been lucky enough not only to maintain but to strengthen over the years. I was very happy when in 1981 I was awarded a high Danish decoration.

On the domestic front, too, much new experimenting was going on. The desire to continue the 'bonfire of controls' started by the previous Government was reinforced by the Conservative Government's more ideological commitment to a reduction of the public sector. I remember, for example, some early and tentative attempts at privatization, including the British Sugar Corporation, but on the whole the pace was moderate. More significant was the attempt to adapt the agricultural guarantee system to the new, freer market conditions. The most ingenious device to this end was undoubtedly the system of deficiency payments. It made it possible to combine a guaranteed return to producers with a relatively (and increasingly) free import regime, and to provide an incentive to greater efficiency by making it possible for lower-cost producers to have a higher return. The system did not always work very well, for example, in the case of fatstock, and among many experiments to improve it we invented a system of 'rolling averages' for determining deficiency payments. This took several weeks to become satisfactorily run in, and during the initial, rather rough, days Heathcoat Amory took to referring to it as the 'rock-and-roll average'.

When in 1957 I was asked to negotiate a new World Sugar Agreement, I looked back on a unique experience in mixing government intervention to secure certain politically accepted economic and social goals with the working of normal economic incentives and market forces, and my strong conviction that this can very often be satisfactorily achieved dates in large measure from that time. Agriculture in Britain is an ever present reminder to the ideologues who, usually without any historical sense, extol the unrestricted supremacy of the 'free market', of what can be done by a realistic and pragmatic approach. Admittedly, it took decades of 'dog and stick' farming, an inter-war-years depression, two world wars, and the two Agriculture Acts of 1947 and 1957 to bring about not only a – usually and generally – prosperous agriculture but also a highly efficient one as well.

With the Sugar Agreement negotiations, which started in 1957, I returned once more to a form of activity of earlier days, this time in regard to a commodity that had already been the subject of an international agreement, but one which had ceased to function in the new circumstances. For nearly twelve months, during which I travelled extensively – everybody consumes sugar, and a lot of countries produce it in one way or another – I was occupied in sounding out interested parties and in preparing for a Sugar Conference which was held in Geneva in 1958 under the auspices of the United Nations and of which I was elected Chairman. Although I had had some contact with sugar matters, I had never been concerned directly with the sugar division of the Ministry of Food. I asked Sir William Rook, head of the leading sugar-trading firm, and sugar controller during the war, for advice, which he gave in his usual succinct manner. 'All you need to know is that the finest fertilizer for sugar is a high price. You have a high price this year and within a year or two you will have sugar running out of your ears.' A valuable lesson for many other commodities!

The highly complex problem of commodity stabilization, the use of quotas, price ranges, buffer stocks and so on, which we had to discuss, would make an interesting monograph. At least as interesting were the complexities of negotiation and, for me, the opportunity, first to visit about twenty-five different countries, particularly in South America and Asia, which I had not known before and including Japan, which I have since had the opportunity to get to know well. Later, in Geneva, I was able to add to my experience the negotiating techniques and skills of many different nationalities and in a new area of economic interest. The pieces of the kaleidoscope were only partly the same as those of earlier occasions. The USA, the UK, France, Western Germany reappeared. Their interests were, however, not quite the same as they had been before, nor were the constraints under which they acted. For example, the USA, as a very large producer as well as importer, had a very well-established sugar regime, which was designed to balance the domestic and foreign interests but, as so often in the United States, was very much subject to the vagaries of Congress and the influence on it of different lobbies. Beyond these, there were also broader political and economic foreign policy aspects, especially in Latin America and the Caribbean, to be taken into account. Britain too had both the domestic interests of the beet growers to protect as well as the Commonwealth Sugar Agreement to safeguard alongside the refining industry and important interests in refined-sugar and sugar-product exports. But there were also important new participants: the Soviet Union, Czechoslovakia, Cuba (on the eve of the Castro revolution), Brazil (endeavouring to make its entry on the world market), Indonesia (once one of the largest sugar exporters trying to keep a foothold on export quotas for possible future needs), and so on.

After much argument and negotiation (with the incipient European Community already throwing its shadow before), we hammered out the 1958 International Sugar Agreement and the new style International Sugar Council started its operations in London. I agreed to stay on for a year as its Executive Director to see the new Agreement working, but at the request of the members that period was extended to the end of 1959. During that time I continued to visit a number of member countries, particularly the USA, but also Cuba after the Castro revolution. The contrast of life in Havana after the revolution with what it had been before could not have been more striking although, at the time of my second visit, the Castro hurricane had not yet reached its full force. Perhaps the most striking impression left on me was not the brief encounter with Castro himself – in the penthouse of the Havana Hilton, renamed the Havana Libre, the corridors full of heavily armed *barbudos* – but the amazing speed with which many Ministers and officials of the new regime with whom I had to deal disappeared from the scene, to say nothing of the many pre-revolution sympathizers who had risked much under Batista when Castro was still in the sierra. This revolution ate its children as quickly as others have done!

For the first time I also visited briefly the Soviet Union and Czechoslovakia. I was well received and the brief visits to those countries did, I think, contribute to their becoming effective members of the Sugar Council.

The running of an independent international organization that, though formally composed of governmental representatives, had strong business links was a new and highly interesting experience, particularly in the recruitment and management of a multinational staff. I confess that I did not view with much pleasure the prospect of returning, at the beginning of 1960, to the Ministry and what I thought would be a rather subdued Civil Service life. My return was made easier by the Minister, John Hare, who was an extremely understanding and kind man. For example, knowing that my return to a 'straight' Whitehall job would require some adjustment, he took me with him on two occasions to the (abortive) Law of the Sea Conference in Geneva, although this was entirely the business as far as the Ministry was concerned of the Fisheries Secretary.

11

'Joining' Europe:
The Brussels Negotiations

The problem of adapting myself to the new environment did not last long. Within a few months, under a new Minister, Christopher Soames, I had to chair a working party to advise Ministers on the implications of the Common Agricultural Policy as it was then developing for our possible entry into the European Economic Community. The work of this group went on simultaneously with the study by the usual galaxy of Whitehall interdepartmental committees (on which I represented the Ministry) of the general problem of our future European economic policy and in particular of our relation with the European Economic Community.

At this point I must somewhat retrace the story of what had happened in respect of Europe and Britain's relations with her neighbours in the previous four or five years, including the two years in which I had been away from the centre. The first phase of the 'making of Europe' had ended in 1954. By that time, the intergovernmental links and actions through the OEEC had been taken as far as they could while, in the direction of 'supra-national' institutions, the Six (France, Germany, Italy, Holland, Belgium and Luxembourg) had established the Coal and Steel Community but had failed in what would have been the most crucial inroad into the citadel of national sovereignty, the creation of a European Defence Community. Instead of it, Western European Union (WEU), including Britain, was created, primarily as another means of coping with the problem of rearming Germany, but containing also a few, though I believe quite feeble, political attributes.

To some in London, politicians and officials alike, it seemed as if at least a temporary equilibrium in the relations between Britain and her Continental neighbours had been achieved and that an adequate working pattern between the organizations in which their interests were most likely to be subject to stress and tension was emerging. NATO and GATT, in the military and broad commercial policy spheres, provided those wider fora (including particularly the Americans and, in GATT, the Commonwealth) in which the British felt most comfortable and that they considered to be most appropriate for the resolution of the respective problems. The OEEC would continue to push forward the liberalization of European trade and, through the European Payments Union, currency transferability. It would continue to be concerned with macro-economic problems, fiscal and monetary, and soon also with aid to developing countries. As far as any further development exclusive to the Six was concerned, Britain was not unduly worried as it had established reasonable relations with the Coal and Steel Community, thanks largely to the choice of able and experienced representatives. And there was now WEU to satisfy some aspirations for closer co-operation in the foreign-policy field on a European basis.

While I was primarily involved in narrower problems of food and agricultural policy at the time, I was able, through interdepartmental committees and less formal contacts, to see the beginning of a spread of a certain feeling of complacency as far as European relations were concerned, which the increasing preoccupations with our own economic problems did nothing to counter. Indeed, since these preoccupations and their possible solutions, as can be seen from the abortive 'Robot' plan, were inevitably formulated in terms far broader than Europe, they tended to reinforce a certain indifference to any possible changes in the existing pattern of European-British relations.

This phase did not, however, last long. Anyone who thought that it would gravely underestimated a number of powerful factors. First, there was the underlying urge towards unification, which, however difficult to define precisely, was very real, particularly in the Low Countries and in Germany. In the second place, in so far as the leaders of the Continental countries had their own economic worries they far more readily, almost instinctively, thought of solutions, or at least ameliorations, on a European basis. Thirdly, they had already made an important start towards European union, important not only because it related to two basic industries, coal and steel, but also because the structure of the institutions set up to deal with them contained important supra-national elements and foreshadowed to some extent the pattern of the future European

Economic Community. Finally, there was Jean Monnet and his tenacious pressure for further progress in integration. He had become the first President of the High Authority of the Coal and Steel Community, but within a short time, towards the end of 1954, he decided to resume his freedom of propaganda and action. Early in 1955 he resigned, though he did not leave his Luxembourg post until five months later.

In June 1955, the famous 'relaunching of Europe' formally took place. The Six had called a conference at Messina to which the British were invited but in which they refused to participate. Then the Six set up a negotiating team to develop plans for the integration of their economies and for the joint development of nuclear energy. The group met in Brussels and the British decided to send a representative, Russell Bretherton of the Board of Trade, but with instructions that made it inevitable that any hope the Six might have had that Britain would participate would quickly disappear. In fact, already in November 1955 the British representative withdrew. By March 1957, in retrospect a remarkably short time for such a large undertaking, treaties for the EEC and Euratom had been worked out and signed, and by January 1958 the new institutions came into operation.

By this time, I had become occupied with sugar matters, but I had been in Whitehall nearly up to that time and through the period summer 1955 to autumn 1957 I was again involved in respect of food and agriculture (still a most powerful element in the consideration of our international and European economic policy) in European matters. Thus I witnessed the gradual—too gradual—realization in London of the significance of what was happening on the Continent. Once again our reaction was slow, once again we failed to make a realistic enough assessment of our strengths and weaknesses and of our true economic interest, dynamically conceived. It was undoubtedly very late for us to have assumed a leading role, but perhaps not too late. But, for all the reasons that operated six years earlier when the Schuman Plan was launched, we again failed to act quickly enough. Moreover, when the Brussels negotiations that led to the Treaty of Rome were in full swing, we were faced with the Suez crisis, and the adoption by Ministers of a major new attitude towards Europe had become an almost physical impossibility. But the sequelae of the Suez crisis undoubtedly helped to generate a new process of thinking and, eventually, action for some Ministers.

We have some accounts of the evolution of British thinking on how to adapt to the emergence of a customs union (as the European Economic Community was then still spoken of) on the Continent from British Ministers, notably Harold Macmillan and Rab Butler, as well as from some of the less senior Ministers who were directly and heavily involved, particularly Reginald Maudling who was in charge of the Free Trade Area negotiations. But most of the senior officials, such as Frank Lee and Otto Clarke, died without leaving a usable record behind.

The official papers, particularly the Report and the relevant documents on the European Free Trade Area negotiations presented to Parliament in January 1959, bear witness to the enormous and highly skilled analytical and diplomatic work that was accomplished by Maudling and the Whitehall team (of which I was a part for only the earlier period). Rereading them now, particularly Macmillan's memoirs, brings home to me even more forcibly than I felt at the time a sense of frustration at witnessing an unrealistic search for the best of all possible worlds. I suspect that the pleasure and relief I felt when I was asked to do the sugar job must have had something to do with this sense of frustration at the laborious operations in which we were engaged and which in my view never had much chance of success.

Still, the Whitehall machine worked with its usual well-oiled efficiency. Numerous plans were produced by the Economic Steering Committee and its sub-committees and a good part of the alphabet was used up in providing a nomenclature for them. What finally got united support was the so-called 'Plan G' of 29 September 1956 (reproduced in the fourth volume of Macmillan's memoirs), which became the British brief in the negotiations that had begun two months earlier. There is no point in attempting to set down, let alone analyse, the details of the zig-zagging negotiations that went on for more than two years, but it is, I believe, worth while to reproduce here a few sentences from the crucial paragraphs – 33 to 37 – of the White Paper of January 1959, 'Negotiations for a European Free Trade Area', that summed up the negotiations and were, in effect, the final statement on this failed effort. This also shows clearly what it was that the British plan was attempting to achieve and in what respects (including food and agriculture which are not explicitly referred to) an unbridgeable gap remained.

Two years ago Her Majesty's Government's concept of a free trade area related primarily to the removal of barriers to trade in industrial goods within Europe. The scope of the project was limited to what was needed to carry out this objective – the removal of tariffs and quantitative import restrictions, and the formulation of rules and procedures to prevent the frustration of the objective by other forms of Government intervention or by restrictive business practices.

In the rest of the economic field Her Majesty's Government recognized the great and continuing importance of extended co-operation, for political as much as economic reasons, but believed that this could be achieved best through the existing procedures of OEEC. More particularly in relation to foodstuffs, which they proposed should be excluded from the free trade area . . .

It proved to be the general wish of the participating countries that the scope of negotiations should cover the whole range of these subjects – so embracing most of the subject-matter of the Rome Treaty – and Her Majesty's Government gladly modified their original attitude to meet the views of their OEEC partners. In the case of agriculture Her Majesty's Government suggested that there should be a simultaneous but separate agreement to strengthen European co-operation and to expand trade in agricultural products . . .

Moreover, once the Treaty of Rome had been signed Her Majesty's Government recognized the importance of reducing to a minimum divergencies between its provisions and those of the free trade area. They therefore readily undertook to modify their original proposals to meet this situation . . .

The Secretariat summarized the fundamental matters on which agreement could not be reached under three heads: namely, external tariffs and external commercial policy; the harmonization and co-ordination of internal economic and social policies; and the institutional system.

We made what we could of the resulting situation. A European Free Trade Area Treaty between the 'Seven' who were not members of the Community (the UK, Sweden, Norway, Denmark, Switzerland, Austria, Ireland) was signed and an organization was set up in Geneva with a British Secretary General; and, as I have already said, the quasi-diplomatic mission sent to Brussels by us – other non-EEC members took a similar step, as did the Americans – was charged with maintaining relations with the Community.

This state of affairs lasted some two years. But when I came back to Whitehall at the beginning of 1960, I was struck by the fact that the whole subject of our relations with the Community – now well established and, as Monnet always forecast, therefore a more important club for the 'realistic' British to consider seriously – was being very actively discussed. The problems were no different: how to fit into the emerging Common Agricultural Policy both as regards the British farmer and our external, particularly Commonwealth, suppliers; the Community's commercial policy towards those outside; and the institutions with attributes that had the effect of restricting national sovereignty.

This time, however, the weight of every one of these problems seemed to be diminished by the gravity of our own economic and potentially foreign policy problems that would have to be faced if a solution on our own had to be contemplated. The burden of agricultural support on the Exchequer, that is the taxpayer, was getting heavier and a sharing of it by the consumer, through action directly affecting prices, seemed less unthinkable. Trading relations with the Commonwealth countries were loosening from both sides while the Community itself was moving in the direction of special trading arrangements with its own ex-colonial areas. The presence of Charles de Gaulle seemed to offer some reassurance, as indeed was proved quite clearly later, that for France at any rate abandonment of sovereignty was out of the question. The special relationship with the United States – though shortly to be given a fresh, almost personal, though not very lasting, impetus with the election of John F. Kennedy – was beginning to seem less effective in practical terms. Perhaps, above all, the problem of managing the British economy within the increasingly troublesome problems of the world economy, as so eloquently described in Mr Macmillan's memoirs, was getting less rather than more tractable, and the brief attempt to manage them on a tripartite basis (USA, UK, Canada) did not get anywhere – except that then, and for some years thereafter, the Treasury representation in Washington tended to be on a more senior level.

More general political considerations were also operating and were probably more decisive in the end than the 'nicely calculated less or more' of the economic equation. The Community showed every sign of becoming an important political fact, and even if federalism was, thanks to de Gaulle, not a serious possibility, the extraordinary personal alliance formed between de Gaulle and Konrad Adenauer, was enough to make many policy-makers in London fear a political isolation that Britain could not possibly tolerate. Fears of the development of a 'third force' had by no means completely died down and provided a powerful argument for those Americans who were pressing us to join the Community.

The process by which all these factors were operating on public opinion, on officials, on academic analysts and, above all, on politicians was complex, as can be seen from a reading of the many memoirs and monographs dealing with this period. However, in a surprisingly short time, within little more than a year, views had crystallized where it mattered: in the minds of the Prime Minister, Macmillan, and of an important number of his principal colleagues and backbench supporters. The last volume of Macmillan's memoirs gives a succinct account of his own growing conviction that membership of the Community was the best course for Britain to follow and of the way in which this conviction was translated into action. While it was to be more than ten years later that this goal was reached (and while this result may still be debatable and, indeed, of uncertain duration) the years 1960 to 1963 mark one of the most crucial phases in modern British history.

For me, personally, they were far more: they were perhaps the high point of my work in the public sector, at any rate in the international sphere. Although, with the exception of the period 1953 to 1957 when my life was most akin to that of the traditional Civil Servant, I had had numerous 'special' assignments, up to that point none could compare with the Brussels negotiations (the first of our attempts to become members of the European Community) in acute inherent difficulty, in the variety of the specific tasks it imposed, in the intermingling of political and technical considerations, and in the pressures to which I and my fellow negotiators were subjected.

Once again, in view of the importance of food and agriculture, both in its domestic policy and its international trading aspects, I was very quickly drawn into the centre of the Whitehall discussions. Throughout the early months of 1960 we were trying hard in the Ministry to keep track of the discussions that were going on in Brussels to agree the main principles of the Common Agricultural Policy. At the same time we were coping with our own problems of determining the appropriate level of agricultural support, dealing with our Commonwealth and foreign suppliers (for example, Danish bacon imports against the background of an attempt to improve the productivity and marketing of home produced bacon), retaining quotas on some foreign produce (e.g. from the USA) and, more generally, comparing our own support levels with those of other countries. On this last point we had to participate in a group, set up I think at our initiative, in Geneva with the improbable name of GOMAP – Group for the Measurement of Agricultural Protection!

In the spring, the Ministry, on the initiative of the Prime Minister, turned its attention to the emerging Common Agricultural Policy (CAP). It was decided that although this was not yet finally settled, it had become sufficiently clear in principle to enable us to form a view on what would be the consequences, at least as far as the CAP was concerned, if we were to join the Community. In the usual Whitehall tradition, a working party was set up. I was made Chairman. The speed with which it had to work, closely geared to the general Whitehall work on Europe, was given a considerable boost by the appearance, in July 1960, of Christopher Soames as Minister. He was not only by temperament a 'doer' but also one of the earliest convinced 'Europeans'. Behind his ebullient manner, I soon discovered a quick mind, a shrewd sense of men and affairs and a readiness to add to his already considerable experience at the heart of government – particularly after Churchill's stroke – new experiences, new influences and advice from new quarters. He, as several others, would have liked to have been put in charge of the negotiations, which were to begin the following year. It is idle to speculate how his approach, often likened – perhaps exaggeratedly – to a cavalry charge, would have worked out. In any event, the Prime Minister decided otherwise, *inter alia* no doubt because of the importance of not making a change at the crucially important Ministry of Agriculture, where Soames had already begun to gain the confidence of the farmers and the food trades. Given the complexity of the looming negotiations it was probably in any event thought wise to create a ministerial group in which the broad political aspect was paramount, leaving agriculture, food, finance, trade and the Commonwealth interests to make their sectional contributions to a well-coordinated team.

But before the team, ministerial and official, could be constituted and all the other organizational details settled, major decisions of principle had to be prepared and taken. This process occupied at least a year: from the spring of 1960 to the summer of 1961 when the application to negotiate to join the Common Market under Article 237 of the Treaty of Rome (which provided for new accessions) was formally presented.

Before the very elaborate official and ministerial considerations of the issues posed by the apparently rapid development of the Community (despite the reappearance of General de Gaulle with his well-known dislike of it) began in earnest, I had an almost fortuitous opportunity to get a glimpse of the new American Administration. In the early months of 1961 the Ministry's decision to foster domestic beef production by importing Charollais cattle from France (a decision taken against a certain opposition inside the department) came up against American veterinary regulations that might have had an adverse effect on our important exports of pedigree cattle to the United States. I was despatched to negotiate an agreement with the new Secretary of Agriculture – which proved to be less difficult than we had thought. But, in the process, I was able to meet a number of members of the Administration, mainly at sub-Cabinet level, a good many of whom I had known in earlier days and in a variety of bilateral and multilateral encounters. These contacts proved extremely useful in the troublesome period before our negotiations and even more so during the negotiations themselves.

The mobilization of the various strands of interest and opinion in Whitehall departments took the well-tried form of committees and working parties, centralized in the Economic Steering Committee under Frank Lee, the Permanent Secretary of the Treasury, one of the most effective senior officials in the post-war period. He had had a great variety of experience, including the Colonial Office, the

Treasury, the Ministry of Food, the Board of Trade and, finally, as head of the Treasury, and his close association with Keynes in the Washington negotiations had added an invaluable international dimension to his practical mind. His greatest strength, I think, lay in his talent for focusing issues for Ministers and in his energy and tenacity in insisting on decisions being taken. These abilities, which are supposed to be the distinguishing characteristics of the best of the senior Civil Servants were, in his case, supplemented – somewhat unusually in the case of so political an issue – by a strong and readily expressed belief in what he considered to be the right solution of this particular problem: he was a firm supporter of the proposition that, for economic as well as political reasons, we should join the Community.

Under his guidance the vast array of problems – the pound, the balance of payments, commercial policy both within the Commonwealth and outside, the impact on the level of economic activity and on prices to consumers, on the farmers, on parliamentary processes and legal principles and practices, to name only a few – was gradually sorted out and comprehensive briefs prepared for Ministers. The report prepared by my Working Party on the Common Agricultural Policy, which I have already mentioned, constituted an important part of this brief, touching as it did on politically sensitive domestic and international issues. Moreover, it gave the opportunity for a comprehensive review of our agricultural and food policy of a kind that had not been attempted for many decades – as Macmillan pointed out at a decisive Chequers meeting (17 and 18 June 1961) at which these problems were discussed.

Although the report did not in any way underestimate the difficulties – I emphasized in my cover note to Ministers that it was 'impossible to square the circle' and please Commonwealth and other overseas suppliers, our own farmer, the consumer, the food trades and the Exchequer, all to the same extent – it concluded that most of them were manageable, particularly when considered against the alternatives open to us if we stayed out. However, great emphasis was placed on the need for speed if we were to seek to enter – given the fact that the CAP had not yet been set in concrete. I ended my note with 'If it were done, when 'tis done, 'twere well it were done quickly' – an injunction that even Rab Butler (later to preside over the ministerial committee that supervised the negotiations and who was regarded by his colleagues, and publicly, as the great guardian of British agriculture) accepted. As it turned out, for reasons which may have been insuperable, speed in the negotiations was exactly what could not be achieved.

Macmillan had urged me to discuss the agricultural problem with Rab Butler, as I seemed to have acquired a reputation for being a stout defender of our agricultural interests in international encounters. (Hans Schaffner, Swiss Trade Minister, later President of the Confederation, had dubbed me 'the Protector', and this may have got to Ministers' ears!) I had a number of long conversations with Butler and in one of them he showed particular understanding of the argument that ultimately the only true safeguard for British agriculture was a prosperous economy. He felt that this, on the whole, could most effectively be assured within rather than outside the Community. I ventured even to suggest to him that the prospect of a relatively more prosperous economy together with continued agricultural support – which with skilful and rapid negotiation need not become any less under the CAP than it was under our own arrangements – provided a 'belt and braces' assurance for the British farmers. This line of reasoning had, I think, some influence in making him, in the end, a supporter rather than an opponent of the Prime Minister's own policy towards the Community.

Similar analytical processes were applied to the other problems that prospective membership posed. Clear-cut answers were, however, not arrived at in most cases, nor could they be, particularly in the more complicated fields of international financial arrangements, exchange rates and so forth. Moreover, since many of the issues (like the CAP itself) had not yet been clearly resolved between the existing members of the Community, and since many of the problems worrying the British Government arose from the to-be-expected reaction of other, particularly Commonwealth, countries, as well as domestic sectional interests and opinions, it was impossible to provide final proof one way or the other in advance. The negotiations themselves were to be the test, and the initial question, therefore, was essentially whether the 'betting odds' were sufficient to favour the start of negotiations or not. In the event, as we shall see, the attitude that resulted from this way of approaching the problem had some very important – in the minds of a number of us in the negotiations totally damaging – consequences.

However, the year or more that passed between the revival of the issue of Community membership and the final decision to start negotiations was not spent only in study and discussion among British Ministers and officials of the substantive issues. A series of actions was taken from early 1960 onwards to test (and thereby prepare) public opinion, as well as to probe European attitudes and those of Commonwealth and other countries. As early as February 1960 the then Foreign Secretary, Selwyn Lloyd, in a public speech gave the first hints that the question was not closed, as had been generally supposed. Again, in May 1960 and on a number of other occasions, ministerial statements showed clearly that the Government was preoccupied with the European question. Some bilateral probing also took place, the most important, however, not until May and June 1961 when there were discussions between officials of the Foreign Office and the Quai d'Orsay.

It was not clear at the time, and it is impossible to say with certainty now, but it seems that these particular conversations, conducted on the French side by Olivier Wormser, the head of the economic department of the Ministry of Foreign Affairs, were not fully analysed and properly integrated into Whitehall thinking. Had they been, they would have provided a highly accurate forecast of the French attitude on the most important aspects of the negotiations that were to follow: the common tariff, the basic principle of the Common Agricultural Policy and the association of overseas territories. The 'probing' talks with Germany that had been held late in 1960 and had produced a much more forthcoming impression may possibly have influenced London to take the French attitude less seriously than it was meant to be.

Opportunity was also taken when it presented itself to have some informal and very preliminary talks with Commonwealth countries and with the USA, represented particularly by George Ball. But the essential work was domestic – in Whitehall, particularly after the Prime Minister had, in June 1960, drawn up a questionnaire that listed the most important questions on which the Government would need to be clear.

A major impetus was given in July 1960 by important Cabinet changes. To one of these, the appointment of Christopher Soames to the Ministry of Agriculture, I have already referred. Two other appointments were also of critical importance: Duncan Sandys to the Commonwealth Office and, above all, Edward Heath as Lord Privy Seal, with a seat in the Cabinet and charged, in the Foreign Office, with European affairs.

It has naturally been widely assumed that the appointment to these crucial ministerial posts of politicians known to be strongly in favour of our joining the Community was part of a deliberate strategy by Macmillan, perhaps even related to the 'Grand Design', a phrase used later to describe a total conception of Western foreign policy as espoused by President Kennedy and largely supported by Macmillan. That may well have been the case, although, since it took another twelve months to reach the vital decisions, there may be an element of hindsight in this view. What is certain is that after the Cabinet changes (and some changes in the official committee structure) the work of the governmental machine was directed more clearly towards determining the 'betting odds'. The Prime Minister himself was leaning towards taking a chance, and with the active work mainly in the hands of these young and equally favourably inclined ministers, supported in the critical departments – Treasury, Foreign, Commonwealth and Colonial Offices – by officials of similar views (and at least by some in the Ministry of Agriculture and the Board of Trade), the psychological element in arriving at favourable 'odds' was not lacking. It is not now of material significance – or even of interest – to identify those groups among Ministers, backbenchers and officials who were hostile or at least very hesitant. As far as their reasons for being so are concerned, many of them showed up, in one form or another, in the issues dealt with during the negotiations (and indeed continued to weigh throughout the next ten years).

By the spring of 1961, these preliminary and preparatory soundings and analyses had been taken about as far as they could without the Government being forced to declare itself publicly. Public opinion had, I think, long since sensed that something was afoot. Parliamentary opinion was lining up on two sides: for and against Europe. Commonwealth opinion was beginning to be restive about the absence of more specific discussion, which would have revealed the way the British Government was thinking. Within the Community, the Commission, Germany, the Low Countries (generally in favour of our entry) and the Italians (on balance also in favour but anxious to be sure, as were in the end also the

Germans, of French reactions) were beginning to be impatient at our slowness. Finally, the French were already beginning to use the argument – one of the continuing motifs of the subsequent negotiations – that the British were clearly 'not ready'.

More decisive moves had, therefore, to be taken, and from the spring to midsummer 1961 the 'pace' was 'quickening' as Macmillan recorded on 16 May. Already in February Heath had given the Council of Ministers of Western European Union an indication that Britain was willing to contemplate a fundamental change in its approach to the problem. On his first visit to the new American President, Kennedy, in April, Macmillan was also able to ascertain that the American Administration was very favourably disposed towards an attempt by us to negotiate entry into the Community and this was communicated to some heads of Commonwealth Governments with whom there had not been much chance of discussing the matter at the Commonwealth Prime Ministers' Conference in March. As far as the American attitude was concerned, it remained steadily favourable. It is therefore a little surprising that Macmillan, as indeed other Ministers and many officials, should have been critical of George Ball, the American Deputy Secretary of State. Macmillan thought him 'determined to thwart our policy in Europe and the Common Market negotiations'; in fact Ball was very much in favour of our joining and one can say – at least with hindsight – that he seems to have had a better appreciation of the negotiating position than we did ourselves. What may have caused the hostile attitude to George Ball's views was the fact that at the time, March 1961, there were still substantial traces in parts of Whitehall thinking of the attempt to find the best of all possible worlds – some combination (through an association between the European Free Trade Association (EFTA) and the EEC) of the advantages of a Common tariff within Europe with special trading relations outside. The attitude of the Americans was basically very simple: they were prepared to tolerate discrimination against themselves by a European Community of which we were part for the sake of strengthening Europe politically. They were not prepared to accept trade discrimination as an end in itself.

A series of ministerial meetings and Cabinets in May and June brought a number of decisions. At the end of May it was agreed to send messages to Commonwealth Governments proposing ministerial visits to discuss the European problem and this was announced to the House of Commons on 13 June. Later that month, after the briefs of the travelling Ministers had been approved by Cabinet, the visits took place. Duncan Sandys went to Australia, New Zealand and Canada; Edward Heath to Cyprus; Peter Thorneycroft to Asia; John Hare to Africa and Lord Perth to the West Indies. Each was accompanied by a number of officials. I was in Duncan Sandys's party. The EFTA countries were also formally consulted at a meeting at the end of June at which Heath informed the other members that Britain would initiate talks with the Community on her own, but at this meeting we were also forced to accept the condition that all the Seven would have to enter the Community at the same time. This was later to prove one of the constraints, which, however, was not vital.

Finally, after informing Commonwealth Governments and President Kennedy of what the Government had decided, the Prime Minister in the House of Commons on 31 July stated that Britain would be applying for membership of the EEC under Article 237 of the Treaty of Rome. A motion approving this course was debated on 2 and 3 August and passed. The letter asking for official negotiations was sent on 9 August, followed (or, in the case of Ireland, preceded) by a similar letter from Denmark and, many months later, Norway.

The preparations had taken us into August. A heavy autumn lay ahead, so a number of us kept to our plans and took our holidays as soon as we could. My family and I went to Menton together with the Marjolin family. While relaxation on the Riviera was the main objective, inevitably Robert Marjolin and I spent a certain amount of time on our walks and on the beach in speculating on the impending negotiations. He was fundamentally in favour of our accession, but having participated in the negotiations leading to the Treaty of Rome and being a Vice-President of the Commission, he was also strongly imbued with the *communautaire* spirit. As a result, I was left under no illusions about the limits to which concessions might be granted to ease our path, limits that were determined – in his mind and that of the Commission generally as it turned out – by what would or would not in their opinion seriously impair the foundations of the Community. Without in any way breaking any confidences, I was able to explain to the Whitehall machine what I thought would be involved. In the light of subsequent developments, I doubt whether this was as fully taken into account as it should have been except probably by Frank Lee — but the path from officials, however powerful, to ministerial decisions is long and sinuous!

When I returned from holiday early in September I was summoned by Norman Brook, Secretary of the Cabinet, who asked me to become deputy leader of the delegation at the official level. This meant that I was no longer to represent the Ministry of Agriculture alone, but Whitehall generally. Both the Minister, Christopher Soames, and the Permanent Secretary, John Winifrith, agreed to release me, and I accepted. The delegation was to be led at the ministerial level by Edward Heath and at the official level by Pierson (Bob) Dixon, our Ambassador in Paris. Harry Lintott came from the Commonwealth Relations Office, Bill Gorrell-Barnes from the Colonial Office, Roddy Barclay from the Foreign Office, Herbert Andrew from the Board of Trade and, at a slightly later stage, Freddie Bishop from the Ministry of Agriculture.

It has been suggested that there had been some difference of opinion, particularly between the Foreign Office and the Treasury, about the composition of the official delegation. I do not know whether this was so. What is more important is the suggestion that it was a mistake to make our Ambassador in Paris the official head. One of the arguments in favour of the appointment had been that he was both highly esteemed and liked by de Gaulle, and this was certainly true. The point has, however, been made that precisely for this reason he should have been kept away from the technical details of the day-to-day Brussels wrangle, so that when it came to keeping in touch with the General on matters of high policy he should not be tainted with the inevitable haggling over details. This view was also held by a number in the delegation. It had of course, nothing to do with the abilities or personality of Bob Dixon himself, one of the most senior, experienced, erudite and skilled diplomatists imaginable. In retrospect, I think there is weight in the criticism of his being compelled to play a dual role (a view also expressed by Rab Butler in his preface to Piers Dixon's charming biography of his father) for, though he did not appear in Brussels continuously, he obviously had, from time to time, to make strong statements of our position, which may well have caused some displeasure to the General. It is of course quite another question whether, if Dixon had not been involved in Brussels, it would have made any real difference to the General's final position, and this cannot be answered, particularly as views have been and will continue to be divided on the basic question of the General's real intentions.

I have mentioned this matter as it was a not insignificant organizational problem, the kind that Whitehall is usually rather good at resolving unless some strong departmental *amour propre* gets in the way. I must repeat that personal relations between Bob Dixon and me could not have been better. Often when he came to Brussels we used to dine quietly (and modestly!) together, and during the tedium of some of the negotiating meetings we amused ourselves by passing notes to each other. One such is mentioned in Piers Dixon's biography of his father.* I remember another occasion when we had been speculating whether 'Europe' would ever really be born, and had then witnessed a deplorable exhibition by the Six of a complete absence of the Community spirit. He was greatly pleased with my note quoting Virgil's 'Tantae molis erat Romanam condere gentem.'

The most important appointment, however, was the expected one of Edward Heath as Minister in charge of the negotiating delegation, the full composition of which was announced on 12 September 1961. So much has been written about him, both at the time and since, that it would be otiose to say a great deal here. As far as the year and a half of the Brussels operation were concerned, Heath proved to be an outstanding leader. He combined in a unique way the qualities of a first-rate official having complete mastery of complex technical details with the necessary political touch in his contacts with Ministers and officials of other countries (within and outside the Six), with the press, and with London. He was the sort of Minister British senior Civil Servants particularly admire and like to work with, always ready to listen to advice yet quite clear in the end as to what ought to be said and done – a combination that showed up to particular advantage when it came to the drafting of the many statements and speeches addressed to

*Double Diploma: A Life of Sir Pierson Dixon, Don and Diplomat, London, Hutchinson, 1968, p. 289.

different audiences and on different occasions. There is no doubt that he (and with him the rest of us) were highly respected by our negotiating partners despite many sharp and sometimes even disagreeable passages. Heath was equally good in small encounters, often over lunch or dinner, with one or two of the other delegations as he was in larger, more formal meetings, including the plenary ones.

A particularly notable feature of the negotiations and of his achievement in them was the relations established with the press, both British and foreign, which was very heavily represented in Brussels throughout the period. It was quite clear from the beginning that anything like a confidential, let alone secret, atmosphere was out of the question. A number of factors was responsible. First of all, the Community itself had from the outset operated in a considerable glare of publicity. The novelty of the institution and its actions, the often still highly disparate objectives of the members, the complexity of the constituent parts of the Community, particularly a sort of contrapuntal relationship between Commission, Council of Ministers and Council of Permanent Representatives, later also the European Parliament, made it inevitable that the press would have ample opportunity for gathering news and gossip. Indeed, the press became a very useful instrument to be employed by different interests for their own purposes.

Naturally, the press had a field day. Great interest had been aroused and it was widely realized that the possibility of the Community being enlarged would raise all sorts of conflicting interests not only between all the countries directly involved (many more than the Six and the new candidates) but also within each country. Brussels was swarming with correspondents, general and specialist, regular and visiting, including some of the most distinguished names among the international corps of reporting and commenting newspapermen and -women. In this situation, and given the variety and complexity of the audiences to whom we were addressing ourselves, establishing and maintaining the right sort of relations with those who were distributing information became a matter of the utmost importance.

Fortunately, we were able under Heath's guidance to do just that, and the regular evening gatherings of a group of us in the basement bar of the Metropole Hotel became an important feature of our activities. These meetings, incidentally, should have proved to anyone present that the widely supposed coldness and unapproachability of Heath was and is a complete myth. He is, to be sure, a very reserved man, but he is entirely capable of the warmest and friendliest feelings and of great personal kindnesses. He is also quite capable of losing his temper, though in my experience this was more likely to happen with his own ministerial colleagues than with officials. After one particularly stormy midnight session with one of them, I tried to argue with him that he would more effectively carry out his task as 'conductor' of the orchestra by allowing some of his colleagues an occasional 'solo'. He listened patiently enough, but it made little difference in practice. As far as the delegation itself was concerned, any internal differences of opinion that appeared as the negotiations progressed was due to the difficulty of the situation itself and to the problem of keeping closely in step with Ministers in London but in no way to clashes with the leader who won his team's complete respect and affection.

I will have more to say about the manner in which our performance might be assessed, but first I will say a few words about the organization of the delegation and its work and then give a brief summary of the negotiations themselves.

Macmillan and other commentators and historians have spoken very kindly of the quality of the delegation – 'Never before in our history had we mustered so powerful and intelligent a number of men to serve so great an enterprise' – and the collection of 'flying knights', as they were soon called (a sample of the 'Rolls-Royce minds' to be found in Whitehall, as some extravagant journalists said), was certainly designed to impress our interlocutors with the seriousness of our intentions. Whether these encomiums were justified or not, Land-Rovers might have been a more apt description of what was needed to traverse the difficult terrain of Brussels (as I said at the time to my colleagues), and we all hoped that we would qualify in this capacity. The Rolls-Royce analogy seemed to me perhaps too reminiscent of the traditional relationship between Ministers and Civil Servants in their Whitehall habitat, and the practice of the delegation of reporting to London after each negotiating session certainly contributed to maintaining a sort of 'Whitehall exercise' illusion that was inappropriate in the circumstances. In this respect, the operation differed considerably from the practices adopted during the early days of the Marshall

Plan. In retrospect it was considered by the delegation as having
been disadvantageous.

Between the application in August and the constitution of the
delegation in September, and the beginning of negotiations a month
later, some further soundings took place: the most important of
these were first with Commonwealth countries at the Accra meeting
of Commonwealth Finance Ministers (September 1961), which
produced on the whole a negative reaction, indeed a hostile one
from Canada; and secondly the bilateral conversations on agriculture which were begun in April with M. Rochereau and continued
with his successor, M. Pisani, who was to continue in the office of
Minister of Agriculture during the negotiations. M. Pisani paid a
visit to Christopher Soames's home in the country where the
discussions that took place in this very relaxed atmosphere seemed
to indicate the possibility of a series of compromises between the
UK position and the incipient Common Agricultural Policy.
Conversations also took place with Dr Mansholt, the powerful
Dutch Commissioner for Agriculture. But even after the negotiations had started, we did not ask for, nor is it certain that we would
have been given, the right to participate in the working out of the
essential principles of the CAP.

Meanwhile the process of preparing the brief for the delegation
went forward speedily. The most important part was the opening
speech to be given by Heath at the first meeting, which had been
arranged to take place at the Quai d'Orsay in Paris on 10 October.
It was a difficult speech to write. It had been generally agreed that
not only had we to be forthcoming but that there had to be an
explicit acceptance of the basic provisions of the Treaty of Rome. It
was also considered essential to state at the outset the main points
of difficulty on which negotiations to accommodate the British
position were necessary. The speech committed us to eliminate
internal tariffs, accept a common customs tariff, a common
commercial policy and a common agricultural policy. We also
committed ourselves to accept and to play our full part in the
institutions established under Article 4 and other Articles of the
Treaty. As for the 'easements', 'derogations' or 'adaptations' that
we might require, they related primarily to trade with the
Commonwealth, including particularly in what came to be called
'temperate foodstuffs', and the reconciliation of our domestic

agricultural support arrangements with the Common Agricultural Policy.

It was accepted in Whitehall that we could not produce a credible statement of acceptance of the Community principles if we were at the same time to state a negotiating position in any detail. As it turned out, the statement leaned more in the direction of detail (the White Paper ran to nearly eighteen closely printed pages) than the subsequent course of the negotiations showed to have been wise. On the other hand, while it had not been intended to publish the full text of the speech – even Commonwealth Governments were shown only a summary – a series of leaks made it necessary to publish it in November 1961, and, while the details it contained were obviously of help *vis-à-vis* Commonwealth and domestic opinion, this conflict between these aims and the acceptance of Community principles was to dog us right through the negotiations.

I should perhaps recount here a conversation I had with Olivier Wormser in his office at the Quai after the end of this first meeting. He expressed general satisfaction with the speech, but was not slow to point out the difficulties that we would encounter in trying to secure concessions for our special problems – rather on the lines of his talks with the Foreign Office earlier in the year. This led me to ask him whether there was any point in going on with the negotiations, whether there was any prospect of the General agreeing to our becoming members. Wormser said that in a recent conversation with de Gaulle he had received the answer that there was no prior, insuperable obstacle to our joining. The answer was given after Wormser had told the General the story of two Eastern European Jewish families wishing to arrange, through an intermediary, the marriage of the son of the one with the daughter of the other. The son insisted that he could not make up his mind until he had seen the girl without any clothes on. It was finally arranged that he would be able to do so by looking through a keyhole. Having done so, the boy then said that he did not like the shape of the girl's nose. While I was slightly reassured by the General's reported reaction to this story, it made me uncomfortable to think how completely we might have to 'undress' during the negotiations! (The General is widely reported to have said on one occasion, 'Je la [Great Britain] veux nue' – charitably supposed to have related to our Commonwealth, and perhaps American connections.)

However, the difficulties, which showed up quickly, but which continued to be a serious hindrance to success, did not come from General de Gaulle directly, but from the manner in which the negotiation was organized. This was different from what we had hoped. We had been expecting to have a negotiation with six member countries individually represented, as would also be the Commission, with a permanent chairman – Paul-Henri Spaak, the prominent Belgian statesman, Foreign Minister, Prime Minister in turn, who had already crossed our paths in the Marshall Plan days, wanted to play this role and would have been our choice – and a proper secretariat. In fact, the chairmanship rotated; the secretariat, to which we supplied two members, was not an independent force that could be relied on, with the chairman, to push negotiations forward, to be constantly on the look-out for agreement and, generally, to act as a catalyst. Most important of all, the Six and the Commission concerted their position before each meeting with us. This not only put us in the position of *demandeur*, it tended to bring the Community's position each time down to the lowest common denominator of readiness to meet our problems. Any advantage we might have gained from the more favourable attitude of this or that member country on this or that of our problems was thus largely lost. The position in which we found ourselves could hardly be concealed from outside parties, British opinion and the Commonwealth in particular. Being regarded by hostile outside opinion as *demandeur* went so far that the meetings at official level, i.e. of deputies of Ministers (in French, *suppléants*), was often deliberately misunderstood in order to describe us as 'supplicants'!

I have dwelt on these organizational aspects because now, almost two decades later, they appear as significant – perhaps even more so – than the substantive issues for which they provided the stage setting. In the environment in which we found ourselves it became virtually impossible to conduct a negotiation between seven governments trying in common to find a solution that would permit British entry. Even if the conference had been organized to make this possible, much would have turned on the attitudes and personalities of the different Ministers and officials involved and much discussion and quasi-negotiation would have had to take place outside the meetings. As it was, there were really at least two negotiations going on. One was among the Six, first in regard to their own unfinished business of which the Common Agricultural Policy was the outstanding example, and second in regard to the attitude to be adopted towards us. The other negotiation, the one in which we took part, was meant to, and very often did, present us with a common front – each time a spokesman for the Six expounding the position they had reached.

Nevertheless, differences between them about their 'own' affairs and their position on our problems (almost always inextricably combined) could not be entirely concealed from us. On these occasions, while we naturally tried to benefit from the more favourable posture of this or that country (often Germany, or the Netherlands, or Belgium), we had to be extremely careful not to try to, or even appear to try to, exploit differences between the Six. This would have earned us immediate odium as being non-*communautaire* and would have supplied powerful ammunition, particularly to the French, and also to some elements in the Commission, who were always on the look-out for British unreadiness to play a proper role.

The meetings with the Six and the Commission were not the only occasions for negotiation in the widest sense. There were also contacts between individual members of delegations and smaller groups from among them, ministerial, official and mixed, involving also others, not part of delegations, who visited Brussels from time to time. I should perhaps record that one small specific benefit resulted from these informal encounters: a small dinner party at the Quai with Heath, Couve de Murville and Wormser at a time when certain British interests were trying to buy the Château Latour Vineyard. There was some – apparently nationalistic – opposition and I like to think that our pressure on that occasion helped to sway the official decision!

There were also frequent contacts in capitals, through normal diplomatic channels as well as through peripatetic Ministers and officials, including meetings at the highest levels, for example with Adenauer or with de Gaulle (notably between Macmillan and de Gaulle at Rambouillet in December 1961). The Commonwealth countries frequently sent missions to Brussels – in some instances to present their case to formal negotiating sessions between the Six and ourselves and sometimes, in a more formal way, to obtain first-hand news on the course of the negotiations and to try to bring influence to bear. The members of these missions were usually of senior status and outstanding ability – Alan Westerman from Australia, John Marshall from New Zealand, Jake Warren from Canada (with Sidney Pierce as the permanent representative) and a bevy of Americans. The Indians had a particularly able permanent representative, also Ambassador to Belgium, K. B. Lall, about whose important part in one respect I shall have something to say presently.

Those with whom we were more regularly in touch in the official negotiations were generally men of considerable authority in their own countries, whatever their position. The French were represented by their Foreign Minister, Couve de Murville (one of a number of Inspecteurs de Finance who had reached ministerial position) and by outstanding officials – Olivier Wormser, Jean Pierre Brunet, until recently head of the Compagnie Générale d'Electricité, from the Quai; Bernard Clappier (later Governor of the Banque de France) from the Inter-Ministerial Committee, and many others, particularly from the Commissariat au Plan and officials of the Ministry of Agriculture who supported M. Pisani. The Germans had the Foreign Minister, Dr Schroeder, and Professor Ehrhardt, Minister of Economics (later Chancellor), supported by his powerful State Secretary, Müller-Armack. The Italians had Emilio Colombo (who occupied a number of ministerial posts, including Foreign Affairs and the Treasury and was later to become Prime Minister) and the Agriculture Minister, Rumor, supported by outstanding diplomatists such as Attilio Cattani and Roberto Ducci (later to be Ambassador in London). Equally strong delegations were present from the Benelux countries, of whom Paul-Henri Spaak deserves special mention. From the Commission a number played major roles: Walter Hallstein (the President), Marjolin (a Vice-President) and a number of others, notably two Frenchmen, François-Xavier Ortoli (later head of the Commissariat au Plan, Finance Minister, and now Vice-President of the Commission) and Jean-François Deniau, who later embraced a political career.

I mention these names among a large number of others, partly to illustrate the quality and standing of those with whom we had to deal and partly to illustrate the enormously complicated criss-cross of channels of information, opinion and downright gossip, of which we had to keep track. After it was all over, one of the many doubts I had about the way the whole operation had been conducted was to wonder whether we did not fall too readily into a sort of quagmire of information leading to endless speculation as to how to interpret this or that titbit and what weight to attach to quite disparate sources (which included friendly sources from the media).

As I have said, attempts were made to keep in touch with authoritative sources at the highest levels. As far as de Gaulle was concerned, the information he conveyed varied, though in general his utterances were enigmatic, and with Adenauer, I believe, we never managed to establish the kind of relationship that would have been needed to counterbalance his deep attachment to the newborn alliance with France and with de Gaulle personally. Macmillan records both an account from Adenauer of his conversation with de Gaulle on the question of our entry in July 1962 and one from de Gaulle in December of the same year after his visit to Germany. The former was somewhat encouraging, but the latter was hardly so, since it spoke of Great Britain joining 'one day'. I believe that it was during this visit that the General, speaking in front of Cologne Cathedral, mentioned the three literary giants of European culture, Goethe, Dante, and Racine. I said to my French friends after the General's 'veto' that while I might forgive him for keeping us out of the Common Market, I could not forgive him the omission from his list of Shakespeare, especially in a speech in Germany, where, thanks to the great eighteenth-century translations, Shakespeare is virtually naturalized! Some of my French friends did not react very favourably, which led me, perhaps unwisely, to question the inclusion of Racine, but I am glad to say that the majority of them did agree with me.

I have already referred to the crucial role played by Edward Heath but before I go further I should emphasize the vital part in this enterprise of Harold Macmillan. There can be little doubt that whatever importance one attaches to circumstances or to the many individuals who were impelling policy in the direction of Europe, without Macmillan's leadership the decision would not have been taken. Without his continuing concern throughout the negotiations, these might well have run into the sands long before de Gaulle could apply the veto. I should also add that the skill, humour and grand humanistic style in which Macmillan handled these (as so many other) affairs made an extraordinary impression on those of us who were in contact with him. I remember for example his performance at the September 1962 Commonwealth Prime Ministers' Conference when early in his opening speech he made a digression (not recorded) on the nature of nationality and in particular on language as its essence. I am not sure how the assembled Prime Ministers reacted (one of them, near whom I sat, read the *Labour Monthly* most of the time) but it made a deep impression on me.

The negotiations, allowing for an interval after the 10 October speech and a fateful pause in the summer of 1962, took about one year, roughly divided as follows: November 1961 to March 1962; April to August 1962, and October 1962 to January 1963. Between the August adjournment and the resumption in October, the vital Commonwealth Prime Ministers' meeting took place between 10 and 19 September. It is, I think, unnecessary to deal in any detail either with the issues as originally defined or their treatment during the twelve months of negotiation. Nor is there any point in describing in chronological detail the ebb and flow of discussion and the progress or deterioration in our position. A few words may, however, be said about the principal points in dispute, the evaluation of our attitude and that of the Six in regard to them and the stage reached when the negotiations ended. The purpose is not so much to give a historical account, even if only summarily, but rather to indicate the problems, most of which remained to be tackled in the following ten years. More important, both as a historical account and perhaps as a general lesson, is it to indicate the relative position of the chief actors, particularly the UK and France, and to arrive at some conclusions about the good and bad points of our own performance.

The basic problem was to fit the United Kingdom's trading system into a new customs union, i.e. an arrangement by the Six that would develop rapidly into (a) a customs-free area for trade within the Community and (b) a common commercial policy (including tariffs or other trade restrictions) towards countries outside. This policy would, however, be subject to a series of derogations designed to take account of special relationships largely deriving from previous colonial associations, mainly with underdeveloped countries mainly in Africa. Recognizing that a regime of totally free trade within the Community could not be maintained without continuous progress towards a common policy in many other respects designed to ensure free competition, the Treaty of Rome (and regulations subsequently to be based on it) also provided for a whole series of measures concerned with the mobility of capital and labour, rights of establishment, and so forth. The final aim was to create a single economic unit – in the minds of many of its advocates, as a first, but major, step towards political federation.

At the time of the negotiations many of these objectives were only a distant dream, even though they served to intensify hesitation and sometimes to produce outright hostility since they seemed to hold out the prospect of a progressive abandonment of national sovereignty – something that was repulsive, both to the Right and the Left of the British political spectrum, though for different reasons. While this formed an important background of difficulty for the British Government, the negotiations themselves were concerned with the more mundane matters of free entry for manufactured goods from the developed Commonwealth countries, the treatment to be given to underdeveloped Commonwealth countries (many still colonies, or just ceasing to be at the time) and to the incipient industries of developing countries such as India.

A special problem was created by the particular trading arrangements with Canada, Australia and New Zealand in respect of foodstuffs where both the British consumer and the overseas producer had long-standing relationships based on developed market preferences on the part of consumers and food manufacturers (e.g. New Zealand cheese and lamb, Canadian hard wheat, Australian beef and dried fruits). Moreover, these were based on prices generally lower than those in the Common Market. The Commonwealth had been given assurances that we would seek to secure for them 'comparable outlets' under any new arrangements, and this became one of the crucial phrases throughout the negotiations.

This question was intimately linked with the other great issue, the support of British agriculture. The post-war British system, after the dismantling of centralized bulk buying at negotiated prices from British and overseas producers, was designed, for the principal foodstuffs at least, to maintain a market for the overseas supplier and to support the earnings and standard of living of the British farmer directly by subsidies from the Exchequer. As I have mentioned earlier, this system, based on the Agriculture Acts 1947 and 1957, was progressively refined and could justly be claimed to reconcile to a considerable degree the varied interests involved. However, it was a system peculiarly suited to a country with a small and declining rural population (even at that time little more than 3 per cent were engaged in agriculture), with an industrial economy historically strongly dependent on cheap food and with still highly important (though diminishing) Commonwealth trading links dependent on reciprocal markets.

The Continental system, traditionally and even more so under the CAP (which was much influenced by Dutch experience) consisted basically of managed markets within – which implied strictly regulated imports from without – while the principal burden of supporting a politically acceptable agricultural standard of living was borne by the consumer. Not only was this the traditional Continental system (the development of the beet-sugar industry under the Continental blockades in Napoleonic times being an outstanding example), but it was well suited to countries with substantial proportions of the population engaged in agriculture, many of whom, in difficult regions and suffering from backward techniques, were incapable of withstanding foreign competition.

To fit all this together was the core of our negotiations. Besides these issues, such questions as subscribing to the institutional patterns that the Treaty of Rome was creating or how to deal with our obligations to EFTA once our negotiations had been successful, though not easy were of a quite different order, requiring mainly diplomatic and political solutions. These were not absent from the trading and agriculture issues either, but the sheer complexity of finding practical economic and commercial devices that could offer a compromise between the two systems was the overwhelming problem. As far as domestic agriculture was concerned, probably the outstanding mainly political problem was that of the 'access' of the farmer to his own government. Under our own system, an annual review brought together the Ministry and the National Farmers' Union, and though the Government eventually laid down the terms for implementing the statutory guarantees for each ensuing year, the annual review had much of the character of a negotiation between two parties. Under the CAP the scope for direct representation to, and negotiation by, the farmers, with their 'own' ministry would naturally have been much restricted.

Intimately connected with the agricultural question was also that of financing the Community's budget. This was a highly complicated issue as it has remained to this day. It involved taking positions on the size of agricultural levies (dependent on the level at which prices were fixed and on the size of the imports from outside the Community), on the extent to which these levies were to be appropriated to the Community's budget, on the relations of those contributions by individual countries to any other criteria for sharing the cost of the Community (such as GNP) and on the level at which, and the purpose for which, members were to be entitled to draw on the Agricultural Support Fund, to which part of the levies was destined.

There were many subsidiary issues, but it can readily be seen what a bone of contention these financial regulations were to become, involving as they did powerful financial interests as well as matters deeply connected with agricultural support and trade policy as such. Moreover, they found different countries, notably France and Germany, on different sides and the British negotiators were often in the middle – as, for example, on the level at which cereal prices should be fixed. It would have been difficult enough in this situation for us to have made reasonable and reasonably rapid progress if our brief had been sufficiently flexible to allow our own recognition of what was and what was not negotiable at any moment to have been reflected quickly in our instructions. These, however, were inevitably framed within the constraints of various commitments, particularly to the Commonwealth. Even after the Prime Ministers' Conference of September 1962, which, thanks to a masterly performance by Harold Macmillan, was relatively successful, we in the delegation felt that we still had to fight on a vast range of specific items, many of them quite trivial.

Another constraint was British public opinion. In this connection I should mention that we had from time to time Parliamentarian visitors from both parties, which tested considerably our ability to speak in the manner proper for Civil Servants. On the whole, we found this more difficult with members of the Opposition, of whom we saw generally only those who were hostile to the Community though, on occasions, as when Fred Peart, later Minister of Agriculture, led a delegation to Brussels, we had very stimulating and balanced discussions. I remember, in particular, talks with Hugh Gaitskell whose attitude on the European question seemed to me quite out of character. We had been personal friends for about thirty-five years and I had always found him a man with the broadest international interest and sympathy. With his pre-war contacts with the Austrian Socialists, his unusually extensive knowledge of Continental, especially German, economic literature, and his devotion to NATO, he seemed to me to be a natural supporter of European integration and British participation in it. This was, however, one subject on which we exchanged very sharp words. I remember one such exchange, the last time I saw him before his death, on 1 December 1962, at a dinner at All Souls. Nothing I could say could budge him and, in seeking for reasons for his attitude apart from the obvious one of the Labour Party's fear of loss of power in national planning, I became convinced – and so told him – that he had been much influenced by K. B. Lall, the Indian Ambassador in Brussels. For a variety of reasons, including family traditions, India and Indian opinion played a specially strong part in Gaitskell's thinking.

While the main task of negotiating in Brussels, reporting in person in London, and keeping in touch with the press fell to the leader and his two principal aides, all the senior members of the delegation had their part to play with their particular opposite numbers, their home departments, and specialist correspondents. In this process we were all labouring under the same handicaps. We had a constant concern to say the right thing to two different audiences: in Brussels we had to be hard negotiators – always, however, being careful to demonstrate not only our reasonableness but also our sincere desire to become members – while, at home, never appearing to give way to unreasonable demands from this 'foreign club'. This dual presentation was the major frustrating factor to which we were subject. Nevertheless progress was made. Despite the long interval between August and October, once the negotiations were resumed a good many of the problems began to look capable of solution. Even on agriculture in the very final phase when a special mandate was given to a committee under Dr Sicco

Mansholt, too late as it turned out, a report was produced that could have led to agreement.

In the later part of December a spirit of great urgency seemed to animate all the delegations – to some extent even the French. On 15 and 16 December, however, when Macmillan visited de Gaulle at Rambouillet, he received a highly negative impression of the General's attitude, so much so that he records his conviction that if de Gaulle could, without incurring intolerable reactions from the other members, he would resist our entry. Macmillan's subsequent meeting with President Kennedy at Nassau, which led to an agreement on nuclear weapons, did not improve the atmosphere as far as de Gaulle was concerned. Some of us in the delegation began to have a kind of 'make-or-break' feeling as far as the next few weeks were concerned. On 11 January, Heath, Dixon and I had Couve and Wormser to lunch at the Embassy in Paris. It was known that on 14 January the General would have one of his famous press conferences and it was widely supposed that he would deal with the Brussels negotiations. Heath asked Couve directly whether the General would say anything at his press conference that might bring the Brussels negotiations to an end. Couve said that he did not expect this. He was further asked whether, even if we were able to solve the economic problems in Brussels, French political objections to our entry would still lead them to oppose our membership. To this Couve replied emphatically that if the economic problems could be solved nothing could prevent our entry.

Despite these assurances, the General did, in fact, speak on 14 January, 1963 in terms that made it quite clear to all the world that France was not prepared to agree to our becoming members of the Community. It is not necessary to describe here the reactions in Brussels by the different countries to which this gave rise, or the abortive attempts made during the next fortnight to keep some kind of negotiation going before the Conference had to recognize, on 29 January, that it had come to an end. I will record only that late on the evening of 14 January Wormser and I left the conference room in search of coffee and had a conversation in the corridor. I did not remonstrate, but expressed surprise at the General's statement, in view both of what Couve had said in Paris a few days earlier and in view of the more hopeful atmosphere that had become apparent in the negotiations. 'Indeed,' said Wormser, 'you don't know how close to success you were.' He would not be drawn further, except to add cryptically that he hoped we would not make the opposite mistake to that we had made in 1958 (when we had broken off the free trade area negotiations).

The question naturally arises whether the result was inevitable and, if not, how it could have been avoided. As far as the second half of the question is concerned, this involves a close look at our own conduct, and I have already indicated here and there some points that give rise to doubt. Perhaps I can do no better than to mention here some of my own comments, which I made in February 1963, to my colleagues on the delegation. I think even now, that these contain all that can usefully be said about that aspect:

I

We shall not get very far by looking at the actual course of the negotiations alone. There are two other areas: one major factor was the basic strategy adopted (consciously or unconsciously) for acquainting (a) Ministers collectively, (b) Parliament, (c) the country, with what was and what was not negotiable. I am not suggesting that those responsible, whether at the ministerial or official level, knew from the beginning exactly what this was. But as the negotiations progressed those of us in touch with them got a clearer idea of our limits of manoeuvre. What I am not certain about is whether our own 'education' was passed on at the right pace so as to affect in turn the negotiating limits imposed on us by Whitehall. The pace at which we took the various problems in the negotiations, the order in which we took them, the posture in which we consequently found ourselves *vis-à-vis* our negotiating partners, and the relation between that posture and the objectives which the Government proclaimed at home were all determined by this relation between what we knew to be possible and what Ministers as a whole, and the country, thought we were aiming at.

I would say that this factor may have had an influence on the speed of the negotiations and, therefore, on the point of time at which, and the circumstances in which, the climax was reached.

This brings me to the second major subject. It can be argued

1 With my brother in Vienna, 1916. (He is wearing the uniform of the Austrian Navy League)

2 With my mother, Czernowitz, 1933

3 With my father,
Czernowitz, 1936

4 Freda when I first
met her, October
1930

5 With Freda,
Czernowitz, 1936

6 Freda, Joanna
and Elizabeth,
Beaconsfield, 1948

7 Marshall Plan. Giovanni Malagodi, Roll,
Robert Marjolin, Sir Edmund Hall-Patch, 1949

8 Negotiations for United Kingdom entry into the EEC; with Edward Heath
and Sir Arthur Tandy (UK Ambassador to the EEC), Brussels, 1962

9 With Sir Alec Douglas-Home (Prime Minister) and Lord Harlech
(Ambassador) at the British Embassy, Washington DC, 1964

10   With George Brown (First Secretary of State)
and Herr Kurt Schmücker (Minister of Economic Affairs,
Federal Republic of Germany), 1965

11   With Lord Thomson and David Rockefeller, London, 1968

12 With Robert Macnamara (President of the World Bank),
Washington DC, 1972

13 The Court of the Bank of England, 1974

14 With Lord Carrington and
Edward Heath at a lunch at the
Royal Lancaster Hotel, London,
organized by Business
Perspectives, 1981

15 Eric Roll: photograph
by Philip Sayer

that the breakdown that occurred on 29 January was not so much a failure of our negotiations *per se*, but a failure of a major aspect of our foreign policy. In some way or other we should try to get a clear picture of what analysis was made (and what action taken upon that analysis) before and during the negotiations in regard to fundamental factors of foreign and defence policy which surrounded our economic negotiations. In this connection, it would be useful to know what advice was received from Paris throughout the negotiations on the general foreign policy objectives of the General and how these fitted in with the French position in our negotiations. An analysis of the discussion at home regarding the prospective French attitude before our application was made (and, of course, of the attitude in the other capitals), together with the advice received from the Embassies, should also be made. It seems to me vital for a real understanding of how the negotiations concluded that there should be a careful analysis of advice received from Paris and from Bonn about de Gaulle's trip to Germany, about the discussions relating to the Prime Minister's visit to Rambouillet and about the discussions of our policy regarding Skybolt, Polaris and the Nassau Agreement (above all, its timing) was settled.

All this may be going rather far afield, but these matters must be looked at.

II

As regards the negotiations themselves, there are some points, mainly on organization:

(1) Should we, and could we, have done more at the beginning to organize the negotiations in such a way as to ensure *continuous* discussion by officials in Brussels?

(2) Would we have done better to have got domestic agriculture hived off at an earlier stage? In other words, should we have had the Mansholt Committee in the early summer? There was some suggestion to this effect at that time.

(3) In general, would we have done better to have devolved more by creating more special groups?

This might (a) have speeded up work, thereby bringing the climax on much earlier, and perhaps with a better chance of avoiding the French veto, and (b) have spread the educational process to which we were subjected a little more widely in Whitehall.

(4)   Could we have got busy much earlier with real negotiation and was there any way in which this could have been done? I know that several of us felt that the first six months were terribly slow and that we were, in the end, not doing ourselves good by proceeding by means of elaborate formal statements. Was this inevitable?

(5)   Was the official side of the Delegation sufficiently tightly organized?

(6)   In this connection, was it wise to have organized ourselves in a way that created an at times quite perceptible gap in thinking between the relatively junior permanent Delegation, almost entirely composed of Foreign Office elements, and the (rather more senior and more widely drawn) 'commuting' part of the Delegation which, because of its commuting, was in closer touch with Whitehall thinking and with the political situation at home?

(7)   Is it possible that this situation was reflected in some divergencies in the way in which we spoke to our negotiating partners – and to the press? Stories have been told from time to time of differences of view inside the British Delegation.

(8)   Was this an inevitable price to pay for the size and set-up of the Delegation?

(9)   Were we wise to encourage as much as we did so much 'gossiping' with all and sundry and the consequential flood of records of conversations? Is it quite clear in retrospect that we gained more than we lost by this process (a) in acquiring information in exchange for giving information (and perhaps presenting at times a confused picture of our negotiating position) and (b) confusing our own minds by this multitude of 'information' instead of taking a clear and cold look at the situation undeterred by what Messrs X, Y and Z down the line in different delegations, whether from among our 'friends' or from others, thought at any moment?

I know that the British Delegation, from top to bottom, has earned golden opinions all round, but this seems to me to be an occasion, above all for self-criticism.

So much for what I thought at the time.

Whether a breakdown through a French veto (I do not believe that any other factor could have caused it) was inevitable from the beginning is impossible to state with certainty. Bob Dixon, after the event, thought it was, and certainly from late 1962 onwards, and particularly after the December Rambouillet visit, the number of those who had reached this conclusion grew considerably. I do not myself share this view. Of course, the General was always on a 'double option' either to let us join after we had agreed to conditions that were acceptable to him, or to exclude us even on grounds well known before it all began, such as that Britain 'was an island'! But I do believe that, assuming the Government was really determined to achieve membership, we could have reached our final negotiating position more quickly, thereby maintaining the momentum that the favourable attitude of five of the Six had created at the beginning and that got eroded over time as far as its practical usefulness to us was concerned. Moreover, the self-assurance that the General never lacked was considerably enhanced for practical purposes by his increasing closeness to Adenauer (culminating in the Franco-German pact signed on 20 January 1963) and by the very large majority that he received – somewhat unexpectedly – in the November 1962 elections. But I recognize that to say this is to indulge in speculation, and to emphasize the need for greater speed is to ask for a degree of political boldness even greater than the exceptional one actually deployed by the Prime Minister and his principal colleagues.

The 'European idea' survived the breakdown, but although there were further explorations looking towards membership, including one in which I was briefly involved in 1966 before I left the public service, it took another ten years before we became members. For myself, I continue to believe that the balance of advantage lies inside rather than outside the Community, even though I recognize that there is much ground for disappointment. Most of the criticism of the Community has some element of truth in it: the overgrown bureaucracy, difficult to manoeuvre and expensive to maintain, the continuing evidence of narrowly conceived national interests frustrating 'European' attitudes on many matters but, at the same time, a recurrent urge to uniformity of regulation or policy in areas where progress could safely be left to come more slowly and organically. Even though many of the problems that caused the prolonged and sometimes fierce battles twenty years ago seem to have melted away, some of our own special problems remain – the budget contributions or the effects of the Common Agricultural Policy, which is a general problem affecting the Community as a whole. Indeed, jobbing backwards, one may wonder whether, if Monnet was right to start with the 'sector' approach, the transition from coal and steel (and leaving the less significant Euratom on one side) to the full-scale attempt at economic union was not too abrupt, particularly since, given the political realities of an inevitable German-French 'deal', it came down in the end to a series of sector approaches with agriculture the most prominent, and most troublesome.

Some practical achievements are undoubted. I include in these the European Monetary System, which we should now seriously consider joining, whatever may have been the arguments against doing so in the beginning. Certainly, without going forward, the Community is in danger of a slow lingering death, and it will not go forward without a more active British participation. Some of my friends, including French ones, at one time deeply committed Europeans, looking at the last twenty-five years or so, are beginning to wonder whether de Gaulle, rather than Monnet, had the correct view of how progress on European unity could be achieved. They may have a point.

12

Economic Diplomacy: Washington 1963–5

The end of the Brussels negotiations inevitably caused a pause in the determination of the Government's foreign economic policy. On a more mundane level, the elaborate apparatus that had been in place for nearly two years, the Whitehall committees and departmental 'rear links' – and for nearly one and a half years as far as the delegation was concerned – had to be dismantled and the senior personnel dispersed to other tasks. After a few months at the Foreign Office, Edward Heath became Secretary of State in the newly created Department of Industry, Trade and Regional Development, an enlargement of the Board of Trade. The chief officials, all in their mid-fifties, went different ways: Roddy Barclay became Ambassador to Belgium, Harry Lintott High Commissioner in Canada, Herbert Andrew, after a few years as Permanent Secretary of the Department of Education, took holy orders, and Bill Gorrell-Barnes retired from the public service and went into business.

I returned to the Treasury to help with the tidying-up process, but a decision had soon to be taken of a more long-term nature. When I was made deputy leader of the delegation, I remained 'on the books' of my old department, but I was told clearly by Norman Brook that the Treasury regarded itself as responsible for me and that if in the end I returned to Whitehall, some 'central economic work' would be found for me. This, I know, was also Frank Lee's wish but he was retiring, and in the autumn of 1962 the Treasury had undergone a major reconstruction. This, the work largely of Otto Clarke and William Armstrong, resulted in the latter becoming Permanent Secretary in succession to Frank Lee while the former took over the whole of the expenditure side. A new 'national economy' group was created under a Deputy Secretary, my old colleague from the planners, Douglas Allen, and, as a result of a more widespread reshuffling, another Deputy Secretary, David Pitblado, was due to come back to Whitehall from Washington.

I was myself rather uncertain about what I wanted to do, perhaps in part because of the fatigue and frustration following the Brussels negotiations. So when I was approached (I suspect at Frank Lee's instigation) by the University of Liverpool and asked whether I would be a candidate for the Vice-Chancellorship, I was very tempted to re-enter academic life by this route. I was then 55, the normal retirement age at the University was not less than 65 (as opposed to 60 in the Civil Service), and a ten-year stint in a new but not unfamiliar environment was quite alluring. All my old doubts and the varying kinds of advice I had received at the end of the war when I had to make a similar decision came back to me and I remembered particularly that many of those whose views I respected had urged me to prefer the academic world to that of action.

I visited Liverpool and had an extremely kind reception from the Chancellor, Lord Leverhulme, and members of the Council and Senate. On my return, my wife and I were very much inclined to accept the Liverpool post. Just at that time, the Treasury, through the new Joint Permanent Secretary in charge of the Civil Service, Laurence Helsby, with whom I had worked fifteen years earlier in the old Ministry of Food, asked me whether I would be interested in going to Washington. I had arranged to call on Helsby one morning at eleven to give him my answer (he knew about the Liverpool offer) and I went to the office, my wife and I having definitely decided to go to Liverpool. At ten forty-five I telephoned her to say that I was now rather uncertain about our decision and discovered that so was she. We quickly agreed on the opposite course to the one we had chosen! Fifteen minutes later I told Helsby that I would go to Washington and it was arranged that I would pay an early visit there to talk things over with Pitblado. The University authorities in Liverpool, I am happy to say, were completely understanding.

Through my various official assignments I had been fortunate enough to be able to visit Washington frequently after we left at the end of the war in 1946, but my wife had not been back at all. We both had vivid and happy memories of the city and the country, and the prospect of going back and being near to so many of the friends we had made was undoubtedly one of the reasons that inclined us to the choice we made. As far as the job itself was concerned, it was not easy, either for me or I believe for those in the Treasury primarily concerned, to be clear about what it would amount to. The post spanned three functions: to be Economic Minister in the Embassy, to be Head of the Treasury and Supply Delegation (a title that had survived from the war and by this time amounted in the main to being the Treasury representative as distinct from being the Ambassador's principal economic adviser, and, in this connection, also having some residual establishment functions in relation to UK representation in the United States); and finally to be the UK's Executive Director on the Boards of the International Monetary Fund (IMF) and the World Bank.

Particularly in these last respects the history of the post went back to Bretton Woods, and it had had a number of senior representatives including, among others, Edmund Hall-Patch, Lord Harcourt, Lord Cromer, Leslie Rowan and Denis Rickett. The post alternated as a rule between a nominee of the Bank of England and one from the Treasury, the deputy representative (or representatives if there was one for each institution) being chosen the other way round. I had known many of the previous incumbents and through my frequent visits had acquired some idea of what the job involved. As I have mentioned earlier, I had also met many members of the new Kennedy Administration, including, within it or advising it from the outside, a number of economists with whom I had been in contact for more than twenty years. This contributed to making the projected transfer not only far from strange, but positively inviting. But, as I say, neither I nor my colleagues in Whitehall or the Bank of England (with whom in this new post I had also to keep closely in touch) had any idea of what within a very short time the work of the post would develop into.

We went with our two daughters to the United States on the *Queen Elizabeth* in August 1963 and after a short stay in New York went to Washington. For some months we lived in an apartment in the Wardman Towers where we had among our neighbours the President of the World Bank, George Woods, and Pierre-Paul Schweitzer, Managing Director of the Fund. It is worth mentioning that the successive British Ministers in this post had all lived in rented accommodation and we too, after a period in the apartment, moved into a very attractive rented furnished house. The Treasury and the Ministry of Works had been searching for a house to buy (the Foreign Office Minister, the Ministry of Defence representative – our General on the NATO Standing Group – and, I believe, the Commercial Minister, all had government-owned houses) but the search had not so far been successful. The Ministry of Works representative was something of a perfectionist, and when it was not the risk of dry rot – which almost automatically excluded much of Georgetown – it was the size of the dining room – which had in his opinion to seat sixteen comfortably – and that ruled out many very desirable houses! We finally found one that we thought particularly suitable, but if it had not been for the chance visit of the then Minister of Works, Geoffrey Rippon, and the Ministry's chief architect, Eric Bedford, I doubt whether even this house would have found favour. It has now been the Washington 'Treasury House' for twenty years and has also turned out to be an excellent investment.

The Ambassador was Lord Harlech, for me a particularly good Head of Mission, not just because of the personal relationship we soon established, but because of his quite exceptional position with the new President and many of his close advisers. As one of them said to me, 'We look upon him as our tutor'! The Minister at the Embassy was Denis Greenhill whom I had already met during his first spell in Washington between 1947 and 1949. We were colleagues not only then but also in more recent years in the City, and have been friends ever since our Washington days. In my own delegation the number two from the Bank of England, Raymond Bonham-Carter, was just about to leave, but I was very happy to find him as a colleague some years later when I went into the City. He was succeeded by John Kirbyshire who already knew many of the Americans we had to deal with and quickly added to his circle. His knowledge and stalwart common sense were invaluable.

Among the members of the US Administration I soon got to know Douglas Dillon, the Secretary of the Treasury, and Henry (Joe) Fowler, the Under-Secretary. The Under-Secretary for Monetary Affairs, the most important official from the point of view of my own function, was Bob Roosa whom I had met during one of my wartime visits to London when he was in uniform there. The story is told by Arthur Schlesinger, and confirmed by Roosa and Samuelson, that when Paul Samuelson (who refused to take a Washington post) was asked by President Kennedy to advise on the appointment of the Under-Secretary, he recommended Roosa in superlative terms. Kennedy, who had at the time not yet appointed the Secretary, said, 'If he is that good, why don't I make him Secretary?' 'You can't do that,' said Samuelson. 'He is too young' – forgetting that the President himself was only one year older.

Another man with whom I had to be in close touch and whose friendship I have valued ever since was the Chairman of the Federal Reserve Board, Bill Martin. George Woods was President of the World Bank and brought his exceptional Wall Street experience and prestige to bear on a post the wider economic, social and political significance of which held no mystery for him. The Managing Director of the Fund, who had just been appointed, was Pierre-Paul Schweitzer, an outstanding *Inspecteur* with whom I had worked closely in Paris when he was the chief official of the interministerial committee on international economic co-operation. I started, therefore, with some advantages through these personal relations. In the heady atmosphere then prevailing in Washington, in which an intellectual approach to problems of public policy was not only not shunned but welcomed, there was again a free and easy movement from universities into government and out again as there had been during the war. This was probably the high point of the 'in-and-outer' so characteristic of American society, and my contacts in the academic world – Harvard, MIT, Brookings and so on – were, therefore, especially valuable. Many familiar and friendly figures reappeared, including Ken Galbraith, for a short time advising the President, but very soon to go off to India as Ambassador – though this certainly did not put a stop to his general advice as his *Journal* so eloquently demonstrates.

Visitors from London were particularly struck by the atmosphere, which was so different from that of Whitehall and Westminster and the relations between them. William Armstrong was both surprised and gratified by the ease with which I was able to arrange for him to see everyone he wanted to see and the very frank way in which he was able to discuss even the most confidential matters. Otto Clarke could hardly believe it when I told him that I was occasionally invited to meetings that Dillon and his colleagues had with their economists' advisory group (organized by Harvard's Seymour Harris) and that I was allowed to take him along, too! The atmosphere must have resembled very much that of the early days of the New Deal (which I only knew in its final phases) and foreshadowed, in its impression of something excitingly new happening, the first hundred days of the 1964 Labour Government.

There was experimentation and there was much discussion about possible new experiments, particularly in economic policy, in which comparisons between the American and the British ways of doing things, partly at least flowing from differences in constitutions, despite their apparent – but misleading – similarities, played an important part. One such discussion with McGeorge Bundy, the President's National Security Adviser, turned on the ease of making tax changes. He had bemoaned the difficulty and slowness of getting the 'Kennedy tax cut' through when, in Britain, the Chancellor had 'merely to get up in the House and it was done'. I told him that it was not quite as simple as that and, in any event, it was not an unmixed blessing. I had cause to remember that conversation during some of the more experimental moments of the 'hundred days'!

I had a number of interesting colleagues among the other economic and financial representatives in Washington, including those on the executive boards of the Fund and the Bank, as well as among the officials of the two institutions. Many of them had been there for a long time, including the formidable Dutch representative, Pieter Lieftinck. Among others, newly arrived as I was, was the French representative. The French authorities were then just changing over to our system of having the same person representing them on both boards, and the new man, René Larre, later to be General Manager of the Bank for International Settlements, turned out to be not only a very able but also very agreeable colleague.

For reasons connected largely with our own economic developments in the next fifteen months, my main and most important contacts were with the Fund officials (including the Deputy Managing Director, Frank Southard, and the Head of the Exchange Restrictions Department, Irving Friedman) and with those of the American Administration. The situation as far as the World Bank was concerned was slightly different in that strictly national British interests played a distinctly smaller part in the problems and operations that came up from day to day. Thus, my contacts with George Woods and his two principal deputies, Burke Knapp (whom I had known from his much earlier post at the Federal

Reserve Board) and Geoffrey Wilson, a former, and again later, Whitehall colleague, were largely concerned with the broader general aspects of the Bank's lending and borrowing policies.

A very important range of relations was that with the financial community, particularly in New York, though, to the extent that I was able to travel, also in Chicago and San Francisco. Through the Treasury, and even more so through the Bank of England, I was able to add many new contacts both in the large commercial banks, as well as in the investment-banking community and in the Federal Reserve Bank of New York, then under the leadership of Al Hayes, with Charlie Coombs his principal operator in exchange markets. I received also extremely valuable introductions from Siegmund Warburg, who knew Wall Street like the palm of his hand, being at the time not only head of the merchant bank he had founded in London, but also associated with Kuhn Loeb, one of the oldest and most distinguished investment banks in New York. I had met Siegmund Warburg some years earlier when I was still in the Ministry of Agriculture. He had called on me a number of times to discuss agricultural problems both before and after we started the Common Market negotiations. This was a subject in which he had a keen interest, as far as I could judge, hardly at all for business reasons. The broad political, economic and social aspects, including the international ones, fascinated him. The fact that his father, unlike other members of the family, had not chosen a banking career, but had been interested in farming, may also have had something to do with it.

As I have already said, neither I, nor those in the Treasury to whom I reported, were clear as to what I would be called on to deal with during a tour of duty in the post, which normally would have lasted three or four years. In fact, my own turned out to be only sixteen months, the last two or three divided between Whitehall and Washington. The content of the job turned out to be something other than 'normal'. The last half of 1963 and the first nine months of 1964 were the final phase of one of the longest periods of government in England by the same party in recent history. The Conservative Government elected at the end of 1951 and re-elected twice thereafter was due to face an election some time in 1964. Before that, however, a number of important political and economic events took place that were to affect profoundly the political and economic climate of the country and with it the British position in the field in which I was to operate – the economic relations with the United States and with the international financial institutions.

I must recall here that while some of us were busy on the Common Market negotiations in Brussels, important developments were taking place on the home front. Already in 1960, the Conservative Government re-elected in the previous year had embarked on a complex of economic policies that was to leave its mark long after that Government had departed from the scene: indeed some of its characteristic features remained valid – with the exception of the first two years of the Heath Government – until the election of May 1979. Broadly speaking the general principles on which the Government tried to steer the economy were based on latterday Keynesianism, a form of macro-economic 'keeping the economy on an even keel', which was conceived in a not fundamentally different way by both parties.

It is well described in non-technical language by Macmillan when talking about the background to the new ideas he was beginning to toy with in the summer of 1962.

If, as the phrase then ran, the economic system became 'overheated' it had to be cooled down by deflationary touches of various kinds, ranging from open-market operations by the Bank of England to economies in government expenditure in every field. The signs of this malaise were said to be easily recognizable – over-employment, an unfavourable balance of payments, pressure on sterling, rises in wages unjustified by any increase in productivity and a corresponding increase in prices.

The opposite remedy would be applied if the symptoms pointed the other way.

I myself, though writing of a slightly later period, but one in which the same conventional wisdom applied, related these principles to the actual operations of the governmental machine, with its centre at the Treasury.

There is something almost automatic about the technique . . . that fits in admirably with the demands of an official machine with its regularity of timetable, its elaborate system of clearance through departmental and interdepartmental committees and its production of papers for Ministers in standardized form.

The process had become so stereotyped that I saw some danger in its creating the illusion that one 'could read off, as on a dial, the correct adjustment of the economy needed at any moment'. I would add that while Macmillan listed a number of 'clinical' symptoms to be observed, in practice the one that was most alarming was the balance of payments situation (for so many post-war years our major policy constraint) with its effect on the sterling exchange rate and/or the reserves.

In the period 1960–2 when Selwyn Lloyd was Chancellor of the Exchequer in Macmillan's last Adminstration, this major form of economic management came, for a variety of reasons, to be regarded as less than wholly satisfactory. Some observers in early 1960 – and even more in retrospect – regarded the symptoms of 'overheating' as pretty evident, but the then Chancellor, Heathcoat Amory, was not able to get as restrictive a budget accepted by his colleagues or the Prime Minister as he thought desirable. When he left office in July 1960, the signs of trouble ahead were multiplying and were beginning to give rise to a re-examination of policy both in the Treasury and among some other Ministers, and this process went on for the next two years during which Selwyn Lloyd was Chancellor. The major reforms to which this re-examination led were not so much in the relation to the preponderant role of demand management by (primarily) fiscal and monetary means, but by the additions of other elements of policy, which became institutionalized and have, despite changes in political rhetoric, remained in one form or another part of the armoury of government in the economic field to this day.

These reforms included (from the summer of 1962 onwards with the strong support of the Prime Minister), first and foremost, the concept of an incomes policy. While this had existed in embryonic form before and was supposed to be implemented in practice by a Council on Prices, Productivity and Incomes, which issued periodic reports expected to have an educative effect on employers and unions alike, it had not achieved a great deal. Even later experiments with a pay pause and intervention in individual specific wage negotiations, especially in the nationalized industries, did not achieve much until the doctrine of the 'guiding light' – later to be called the 'norm' – was enunciated at the beginning of 1962 and the National Incomes Commission was set up in the summer of that year.

By that time, for reasons that do not emerge entirely clearly from Macmillan's memoirs, the Prime Minister seems to have lost confidence in Selwyn Lloyd's ability to carry forward this new incomes policy and, in the light of the Chancellor's last budget, seems also to have expected him to be less than fully sympathetic to his own views, which were turning towards economic expansion, with a strengthened incomes policy as one of its main instruments. So in July 1962, in addition to the Cabinet changes I have already mentioned in connection with our European policy, an important change occurred at the Treasury. Reginald Maudling, hitherto President of the Board of Trade, became Chancellor. He inherited a number of other important changes instituted in the preceding two years: a reform of the budget accounts and the introduction of the so-called 'regulator', which made it possible for certain tax changes to be introduced between budgets; a long-term look at government expenditure based on the recommendations of a committee under Edwin Plowden; a revised policy towards nationalized industries; a higher threshold for surtax, and last but not least the setting up of the National Economic Development Council, a body representing government, employers and trade unions.

I had known and liked Maudling from the time he was Economic Secretary at the Treasury and had been involved with him in some of the negotiations for the European Free Trade Area. I now had an excellent opportunity of getting to know him in his new role as Chancellor in my early days in Washington some time after he assumed the post. One of his first international engagements was to lead the UK Delegation to the annual meetings of the IMF and International Bank for Reconstruction and Development (IBRD) in Washington in September 1963, followed by the usual visit of the Chancellor to New York to meet members of the financial community. These encounters had to be somewhat curtailed because Maudling and Tony Barber (the Financial Secretary) accompanied by Derek Mitchell (the Principal Private Secretary) had to return in time for the Conservative Party Conference. This turned out to be more important than had been expected since it marked the end of Macmillan's seven years as Prime Minister. His decision to carry on through a 1964 election, taken against an earlier decision to give up the party leadership and No. 10, was in turn reversed when he had suddenly to undergo a prostate operation.

The resulting contest for the leadership and the appearance of Sir Alec Douglas Home (as he had become) are now well-known parts of the political history of that period. The political background to all that was happening on the economic and financial fronts changed, as it was bound to do, given the struggle for the leadership that had just taken place and also the near prospect of an election. This, however, was not immediately evident. The situation in the United States was also radically altered by the assassination of President Kennedy, which took place soon after Macmillan's departure from the centre of the stage. We were in Washington at the time. I heard the news while at a meeting in the World Bank, and the consternation and grief that followed has already been much written about. Whether history will prove the subsequent exalted view of the short Kennedy presidency to have been justified or not, in the United States the event itself was regarded as a traumatic turning-point.

In the short term, and from the point of view of the events I am describing, the important thing is that Maudling continued to head the Treasury for the next twelve months.

I had only a peripheral knowledge of what was going on in Whitehall and Westminster during the first nine months or so after Maudling first became Chancellor, as I was then still deeply immersed in the Brussels negotiations. During the three months that preceded my move to Washington I had more opportunity to be briefed by Treasury officials and by the Chancellor himself, as well as to become acquainted with the views of the Bank of England. By the autumn of 1963 when Maudling came to Washington, the expansionist inclination of the Prime Minister, which may have been partly responsible for Maudling's appointment but which had certainly been much slower in implementation than some people thought, had begun to assert itself more clearly. This was already evident in a somewhat liberal budget as far as personal taxation was concerned as well as in a greater readiness to involve, and be influenced by, the National Economic Development

Council – the British instrument for French type 'indicative planning' – particularly its 4 per cent growth target. In fact, whether due directly to the reliefs to the home market provided by the budget (much disputed then and later and, here and there, compared unfavourably to a stimulus to exports through devaluation) or not, the economy picked up considerably in the later months of 1963.

Against this background and not least due to the charm of his personality, Maudling's visit to the United States was a success, so much so that some observers thought that the notorious 'stop-go' from which the British economy had suffered so long had at last been banished, and even sceptics of the precise size and nature of the budgetary stimulus were far from certain that the previously oft-experienced unfavourable balance of payments consequences would follow. As far as the United States was concerned, views in the Administration, though mixed, were on balance reasonably favourable to what later came to be looked on as Maudling's 'dash for growth'. The Kennedy Administration had had a strong expansionist bias and, in this respect, the Johnson Administration was, at least to start with, not very different.

Some of those who advised both Presidents – without being directly concerned with economic and financial policy – would, I think, have been reluctant to see the USA urging a more cautious policy on the UK at that stage. Even in the US Treasury, which was more conservatively inclined, there was, as I recall, no sense of worry over any possible 'overheating' of the British economy at the end of 1963 and in the early months of 1964; nor was there such sentiment in the Council of Economic Advisers, headed by Walter Heller or the Budget Bureau, whose director was Kermit Gordon – two highly distinguished economists with whom I not only had to keep in close touch officially, but with whom I had many relaxed, quasi-academic discussions on economic policy.

By February 1964, however, with preparations for the budget already taking place, official opinion in Britain began to be more worried. The estimate of the expected balance of payments deficit ran into several hundred million pounds (though much less than in fact it turned out to be) and some restraint was seen to be necessary. Among the measures that were considered was an increase in bank rate from 4 to 5 per cent. This was a matter that I had to discuss with the American authorities and I encountered considerable resistance, since the Americans were themselves worried about their balance of payments and were at the same time concerned that they might be forced into a higher interest policy themselves. As it happened, the new Prime Minister, Alec Home, visited Washington in February and he too was strongly urged by a number of officials, from the President down, to limit the increase to ½ per cent, but without success. I mention this episode not so much for its own sake, but as indicative of the very close relationship in these, as in many other matters, that then existed between the US and ourselves and that left a special mark on events (as I thought at the time) during the next three or four years.

As far as the British economy was concerned, the 1964 budget was evidence of a touch, but only a touch, on the brakes. The result of what could even at the time be seen as a gamble turned out to be unfavourable: the projected balance of payments deficit rose to something near £800 million. The estimates and their implications for policy were much debated from the spring to the autumn of 1964 and, in view of the election, which by April had become a certainty for the autumn, were a major part of the political debate. Another important part of Government policy – foreshadowing both in its domestic aspects and in the implications it had for the attitudes of the American Administration events that were to occur in 1965 and 1966 under the Labour Government – was incomes policy. Maudling attached considerable importance to making some progress on this front by using the National Economic Development Council (NEDC) and by trying to get the 'guiding light' of a 3½ per cent increase in wages accepted on the basis of a 'Statement of Intent' from employers and trade unions. This, the emphasis on NEDC, and – in a different area – the first attempts at 'structural' policies by Heath in his new department – the reform of resale price maintenance and regional development – were all to have their successors after the election.

Meanwhile, in Washington, both the Administration and the International Monetary Fund were getting increasingly worried about the outlook for the British balance of payments. I, and the visitors from London, William Armstrong, Rowley Cromer and Otto Clarke, were asked many questions about the outlook, about the options the Government was considering and even about the possible actions of a Labour Government, should Labour win the election. These latter questions were naturally also asked when leading Opposition spokesmen, Harold Wilson, Jim Callaghan and Patrick Gordon Walker among them, visited Washington and New York.

One of the occasions when the American concern was most clearly expressed was when Roosa visited London in the late spring of 1964. As a good economist, as the Under-Secretary for Monetary Affairs in the Treasury, and as a former official of the New York Federal Reserve Bank in charge of open-market operations (on which he had written a classic book), he was particularly concerned about the financial consequences that any weakening in the international credibility of UK economic policy might have. A massive short-term capital outflow could be the result and countermeasures such as exchange control and import restrictions, or taking the consequences through a devaluation – particularly if these measures had to be taken in crisis conditions – were all fraught with great risks not only to Britain but to the international monetary system as a whole. Extended 'swap' agreements between central banks were one of the preventive measures he advocated, and indeed these had to be used subsequently.

Although pressure on sterling built up in the autumn, it was inevitable that, once the decision on the timing of the election had been taken, it would be extremely difficult if not impossible to take the deflationary measures that a less optimistic reading of the developing situation would have required – and made impossible – at an earlier stage. For the Chancellor, there was no choice then but to continue to display as much confidence as possible, and this he had an opportunity to do before the best (and largest) international forum just before the election: the annual meeting of the Fund and the Bank in Tokyo. I was in his party, and worried though I was by what I knew to be the real dangers of the situation, I greatly admired the assurance, good humour and skill with which Maudling presented a case in which he may not have had the utmost confidence himself.

When the election came, on Thursday 15 October, instructed opinion on both sides of the Atlantic had no doubt that, whatever the political complexion of the new Government, it would be faced with a critical situation; moreover it would be one in which the sharp antagonism displayed in the election campaign would make a sober and realistic approach to the problems very difficult. As it turned out, the small margin by which Labour won and the fact that it had to carry on for eighteen months with this exiguous majority made the task even more difficult than it was in substance.

13

Whitehall III

THE HUNDRED DAYS

The next phase of my life occupied barely two years. It deserves, nevertheless, a fairly extensive account for two reasons. From a personal point of view, it brought me more closely in touch with the very summit of policy-making in government, and certainly over a much more extensive area than I had been involved in hitherto. In the second place, the economic problems with which the British Government had to deal during this period and the solutions with which it experimented, though now twenty years behind us, are still very much the day-to-day concern of government and of anyone interested in public affairs. I do not, however, think that meticulous detail is needed, not only because much of what happened during these two years has a certain repetitive quality, but also because despite any constraints of official confidentiality most of the events were described and analysed in great detail in the public prints at the time they occurred by investigative journalists. Except for a few highly sensitive matters – including politically sensitive ones – the Government of that time and others since had a fairly welcoming attitude to publicity; moreover since then writers of political memoirs or biographies have added much further material.

In his account of the 1964–70 Labour Government, Harold Wilson has told us that on becoming Leader of his Party, eighteen months before he became Prime Minister, he had developed quite definite ideas on the machinery of government in general and on that relating to economic policy in particular. These included the creation of a new department, separate from, and 'at least as powerful as', the Treasury. It 'would be concerned with real resources, with economic planning, with strengthening our ability to export and to save imports, with increasing productivity and our competitiveness in domestic and export markets.' I knew that for a considerable time there had been discussions among academics and others about the machinery of government and that, especially in intellectual circles sympathetic to Labour, there had been much concern about the role of the Treasury in a future Government dedicated to planning and, in the political language of the day, to 'getting Britain going again'.

However, my own first encounter with these ideas as held by prominent members of the Labour Party had come in the early summer of 1963 before I went to Washington. We had been invited to a large and very agreeable luncheon party by Roy Jenkins at which I was placed (deliberately, as I later discovered) next to George Brown, whom I had met only very briefly many years earlier when he was the Junior Minister at the Ministry of Agriculture under Tom Williams, that great Minister of the first post-war Labour Government, author of the 1947 Agriculture Act. Our conversation, in which Roy Jenkins also occasionally intervened, was on the question of how to organize the economic work of government and in particular whether it could be improved by having a Department of Economic Affairs. I was at the time a Treasury official, but I do not think that this influenced my judgement, particularly as the discussion, as I could judge it at the time, appeared to be entirely academic.

I admitted the theoretical case against having the whole of economic policy run by a department with the 'candle-ends-saving' tradition of the Treasury, one that apart from that had of necessity to look primarily, if not exclusively, at the financial appearances of economic phenomena. But I remember very clearly (and this is significant in view of later developments) stressing three things: first, that it was far from easy for government in practice to take account of all the economic factors that were significant and that finance in the broadest sense could often be the most useful focus of diagnosis and therapy; that the Treasury was so powerful by statute and tradition that any new department would have an almost impossible task in trying to assert itself, and, above all, that traditionally in British government departmental machinery was rarely as important as the relative power of Ministers. A Minister who was powerful by status and personality would soon make his department powerful, too.

I had no idea at the time that this conversation was meant to have, or would have, any practical consequences. The next step in this story has already been told by George Brown in his memoirs. While I

was spending a few days in New York on my way to Washington in
1963, I was walking along Fifth Avenue with my wife and
daughters when to our surprise we met George Brown. In the short
conversation we had he urged me 'not to put down deep roots' in
the USA: there would be an Election the following year and I might
be wanted in London. A further hint came a few months later when
Harold Wilson on a visit to Washington, at a luncheon party at the
Embassy, talked about his intention to create a Department of
Economic Affairs and, winking at me, said, 'And we have even
picked the Permanent Secretary.' Then, some time before I went to
Tokyo with Maudling, it was intimated to me, in that admirable
Establishment language, that it would be 'convenient' if I could be
in London for consultations after the IMF and IBRD meetings.
Thus the Election found me in London, and indeed even a few days
before the Election, Helsby and Armstrong, the two Joint Secretaries of the Treasury, told me of the contingency plans for a new
department (Helsby having got Alec Home's permission to talk to
Harold Wilson about these matters) to be set up if Labour won,
which would have me as Permanent Secretary.

I cannot say that, at the outset, I was particularly enthusiastic
about the prospect, though after acting as the spokesman for our
economic policy in Washington on instruction from the centre, the
chance of helping to shape that policy at the centre was clearly
attractive, and I was soon caught up in the excitement, unfounded
as it later turned out to be, of the 'hundred days' of the new
Government. As most of the major turning-points in my life, this
one came spontaneously and we accepted it without fuss, although
both my wife and I were rather sorry at the thought of leaving
Washington at the moment, when the house we had procured for
the Treasury was at last ready. My wife had to move into it during
my absence in London.

The Johnson Administration was beginning to develop a
character of its own and we were not very keen on abandoning the
many close – and from a British point of view highly valuable – ties
we had made. Still, I readily fell in with the 'planning against the
day' that was going on and examined with interest the blueprint of
the new department, which the Treasury had produced and which
Helsby and Armstrong showed me. It had, as I remember, some
forty people in it, including only one Deputy Secretary and a

somewhat ill-defined role for the Chief Economist. It was quite clear to me from the beginning that the Treasury was going to regard this new department as a very awkward foundling, but one who had inevitably to be taken care of. This, however, had to be done without disturbing the existing household too much, above all at only a minimum cost to the size, quality and power of the Establishment and its existing incumbents. The only sign of generosity was that the Treasury seemed to be prepared to let me have, as a Deputy Secretary, Douglas Allen, then Third Secretary in charge of the 'National Economy Group' in the Treasury.

I did not spend any time debating these matters before 15 October, the date of the Election. Despite my frequent and prolonged absences from Whitehall, I knew enough about the ways of the Establishment to realize that, as I had told George Brown some months earlier, what was going to matter in the end was what Ministers wanted. Any argument I might deploy to my fellow Civil Servants would be so much wasted effort.

Another example of the struggle for 'status' came a little later when Helsby and Armstrong drew my attention to the slight difference in salary between them and other Permanent Secretaries. In the days when the Permanent Secretary of the Treasury (e.g. Edward Bridges) was also Head of the Civil Service, his salary was £500 per annum higher than that of the other Permanent Secretaries, and this difference had continued and been shared between two incumbents (though I believe at £500 each!) when the two functions were divided, as was the case with Helsby and Armstrong. I believe that at some time before or after the salaries of the Head of the Foreign Service and of the Secretary of the Cabinet were similarly raised. They said that they hoped that although George Brown was number two in the Government, I would not claim the same salary as this would cause embarrassment. (They did not explain to whom!) I reported this to George Brown as a matter that could affect the status of the department, but he was in one of his moods and all he could do was to complain bitterly that I was already overpaid – as were all Permanent Secretaries – in relation to himself and other Ministers (which was probably true). I dropped the matter. Perhaps I should not have done so!

George Brown, in his memoirs, says that he thinks he could have got William Armstrong to head the new department and, in that event, 'that battle' (i.e. the one between the 'entrenched Treasury and our new department') would have been 'won before it started'. I do not think for one moment that Armstrong would have left the Treasury. And as for the other part of George Brown's speculation, it shows a surprisingly simple view of the reasons for the problems that the Department of Economic Affairs (DEA) had to face, a view contradicted in fact by his own much more sophisticated account of the history of the department. I shall have occasion to revert shortly to this question of the viability of the new department and also to deal with the question more generally in connection with later discussions of Whitehall machinery.

As for the difficulties that finally resulted in the disappearance of the DEA, it was clear already from the first day that settling its functions was going to be a major problem. We have George Brown's own account as well as that of Harold Wilson of the way in which this was done initially – by means of what came to be known as the 'Concordat', the Treasury presumably cast in the role of the Pope and the DEA in that of a secular power, although George Brown on occasion liked to refer to himself as 'the Pope'! I have nothing new to add to some of the details of the process by which agreement was reached that have already appeared in print. The Prime Minister was presented with a draft by the Secretary of the Cabinet (Burke Trend) and the Joint Permanent Secretary of the Treasury in charge of the Civil Service (Laurence Helsby). The Chancellor at No. 11 was discussing the problem with his advisers. At the same time (the Friday evening after the Election, 16 October), after the appointment of the seven principal Ministers, George Brown (having become First Secretary of State and Secretary of State for Economic Affairs), Donald MacDougall, Tony Crosland, Robert Neild, Thomas Balogh, Tom Caulcott and I were discussing the same question in George Brown's flat. Some attempt was made to negotiate an agreement by means of inevitably rather confused telephone calls between the three venues of discussion. A great deal of almost medieval disputation took place on 'long' versus 'short' -term problems, on the 'real' versus the 'money' economy on balance of payments, reserves and exchange-rate problems versus those of growth, and the result, which was a pretty hopeless mish-mash, was ultimately put on paper. I do not recollect that it was referred to thereafter for the purpose of settling disputes between the two departments, and the whole issue itself was not formally raised until a later stage in George Brown's time.

In any event, there was not much opportunity at that stage for those in the new department to go on worrying about what its functions were to be, and could rationally be expected to be. That came later. The immediate preoccupation was to get some sort of machinery set up and working on what, in industrial terms, would be called a 'green fields' operation. The physical process has been described by George Brown and more recently by Susan Crosland in her biography of her husband. This process, apart from the inconveniences of the first few days – lack of furniture, lack of telephones and, despite the Treasury's elementary forward planning, lack of people – was not a matter of any great consequence. The creation of the top personnel, ministerial and official, was more important, but this was accomplished very quickly, including the establishment of the appropriate links with other departments both directly and through the Cabinet Office machinery. The setting up of these 'networks' or conjunctive tissues, both visible because institutionalized (through ministerial, official and mixed committees) as well as invisible and informal (through personal relationships), is as a rule one of the tasks that the British governmental machine accomplishes efficiently and quickly.

The ministerial echelon at the DEA consisted, in addition to George Brown, of Tony Crosland as Minister of State – he had at first to be named Economic Secretary to the Treasury as the statutory provision for a Minister of State did not yet exist – and Maurice Foley and Bill Rodgers as joint Under-Secretaries of State. At the official level, in addition to myself, Donald MacDougall (who had been Economic Director of NEDC and whom I had known since the late thirties when he taught at Leeds and I at Hull) came in as Director General, and, as I already mentioned, my old friend Douglas Allen as Deputy Under-Secretary. Towards the end of my time in the DEA, when the new grade of Second Permanent Secretary had become fashionable in Whitehall, I persuaded George Brown to have him promoted to that rank, and he later succeeded me as the Head of the department. (He then became in turn Permanent Secretary of the Treasury, and Head of the Civil Service.

Now, as Lord Croham, he continues in a number of important posts outside the official public service.)

The Treasury's original ideas of the size and structure of the department was soon seen to be inadequate, without my having had a long, fruitless and largely abstract struggle. Without any empire-building efforts on the part either of George Brown or myself, by the time the full scope of the work on prices and incomes, on regional development, on industrial policy, on the preparation of the national plan, to say nothing of trying to keep up with the Treasury on general economic policy, had really developed, the department had several hundred officials, including two additional top Deputy Secretaries, Arthur Peterson from the Home Office and Ronnie McIntosh from the Board of Trade, together with a number of economists and a group of specially recruited industrial advisers, whose first chief was Fred Catherwood, on secondment from Tube Investments. Tom Caulcott from the Treasury became George Brown's Principal Private Secretary, to be succeeded later by John Burgh, now Director General of the British Council.

The appointment of both Ministers and economic advisers took some sorting out. As far as the second post in the DEA was concerned, the choice had apparently lain between Roy Jenkins and Tony Crosland. I had some discussion with Roy Jenkins and could not but agree with him when he preferred a (lesser) department of his own against the offer by George Brown to let him have 'half the DEA'. He knew, as I knew, that with the best will in the world no Cabinet Minister could really divest himself of responsibility to this extent, especially in a new department. In the end, Roy Jenkins was made Minister of Aviation and Crosland came to the DEA where, however, he stayed only until January 1965 when he joined the Cabinet as Secretary of State for Education. Roy Jenkins may have felt somewhat disappointed at this stage at still being outside the Cabinet, but he did not have to wait long for the very high posts of Chancellor and Home Secretary for which his exceptional gifts so eminently qualified him. There was much toing and froing about the positioning of economic advisers. In the end Robert Neild went to the Treasury (where Alec Cairncross remained as Head of the Government Economic Service), as did Nicky Kaldor (though for taxation questions only), and Thomas Balogh to the Cabinet Office.

The department's early logistic problems were mirrored in my personal situation. No successor to the Washington post had been appointed immediately as other matters were more pressing. But after a very short time it was decided by the Prime Minister, George Brown and Callaghan that there was advantage in my continuing to hold the Washington post for a while given the continuing, and indeed even more pressing, need for a dialogue with the American authorities.

So for three months, until John Stevens, then an Executive Director of the Bank of England, could take over – on 15 January 1965 – I had a double role to play. This presented not only professional, but also some quite difficult domestic problems. In Washington, my wife had to supervise the move into the new Treasury house and to monitor the considerable work that was connected with that. Our social or quasi-social life, since in the kind of post I held there is very little purely personal social life, suffered considerable disturbances, as it was never certain until the last minute whether I would be on one or the other side of the Atlantic. The 'commuting' was made easier by the excellent arrangements the 'machine' was able to make in both Washington and London – as well as by the fact that I generally travelled without any luggage. If asked why I was travelling back to Washington so often, said Harold Wilson, I could always say that I had gone to collect my toothbrush, etc., which I had left behind!

My dual role had, however, considerable advantages as far as the scope of the DEA's functions were concerned. Through my Washington activities we were inevitably and very firmly brought into the centre of the most acute financial problems – 'the cold war', as William Armstrong called it – which the Treasury would very much have liked to keep as its exclusive preserve. I should, however, at this point emphasize that the jurisdictional sensitivity of the Treasury was wholly institutional and did not extend to personal relations. In particular, those between William Armstrong and me could not have been friendlier or more frank and open. This helped a great deal, particularly on the occasions when relations between Ministers were more strained.

In London, after some fairly uncomfortable nights in clubs, our old friends and neighbours in the Hampstead Garden Suburb, the Gordon Walkers, kindly put me up and I was driven to work with the Foreign Secretary and his detective. Where to live after we moved back to London was another problem, as our house was let to an American General. This problem was solved through the ingenuity of one of our officials who recalled the existence of a flat at the top of the Treasury building (in fact only two floors above my office). This was furnished by the Ministry of Works – much more austerely than the Washington house – and let to me at a 'commercial' rent – which, being in SW1, was quite a heavy charge on my budget. When my wife and I finally came back to London together in January 1965, we moved into it and stayed there for almost the rest of that year – which turned out to be the greater part of my remaining time in the public service.

There were all the inevitable but minor problems to be dealt with and settled quickly. The really demanding part was the professional one, though not so much the setting up and organization of the department (a task in which, especially as a result of my frequent absences in the early weeks, Douglas Allen's contribution was invaluable) but in the policy issues of those first hundred days. In one sense the problems of the economy, and particularly the immediate financial pressures caused by the balance of payments deficit, which by the standards of those days was enormous, were a continuation of what had gone before, what had been developing through the abortive 'dash for growth'. But the setting was quite different. Here was a new Government formed by a Party that had been out of office for more than twelve years and that was now faced with crushing responsibilities while having only an exiguous majority in Parliament.

Whether they could have been foreseen or not, some of the consequences of this situation proved inevitable. There was first a lack of experience: only two of the Cabinet Ministers apart from Harold Wilson had held Cabinet office before. Then, despite the attacks launched during the campaign on the previous Government's economic policy, there was genuine surprise and some alarm at the magnitude of the problem when Ministers were presented with it. Yet there was also highly praiseworthy though injudicious enthusiasm as to what could be accomplished quickly. There was some distrust of the existing body of advisers who had for so long been working for 'the other side' (very reminiscent to me of the attitude that was displayed towards some of my friends in the

Canadian Civil Service when the Diefenbaker Government came into power); yet Ministers were also faced with a multiplicity of counsel from their own unofficial advisers, and it soon became evident that among the top members of the Cabinet the hard-fought battle for the leadership of the Party had left considerable scars. Finally, whatever the Government's own views, qualities or deficiencies, the world, including particularly the financial community – soon lumped into one mysterious and malevolent force and christened 'the gnomes of Zurich' – was, if not wholly hostile, certainly apprehensive and, at best, wondering what was going to happen next.

In the USA, as I have already indicated, the Johnson Administration, ostensibly in the same mould as its predecessor, was developing a character of its own. Some members and advisers changed; new or aggravated problems, such as the American balance of payments deficit, were beginning to preoccupy them even more than before and making them judge our problems in a somewhat different light. The Vietnam War had become even more of a festering political sore and economic drain. In general, despite a broad liberalism, and the President's 'Great Society' programme, the trend was somewhat more conservative, and the 'experiments' of the new British Government, therefore, likely to be scrutinized more carefully. All these factors, domestic and international, small and large, combined to make the 'hundred days' something very different from just the 'next chapter'.

Like all new incoming Governments, this one was presented with elaborate briefs expounding the situation, identifying the problems and indicating choices for action. As far as the economy was concerned, the Treasury brief was available, so the principal actors have told us in their memoirs, to the PM, the First Secretary and the Chancellor on the evening after the Election. Even without any explicit mention in these presentations, it was quite clear that devaluation of the currency had to be one of the options that would have to be considered. Much has been written by those directly concerned and by many well-informed commentators about the manner in which this problem was tackled at the outset and about the fact that the decision reached on the Saturday night (17 October) between the three principal actors was to rule out devaluation. I neither expressed nor, at that stage, held particularly strong views for or against devaluation. However, in my own mind I was also far from convinced that the economic circumstances of the day were such as to make the economic advantages supposed to flow from a devaluation a reality, in particular improved export competitiveness in an inflationary climate; or, perhaps even more important, whether the financial assistance that would need to be forthcoming if it was to be carried out successfully could be secured. I also knew what a powerful political obstacle the memory of the 1949 devaluation, also by a Labour Government, would present. I was in any case sure of one thing, that a decision one way or another should not be delayed. From my activities in the United States and from my contacts in the international financial community (closer perhaps at the time than even those of the Treasury), I knew that markets were in a high state of expectancy, enhanced by the knowledge that many if not most of the new Government's outside advisers were in favour of devaluation. Any prolongation of the state of the uncertainty would, I felt sure, cause considerable upheavals in markets, reduce the credibility of the Government's policies and probably force a devaluation on the Government in circumstances in which it had least control of the resulting situation. If there was to be devaluation, it ought to take place at once (quite apart from the political advantages of speed, which Harold Wilson has pointed out); if it was not to be, the sooner markets knew, the better.

This view was, I know, also held by George Brown but was not shared by everyone at the time, and it has been criticized since. But those who were in favour of delaying a decision were really in favour of devaluation and they hoped that a delay would swing more opinion to their side. In fact, the top three men did take an immediate decision and it was against devaluation. Apart from an occasional and only very brief reappearance, the subject remained off the agenda until the summer of 1966. I am still convinced that it was essential to decide this issue there and then, and while there may be legitimate debate on whether the actual decision taken was the right one, I believe that it was.

The first major examination of what the immediate steps in the Government's policy were to be had, in fact, begun on that Saturday morning when the PM and the other two Ministers met with their principal advisers. In the course of that morning a number of decisions were taken that William Armstrong and I were then left to put on paper. The result was the first draft of the White Paper (soon dubbed the 'Brown Paper' by the press) laid before the House nine days later, on 26 October. Parliament assembled the next day. Although it is easy to criticize the programme, it contained, despite the speed with which it was composed and agreed, a certain degree of internal logic. It consisted of proposals for dealing both with the short-term situation, characterized by the continual pressure on sterling and the reserves due to the balance of payments situation (which was aggravated by the financial consequences of 'leading' and 'lagging') as well as with the longer term factors designed to produce a lasting improvement in our international situation. The most important measure in the first category was an import surcharge on most imports of 15 per cent and, somewhat less effective, a scheme for refunding to exporters certain indirect taxes. To buttress these measures both economically and, perhaps more important, from the point of view of creating the right political atmosphere, the paper promised 'a strict review of all government expenditure' in order 'to relieve the strain on the balance of payments'. Items of low priority such as 'prestige projects' were to be cut out and the French Government had been informed that the British Government wished to review the Concorde project.

On the longer term, the paper could not anticipate the Queen's Speech, but the country was warned that the social programmes 'would have to be paid for'. Other policies were also announced or foreshadowed: an immediate consultation with both sides of industry on a plan to increase productivity, and the setting up of a Price Review body, policies to improve the mobility of labour, and measures to foster regional development. I was at the time still the UK Executive Director of the IMF, and therefore happy to see included 'consultation with the International Monetary Fund on the use by the United Kingdom of its drawing rights'.

The paper was designed to calm international and domestic financial opinion without unduly upsetting the Government's supporters. It did not, however, have the desired effect. I had taken the paper to Washington and although the Americans were no more enamoured of new trade restrictions than anybody else they accepted the whole package with considerable sympathy and, what is more, said so publicly. Later, on 30 November, I made a presentation to the IMF, which was also well received although there were some searching comments on the Government's policy. But the import surcharge ran into heavy fire from our other trading partners, particularly in Europe, largely because there had not been adequate prior consultation, and the Government was forced on the defensive and had to make promises of early reviews. The clear hint that Concorde was to be dropped (the suggestion made here and there that this was included as a result of American pressure is a complete myth!) was soon discovered to be empty. The legal opinion was that there was no provision in our agreement with the French for unilateral cancellation; it was clear that the French would insist on going ahead and that we might have to defend our action before the Court at The Hague with the prospect of a sentence of very heavy damages. (I have heard it argued that this might have been worth paying rather than the heavy further costs that Concorde involved. Now that I am a frequent passenger on Concorde, I have mixed feelings on this matter!)

The Queen's Speech a week after the White Paper on 'The Economic Situation' contained a legislative programme that was naturally tailored to the Government's election pledges and the expectations of its supporters in the House rather than to keeping the 'gnomes of Zurich' quiet. So the drain on the reserves continued and further emergency measures had to be taken including a 2 per cent increase in Bank Rate in November.

I had to explain to the Americans – Dillon, Roosa, Martin and others – the reasons for this move and to get them to accept it. The somewhat dramatic circumstances in which this had to be done (one of my last acts in my Washington capacity) have been described by Harold Wilson and George Brown as well as by a number of contemporary commentators. I was, indeed, on my way to London and was caught by telephone by the Prime Minister and George Brown while changing planes in New York. I returned to Washington late at night and had some difficulty in finding an innocent excuse for my return while a dinner party was going on in our house. At the same time, the Governor of the Bank secured – on the central bank network – facilities amounting to $3,000 million, and for the time being the crisis was over. Shortly thereafter, on 7 December, the Prime Minister, accompanied by a number of

Ministers and officials, paid his first official visit to President Johnson. While defence and foreign policy were ostensibly the main topics of their discussion, economic policy was perhaps even more important and, on the whole, the Prime Minister's problems, particularly in their domestic political manifestations, found a sympathetic hearing in the Johnson White House.

There were, however, some differences of view. I remember dancing with my wife at the White House on the occasion of the Wilson visit when the President, also dancing, stopped me on the dance floor to raise a question about Bank Rate. I told him that Walter Heller had agreed with the points I had made to him, but President Johnson took a note out of his pocket, which turned out to be an analysis by Walter Heller of this subject and which we proceeded to debate while our dancing partners stood there listening in some surprise.

I should add that throughout the remaining eighteen months or so that I continued in the public service, I had ample opportunity to witness the very close relations that existed with the American Administration at all levels. These ensured that the discussion of problems in the economic and financial sphere, even where there where strong differences of view, turned into genuine attempts to arrive at common solutions. Day-to-day contacts were supplemented by occasional meetings for a broader review, for example, a visit by two distinguished American economists, Gardner Ackley, the Chairman of the Council of Economic Advisers, and Kermit Gordon, Director of the Budget and some of their staffs, organized by the DEA, with other departments participating in the meetings.

The remaining weeks of the year and of the hundred days (their end being marked almost to the day by the death of Winston Churchill), while full of important activities for the Government, particularly on the international front with the beginnings of the Rhodesian problem, were, as far as economic matters were concerned, less hectic: the measures and the international financial package had had their effect, and while we continued in the Treasury and the DEA to watch with extreme interest, indeed excitement, the twice daily reports on financial movements, the DEA was able to begin to look at what its other activities were to be. For me, the 'resident' Washington phase was coming to an end, and although I had many more occasions to visit the United States in the next eighteen months, from 18 January onwards I was at my desk in Storey's Gate.

STEERING THE UNITED KINGDOM ECONOMY

The longer term work of the DEA had already begun before the year ended. The short lull as far as immediate financial pressures were concerned, at the beginning of 1965, enabled the department to develop a distinctive range of activities of its own before new financial storms broke. Before I describe these activities, I need to say something more about the relation between the DEA and the Treasury as it evolved after the 'hundred days'. I have already referred to George Brown's own account in his memoirs and to a number of passages in Harold Wilson's report of his two Administrations from 1964 to 1970. Wilson and Brown, together with Callaghan (who has not yet given his own version of this period) were the principal actors, conducting national affairs of the utmost importance in the fullest possible limelight. All three had only very shortly before the Election been engaged in a fiercely fought contest for the leadership of the Labour Party, from which Wilson had emerged as a possible future – and very soon actual – Prime Minister. Since they also had very different and very strong personalities with very different backgrounds, apart from their roles within the party machine, it would not have been surprising if some strain had continued to exist between them after the 1964 Administration was formed.

Even if there had been no background of personal rivalry, the positions that they occupied in regard to the central core of the Government's responsibilities and its most acute problem – the economy – would inevitably have led to tensions. For there was clearly a basic misunderstanding about what the creation of the new department was designed to achieve, a misunderstanding that was only papered over by the 'Concordat'. As First Secretary, virtually Deputy Prime Minister, the head of the DEA could legitimately assume that he was 'overlord' of the whole field of economic policy, with the Treasury, the Board of Trade, the Ministry of Labour and so forth being primarily executive departments enjoying only a limited autonomy in policy making – at least in the sense that they could not pursue policies that were incompatible with the central direction of the economy by the DEA.

It is, to put it mildly, highly doubtful whether such a concept is in practice compatible with one fundamental principle of British Government or with one powerful modern tendency that itself runs counter to the tradition. The principle is the – at least theoretical – equality of all members of the Cabinet, combined with their collective responsibility. The modern tendency is for the Prime Minister, the *primus inter pares* in Cabinet, to become increasingly *primus* with the *pares* becoming less so in so far as the most vital aspect of government is concerned: in modern Britain, except for moments of foreign affairs or defence crises, the economy.

Thus, for what the protagonists of a department of economic affairs believed in to have become a reality would have required, in the first place, a degree of delegation of authority not only by a number of senior Ministers but also by the Prime Minister himself as well, which would not be easy to conceive in a modern government. I do not believe that George Brown, a most sensitive person and one who, except in moments of emotional stress, was mindful of the sensitivities of others, would have expected that. But what he and some of his pre-Election advisers seemed to expect was a much more authoritative position for the DEA *vis-à-vis* the Treasury.

In theory, this could have been secured. There are countries in which the establishment of economic policy is divided between a number of departments, and that concerned with finance not necessarily forming the court of last instance. However, this would have been a major departure in Britain. Not only is the Treasury statutorily in a special position – there are innumerable Acts of Parliament that expressly place responsibility on the Treasury for consenting to implementation of this or that provision or of the legislation as a whole – but, with the pragmatism inherent in British government (and this derives particularly from a time when the economic scope of government was more limited), emphasis has always been placed on the control of the purse strings. Still, given the changes that had already taken place in the preceding thirty years – the pre-war Economic Advisory Council, the Council on Productivity, Prices and Incomes of Selwyn Lloyd, to mention only two examples – the case for a broadly based and superordinate department could have been carried into practice. This would have required redefining in a more limited way the functions of the Treasury and not the other way round, i.e. by attempting to define the functions of the new department. This is precisely what the 'Concordat' attempted to do.

To the conceptual and practical constitution-making difficulties have to be added the problems created by the Prime Minister's own responsibilities, his own conception that the two departments should be in a state of 'creative tension', the residual personal problems between the principal actors and, perhaps most important of all, the fact that the most urgent problem immediately facing the Government (and as someone rightly remarked, 'Governments do the urgent not the important') was financial. It is easy, therefore, to see why the DEA was forced on to a course of carving out a role for itself, rather than inheriting automatically the leading role from the Treasury.

I cannot say that I saw all this as clearly in 1964 as I believe I see it now although, having known the Treasury well for many years, and for at least some time not only from the inside, but with a specially advantageous quasi-'outside' position as well, I was even at the time very sceptical about the exaggerated hopes for the DEA entertained by many others.

There were some who, being not very well disposed towards the whole trend of the new Government's policy, expressed doubts about the new department. One commentator, Nigel Lawson, writing as an independent contributor in the *Financial Times* on 14 April 1965, even produced a 'Requiem for a Lost Ministry'. Though several years in advance of the official demise of the department, it was very percipient in its analysis of the reasons for the continued preponderance of the Treasury.

However, a number of considerations kept me from worrying unduly about these jurisdictional issues in the first few months of the new Government. In the first place, I knew (and had so advised George Brown) that apart from – and usually more important than – constitutional boundaries, was the personal position of any individual senior member of the Cabinet and his relationship with the Prime Minister. In the particular case of the DEA, what this was to be had still to be worked out in practice. In the second place, it was impossible not to be caught up in the excitement of a new Government, formed by a Party that had so long been out of power, trying to cope with problems of extraordinary gravity and complexity.

To this must be added the fact that I was in a somewhat special personal position, additional to and distinct from that of being the official head of the department. I have already referred to the dual role I played during the first three months when I continued with my Washington activities – in an even enhanced way – travelling back and forth representing as much the Treasury as the DEA. This situation continued after my return to London, when thanks to my friendship with Armstrong and the kindly attitude of Jim Callaghan I was often called on, particularly in international negotiations, to deal with many strictly Treasury matters either alone or in double harness with Armstrong. Thus, we both went to Paris to explain to the Organization for Economic Co-operation and Development (OECD) the Government's first budget and its general economic policy. Callaghan also invited me to become a member of his Budget Committee on a personal basis, and although this created occasional awkwardnesses with my own Minister they were overcome.

Another important factor that made it possible in the early months of 1965 to forget the problem of demarcation was the development of important new activities by the DEA, although in retrospect, as I shall show, this can be seen to have been a mixed blessing. These activities fell into four categories: regional policy, industrial policy, policy on prices and incomes and, theoretically at least encompassing all these as well as other central macro-economic policies such as fiscal policy, the National Plan.

The development of all these inevitably led to a considerable expansion of the department. Regional policy included the setting up of a series of regional planning boards with outside chairmen but requiring staffs of Civil Servants to service them, though we tried to economize by associating those with existing regional government offices in the field. Industrial policy was largely in the hands of a group of industrial advisers appointed from outside (headed at first by Fred Catherwood) but these too had to have an appropriate official staff. Prices and incomes policy, though its execution was entrusted to a specially created board again staffed by outside public personalities, needed a substantial and strong division inside the department. The National Plan called above all for a strong group of economists who had to be recruited quickly from universities and elsewhere, and also for experienced Civil Servants to conduct the complex series of interdepartmental discussions and negotiations.

The recruitment and organization of all this additional personnel was accomplished remarkably quickly, as was the integration of this new machine into the broader Whitehall organism of working parties and committees at different levels. When, a little over a year after its formation, I lectured on the department in a series organized by the Royal Institute of Public Administration, I was able to report that it had a staff of 550 (a large number when one considers that it had been going only for twelve months, but still only one-third of that of the Treasury, traditionally one of the smallest government departments) and that it had become an integral part of the Whitehall machine, distinguished from others by two important characteristics: it had no executive responsibilities and it had no 'sectional' interests to defend.

While I had to be concerned with all the department's activities, each one of them was in the charge of one of my senior colleagues who enjoyed a considerable degree of autonomy and complete and direct access to the First Secretary. Thus, the putting together of the National Plan was very much the responsibility of Donald MacDougall who was also much involved in the early stages of the prices and incomes policy, an area that was then taken over by Douglas Allen. Within a few months, as the department's activities developed, the more senior official levels were expanded so that in addition to the Director General (Donald MacDougall) and a Second Permanent Secretary (Douglas Allen) we had five Deputy Under-Secretaries, responsible for industrial policies (Ronnie McIntosh), economic co-ordination, overseas (Derek Mitchell), economic co-ordination, home (Evan Maude), economic planning (John Jukes) and regional policy (Arthur Peterson). In addition, there were seven industrial advisers (seconded by their firms) and eight regional economic planning boards chairmen, by this time all Civil Servants. The quality of the department's staff was widely recognized even by those who had their doubts about the *raison d'être* of the department as such, and is proved also by the very high positions in the public service and in business that so many of them subsequently attained.

As for the activities themselves, one's judgement will be coloured largely by one's views of the proper scope of government intervention in the economy, since each one of them – the Plan itself only by implication – involved some degree of intervention, and in certain instances a very considerable degree. It should, however, be emphasized that with a very few exceptions the department's functions did not include executive responsibility: implementation was left to other departments. A good deal of what was done was not entirely new: regional development policies, for example, were attempted in one way or another by earlier Governments and regional organizations, and offices representing a number of departments had been a feature of the machinery of government for a long time. The Plan, though ostensibly a new development, also had its antecedents in the reports of the National Economic Development Council (NEDC), which had attempted under a Government of a different political complexion to combine various strands of economic policy and to produce something approaching the indicative planning method of the French Commissariat au Plan.

Nor was prices and incomes policy entirely new. It had been attempted before and was to be continued, though in different forms both in regard to the specifics of policy and to the organization for devising and implementing it, by later and politically different Administrations. This aspect of the department's work I had personally regarded both then and since as not only important in itself but as having more legitimacy across the spectrum of different political conceptions of economic policy than any other. It seems to me that in a modern advanced economy, at least if it is a fairly open one in which fluctuations of economic activity and their consequences are much influenced by international economic events, means for influencing the course of incomes – and, to the extent to which incomes influence them, prices – must be included in the arsenal of macro-economic policies at the disposal of government. Even if incomes policy is not explicitly recognized and used, modern Governments inevitably act on incomes not only because they are major employers and must, therefore, have a policy about the wages and salaries they themselves pay, but also because the other, traditional and unquestioned major instruments of policy they employ, fiscal and monetary, inevitably affect incomes directly or indirectly.

Thus in spite of the very great difficulties in securing co-operation from both sides of industry (without which an explicit incomes policy is impossible), in spite of the great technical problems of devising the right system suited to a particular economic climate and monitoring its observance, and despite the hostility (and ridicule) that greeted some of the early attempts of the Government – inevitably more high-sounding than could be sustained in practice, the first 'solemn and binding' declaration of intent by Government, unions and employers was soon known as 'Solomon Binding' – this was one of the areas of the Government's efforts with which I was in entire sympathy.

One amusing incident at a critical moment during the evolution of the policy towards statutory provisions that reached the gossip columns at the time and that is briefly mentioned in Harold Wilson's memoirs is worth recounting because it provided some light relief in a very tense situation. It occurred during the summer of 1965 when there was another anxious period over sterling and innumerable telephone conversations took place between the US Secretary of the Treasury Joe Fowler (who had succeeded Douglas Dillon) in Washington and the Chancellor, sometimes in his London office, sometimes in his holiday home, followed by telephone conversations between the Chancellor and the Prime Minister, who was on holiday, to all of which I was asked to listen so that I could keep George Brown informed.

It became clear that the efficacy of prices and incomes policy was a major element in determining the credibility of the Government's whole policy and, therefore, its ability to command continued international financial support. George Brown had been having discussions with the Trades Union Congress (TUC) with a view to establishing a statutory basis for prices and incomes policy and these were to culminate in his appearance at the TUC's forthcoming Brighton Congress. Before this, he was taking a short holiday on the Riviera as the guest of Harold Lever. I was asked to visit George and, in order that he could have the latest papers on the subject, Douglas Allen and I flew to Nice. By chance, David Howell was on the same plane and on arrival was met by Ted Heath whom he was joining on holiday. Ted naturally asked me what I was doing there. I do not know whether he believed my explanation that I had come for a short holiday: although I was wearing what could pass for holiday clothes, I had no luggage and Douglas Allen wore a business suit and carried the standard Whitehall briefcase! Fortunately, we were whisked away by Harold Lever's driver before we had to offer any further explanation.

Nothing that has happened in recent years, not only in our country, but in others too, has changed my view on the importance of an incomes policy, although I fully recognize the great practical difficulties, not least the problem of 're-entry', i.e. of reverting to a free system of collective bargaining when changed circumstances make the maintenance of controls inappropriate. Most recent experience in a number of countries has shown that those that in one way or another can most quickly adapt incomes to changing circumstances will most quickly and smoothly cope with major disturbances, for example the oil shocks. This has pre-eminently been true of Japan; it has been true of Austria; until recently at least it has also been true of Germany and Sweden, and, for somewhat different reasons, it has been and in a measure remains true of the United States.

I was more ambivalent about the Plan itself, not that I rejected the concept but I did have doubts about the wisdom – in the time span that political necessity appeared to impose and, above all, in view of the enormous and acute disturbances in the financial sphere that demanded immediate action on the fiscal and monetary fronts – of laying down a programme (or at least a conditioned forecast) for several years ahead. When one looks again at the document that emerged, while it is easy enough to show how many of the courses of action and their predicted results were falsified by the substantial changes which were occurring even while the Plan was being printed, the general effect is not as disappointing as one might expect. Nor does it give the impression of an irrepressible urge to interfere with all markets and impose government authority on all economic activity. Indeed, if anything, it suffers rather from an excess of 'exhortation', the most common coin of government policy.

Probably the most controversial part, both at the time and in retrospect, of the department's activities was that relating to industrial policy, though here the department was far from being always the spearhead. Technology and the Board of Trade and a number of others, Transport and Housing among them, were much – and sometimes more – involved. As far as the DEA was concerned, industrial policy writ large was almost non-existent except in the broadest terms always used by Governments, before and since, of urging greater efficiency, productivity, innovation, greater competitiveness, mobility of labour, more training and so on. In most of these areas new measures were introduced to help achieve the desired objectives, but generally speaking they were a continuation, albeit in a more intensive way, of policies already well known and tried, or they fell very much within the scope of other departments. The DEA's role was that of stimulator, particularly through the boundless energy of its Minister.

A good deal more was also done to enlarge the area of direct support in the shape of incentives for industrial arrangements designed to make industries – or firms within industries – more efficient; and, while the scale of this support was very much greater than it had been before, it was not in principle unprecedented. One institutional innovation in the field of industrial restructuring was, however, introduced, the Industrial Reconstruction Corporation, created at the beginning of 1966. The idea for it had been germinating for a long time among Labour's advisers, notably Thomas Balogh who had pre-war experience in the City and similar institutions, and had existed in a number of Continental countries for some time. I chaired a working party, composed of officials as well as representatives from industry and finance and, although there were some fears expressed that a new institution might become a privileged government-owned and -financed merchant bank, the White Paper in January 1966 was drafted in a way that laid most of these fears to rest. Both the first Chairman (Frank Kearton) and the first Managing Director (Ronnie Grierson) were drawn from the private sector and during its limited life before it was abolished during the first 'free-market' phase of the Heath Government it did a good deal of useful work, though perhaps not as dramatic as some of its early protagonists had hoped – and opponents had feared.

In what might be thought to be the central core of policy towards industry of the Labour Government of that day, nationalization, the DEA had practically no part to play. The First Secretary was naturally much involved with this issue in Cabinet but, given his past attitude and closeness to Gaitskell, it is fair to assume that he was not a 'nationalizer'. As a department we were only very peripherally involved. The initiatives here were partly with the particular departments directly concerned – Transport, Technology, Power, Trade, to name a few – and in any event were mainly taken and debated at the political level. I had personally some quite informal discussions with the Chairman of the British Iron and Steel Federation (Ted Judge), who had developed some interesting ideas on alternatives to outright nationalization, as well as with the Chairman of the Iron and Steel Board (Sir Cyril Musgrave), but any alternative policy, though on paper entirely feasible, remained a 'might have been'. I suspect that George Brown would have been sympathetic to a practicable alternative.

In the event, the major preoccupations in the field of industrial policy were concerned with particular instances, including 'rescue' operations for individual firms, which, if they were sufficiently important from a financial, export or employment point of view, always involved the Secretary of State himself and two or three of his most senior officials.

With his extraordinary energy and his determination never to accept an unsatisfactory situation without attempting to remedy it, particularly where employment prospects depended on the survival of an industry or firm, George Brown never hesitated to plunge in and to cajole individuals or companies to participate in this or that venture. This often gave rise to stormy, but also hilarious, sessions with reluctant tycoons in which my own part was necessarily entirely that of an onlooker. One lasting benefit to me of these encounters was to have formed a fast friendship, based on personal as well as intellectual affinities, with that remarkable member of the Wilson and Callaghan administrations, Harold Lever, whom George often brought into these discussions.

George Brown in his memoirs says that one of his mistakes was to allow himself 'to become over-immersed in the working out of prices and incomes policy'. I would not single out this particular part of the DEA's function: I have already said that I regarded it as specially important and without the Minister's untiring efforts, particularly when it came to putting it on a statutory basis, it would never have worked at all.

However, in a more general sense, George Brown is right. I have indicated earlier than I regarded the development of certain activities peculiar to the DEA as a department as a mixed blessing. In this sense it is quite true that the First Secretary of State immersed, for example, in the fight for the prices and incomes legislation with the unions, the Federation of British Industries (FBI) (as it then was) and in Parliament, or in an attempt to rescue the Clyde shipbuilding industry, to say nothing of attending EFTA meetings or conferences of the Socialist International, had, even with his extraordinary reservoir of energy, little time to take a systematic interest in the direction of the more general elements of economic policy.

To all these obvious calls on his time must be added two others, which, in theory at least, need not have come his way. One was Rhodesia; the other Europe. The latter at least could be said to have fallen fairly naturally to George Brown, not only because he had always been a keen 'European', but also because the wide range of the interests involved in any resumption of our attempt to join the Community made it necessary to entrust this to a superdepartmental Minister. Rhodesia, that is to say the management of the policy of economic sanctions, need not have been entrusted to the DEA but, with his usual enthusiasm, George Brown was not at all unhappy at the thought of becoming a 'Minister of Economic Warfare' in addition to his other duties. Both these activities led to some further expansion of the department and therefore involved me personally.

In the case of Rhodesia, this meant a good deal of discussion with the Americans as well as Continentals and negotiation with various industrial, commercial and financial interests. As far as Europe was concerned, this was a very welcome addition to my duties, as it almost meant taking up where I had left off – or so it seemed at the time. In fact, discussion with individual Governments, with the Commission and with influential outside people, such as Monnet, while interesting, did not really lead to any result. The culmination of this phase, a visit by Georges Pompidou and Couve de Murville to London at the beginning of July 1966 showed that the French were as opposed as ever to our entry and, in private briefing to the press, put a good deal of emphasis on the troubles of the British economy, including a possibly over-valued pound – with the obvious consequences in the markets the next day! What made both George Brown and me wonder right from the beginning whether the French had come with any intention at all of doing business was the fact that while each one of us on the British side had a voluminous folder of briefs, not one of the members of the French delegation had a single sheet of paper in front of him!

The First Secretary was involved in major economic discussions whenever critical moments occurred, as they did frequently during 1965 and 1966 – whether through uncertainty generated by tax reforms (arguably justified in themselves, but possibly mistimed), recurrent rumours of devaluation, flights of capital, run-down in reserves, or intimate discussions with the US Administration on the relation between certain domestic policies (particularly on the effectiveness of prices and incomes policies) and the external financial situation. This, however, did not make up for the lack of continuous and systematic participation by him and the department as such in discussions of central policy, even though I personally had some at the official level. My participation in such discussions could not, of course, take the place of intimate discussion between Ministers.

The result was that the gap between the conception of the department's function and the reality became more obvious to many in the department who had not before thought much about it but, more particularly, to George Brown himself. I have said earlier that it was not until a later stage in the department's history that this issue arose again. That stage was reached in the early months of 1966 when George Brown, as he indicates in his memoirs, became more acutely impatient and, with the approach of an Election, more concerned about the future. We had a number of conversations during that time and, on 29 March, two days before polling day, while he was working in his constituency, we met in Derby for lunch and had a thorough discussion. In the expectation that the Government would be returned – as it was, with an increased majority – George had arranged to meet the Prime Minister one evening during the weekend immediately after the poll. In preparation we agreed on the various points that he was to raise concerning the future activities of the DEA with considerable emphasis on the need to clarify relations with the Treasury, indeed the position of the department in the whole process of economic policy-making.

The next few months, however, showed little change and the frustrations that George Brown records were increasingly translated into a partly real, though perhaps more an imagined, fundamental difference of political purpose. George Brown describes it as a situation in which the department was constantly trying to work for expansion while, largely through Treasury influence, the general direction of policy was highly deflationary. I am not certain, looking back on these eighteen months from the beginning of 1965 to the 'July measures' (as they became known) in 1966, whether there was quite so fundamental an incompatibility. Not surprisingly, George Brown and his advisers did not care for the deflationary policies, both on expenditure and on taxation, that were put into action from time to time – and many were of a kind that could reasonably be debated by reasonable men. Some of them were in the fiscal field, such as the timing and some of the details of corporation and capital gains tax or the precise use of the regulator. In this connection some advisers placed an excessive emphasis on the automobile industry, which almost became a kind of governor of the whole economy, by being subjected to alternate sticks and carrots. Later, there was the controversial introduction of the selective employment tax (SET), which was based on a highly theoretical concept of the mainsprings of economic development. Most acutely controversial was the question whether, and if so when, the parity of sterling was to be changed.

It was indirectly on this last issue that according to his own narrative George Brown finally decided to resign. This was at the time of the July 1966 cuts, by which time George Brown himself, some other very important Ministers and most advisers had become convinced that devaluation was necessary. There was, however, heated argument whether this should precede, follow, be simultaneous with, or in place of, further deflationary measures – in the language of the day, whether 'a hole should be dug first'. This, as I recall, meant whether the deflation should come first so as to release resources, which could then, with the extra competitiveness of a devalued pound, be devoted to exports.

As it turned out – and we have the accounts of at least two of the principal actors, Wilson and Brown – the subject of devaluation was declared taboo and the deflationary measures were agreed. Armstrong and I were instructed to work out the details and prepare the first draft of the Prime Minister's statement, which he made to a packed House on 20 July 1966. George Brown was not present, and when Bill Rodgers passing the official box asked me where he was I told him that he was in the department and that I understood he was intending to resign. Rodgers with his usual skill and efficiency immediately organized a round robin of about a hundred MPs urging Brown not to do so, and this must have been a major factor in making him change his mind. However, his time in the DEA was coming to an end and within less than a month he had taken up his new post as Foreign Secretary.

For myself, the last few months had been punctuated not only by a number of particular official assignments in connection with financial negotiations, especially in the USA, or with exploratory discussions about 'Europe', but also with increasing doubts about my continued stay in the Civil Service. I had had a number of approaches, some academic or academic/administrative, an offer from George Woods of a Vice-Presidency of the World Bank and some from business.

A minor complication – indeed it turned out, as I had expected, to be a non-event – was the speculation that had started at the end of 1965 and gathered momentum in the first few months of 1966 about the successor as Governor of the Bank of England to Lord Cromer whose term of office was soon to come to an end. This followed closely on another, quite different, appointment that was in the offing, namely that of Director of the London School of Economics to succeed Sir Sidney Caine. About the latter appointment I knew practically nothing except that, in common with several other Permanent Secretaries, I had been asked by Lord Bridges, Chairman of the School's Governors, for suggestions for possible candidates. I had no intention of being one myself and indeed had no idea whether, if I had been one, I would have had a chance.

The speculation about the Bank of England, which spread in the newspapers like a rash, was something different. It was no secret – and given the openness with which certainly George Brown but also Harold Wilson spoke at least 'for background' to the press, it could hardly have been so – that Lord Cromer was not in the Government's good books. Equally it was known that he himself had little sympathy with the general direction of the Government's economic policy, although he carried out his duties loyally and, indeed, had done a most remarkable job in securing financial assistance at most critical moments. It was, therefore, generally expected that he would not be appointed to a second term and he himself indicated that he wanted to return to private life.

Apart from one or two cryptic remarks made to me by George Brown, I had no knowledge of what discussions – between Ministers, directors of the Bank, City figures, or officials – went on about the succession. I can only suppose that George Brown did mention my name, though, of course, I do not know whether he had seriously 'put it forward'. For my part, I had no illusions; above all because I knew that the rest of the Court of the Bank (as the Board of Directors is known) and many elements in the City would be opposed to the appointment of any Civil Servant, if only, as Cecil King later told me, because of the disparity of pay! This was confirmed to me much, much later by Jim Callaghan who also added that if it had not been so, he would also have had to 'consider his own Permanent Secretary'! The appointment went to the Deputy Governor, Leslie O'Brien, who had been in the Bank all his working life and was universally respected. I had had a good deal to do with him during the various crises and had learned to admire him very much. My respect and affection for him were enhanced when some years later I could see him closely in action after I was myself appointed to the Court during his Governorship.

It was not until the summer of 1966 that the thought of leaving the public service less than two years before I would reach the official Civil Service retirement age began to crystallize in my mind. I told George that although I had not reacted to any of the business approaches that I had had, I was leaning towards making a change in the autumn and that I was thinking primarily of the City. I asked him to inform the Prime Minister, which he did and I then made it clear to both of them that I would be guided entirely by them as to the timing of my departure.

The subject was not referred to again until after George Brown had left the DEA. When he knew that he was to be Foreign Secretary and so told me before the news became public, he also urged me to go with him to the Foreign Office at least until it was time for me to retire. He was quite insistent, but I pointed out to him that this would never work and that whatever my own feelings were and despite my constant readiness to try something quite new, he would handicap himself gravely and unnecessarily by importing an outside Permanent Under-Secretary, even assuming that all concerned could be persuaded to accept so unusual an arrangement. I told him that these transplants are not always easy; as between the home Civil Service and the diplomatic service they were very rare indeed at the highest level. For example, despite Macmillan's support and the great qualities of Roger Makins, his import into the Treasury had been very difficult and, as far as I could tell, had not worked out particularly well. A converse move, an outsider into what was, and I believe still is, internally at least, the best organized and most closely knit department in Whitehall could only lead to frustration all round.

After a final talk over an early morning cup of tea on the terrace of the House, he desisted. I was amused shortly afterwards to receive separate visits from the Permanent Under-Secretary and the Principal Private Secretary at the Foreign Office who wished to be briefed about their new Minister whose impending arrival seemed to have inspired some apprehension. These I was able to dispel. I did not, of course, tell them about the Minister's earlier ideas about myself!

I stayed in the DEA only a short time after George Brown's departure, but had occasion to experience a very different type of Minister in Michael Stewart, whom I had previously known only unofficially. He was quiet, precise, methodical, never given to temper tantrums and always extremely courteous. It is hard to tell whether the work in the DEA, which he had for only a very short time before he was succeeded by Peter Shore, would have suited his talents, because, far from the department's position improving, a real process of decline set in with most of its specific activities gradually moving to other departments and with the Prime Minister taking a more openly direct interest in what remained of its functions.

I myself left the department (and the Civil Service) on 30 September 1966, a little under two years after the DEA had been set up with me as its first Permanent Under-Secretary. Douglas Allen succeeded me and, when William Armstrong left the Treasury to become Head of the Civil Service, Allen was the obvious successor at the Treasury and, subsequently also, the Civil Service Department.

The rules of the Service require in certain cases a period of 'purdah' before a retiring Civil Servant may take on a business appointment. This, in my case, was fixed at six months (twice the period of some who came after) and thanks to the kindness of some friends at Harvard I was invited to spend that time at Harvard at the School of Government in the recently founded Kennedy Center as one of the first batch of Kennedy Fellows (indeed, the only foreign one).

A SUMMING UP

At this point I should like to add a few more words about the personalities with whom I was so closely in contact during this first phase of the new Labour Government. I saw, of course, much less of the Chancellor or of the Prime Minister than I did of George Brown. Callaghan, whom I got to know better after I left the Service, seemed to me always the most relaxed of the three. He was polite to his officials and advisers (and always kind to me), though he could be quite sharp when dealing with people representing outside interests. He had prepared himself with some academic briefing in economics before the Election and he continued to pay a good deal of attention to the advice he received from those who had been recruited on a temporary basis into the service of the new Government. But, at least in the early days, the process of striking the right balance between what continued to be somewhat theoretical advice, his own very shrewd instincts, and the political pressures in Cabinet and Party, was clearly a difficult one for him. It was not helped by the circumstances created not only by the existence of a rival department, headed by a man of more exuberant temperament, but also by the Prime Minister's position and attitude. These factors did not make it easy for the Chancellor to establish his own position, as distinct from that of the Treasury as a department, though had the devaluation taken place in the summer of 1966 I believe that Callaghan's personal record as Chancellor might well have been different.

The Prime Minister was a trained economist who not only as a matter of course had access to the new advisers in the Treasury and the DEA, but had a staff of his own advisers in No. 10 and the Cabinet Office. By nature, I believe, a rather conservative man, one certainly very conscious of the important role that the private sector and markets played in the economy, he was under the inevitable constraint of having to lead a Party divided on many fundamentals of economic policy, tasting power for the first time in many years, but having to govern with an exiguous majority during the initial period. This inevitably gave his Administration its stamp in the perception of the public at home and abroad. He and even more some of his advisers were inclined to blame sinister outside forces for much of the difficulty that the Government experienced and this addiction to a sort of conspiracy theory of history led him to react quickly and decisively but not always with sufficiently well thought out measures. The conspiracy theory was also often invoked where attitudes of colleagues and advisers were concerned, and often intrigues were seen and reacted to where the assumption (even if unduly charitable) of more innocent motives would have led to a smoother working of the governmental machine.

George Brown, though not entirely free from what I have come to regard as an occupational disease to which politicians are often subject, namely to see conspiracies everywhere, was however much less affected by this. He knew, and took for granted, that much of the business community would not be in sympathy with the Government, but despite many angry scenes he managed to establish remarkably friendly and constructive relations with many business leaders. They – and we in the department – had at the same time to put up with an exceptionally volatile temperament, of which colleagues, including particularly his Junior Ministers, his Private Secretary and myself were the principal targets. I think the primary reason for our being so selected was our continuous propinquity, though, as far as I was concerned, too much of a readiness to become emotionally involved, to the point sometimes of a reciprocal loss of temper, had also something to do with our occasional quite tempestuous clashes.

These, however, never lasted long and I should add that I do not remember a single one concerned with any important matter of policy as distinct from sometimes quite trivial administrative questions. The worst one I remember was about access to some secret documents that required special indoctrination, which I had had in my NATO days and which George still had to undergo – a process that took less than fifteen minutes after he finally consented to it! Certainly in my case our disagreements never diminished my high regard for his exceptional intelligence and deep-seated patriotism or my personal affection born of a recognition of the basic kindness of this exceptional man. Douglas Allen, although he also had some stormy encounters, had on the whole an easier relationship, no doubt because he has a more equable temper. Significantly, George Brown established a particularly close and happy relation with Denis Greenhill – an embodiment of good sense – whom he chose to be his Permanent Under-Secretary at the Foreign Office.

I have not much to say of other Ministers, although I had many occasions to see them in interdepartmental committees or when they passed through the First Secretary's office, as most of them did to ask his view or secure his support on many issues, from postal charges to the motorway programme. There is no doubt that whatever view one may take of their politics, they were a quite exceptional group of individuals with many outstanding qualities of intelligence, erudition and character. Despite my proximity to them during the first two years, I find it difficult to judge them as a governing team given, as I have repeatedly emphasized, the background, i.e. on the one hand their inexperience, on the other, the exceptionally unpropitious world climate, of which I have of necessity only mentioned the economic components. In addition, like all Governments, they were, contrary to popular opinion, more loyal to their election pledges than it turned out to be wise to be. I believe it was Chateaubriand who said that the qualities required to achieve power are not necessarily those needed for exercising it. I would paraphrase this dictum (and have so told Ministers from time to time – much to their shocked astonishment) that the promises required to be made to win elections are not necessarily those one should be most eager to carry out after one is elected. This is, I hope, not cynicism but simply a statement of one form in which the dilemma of our type of democracy and electoral system presents itself. Against the well-known assumption that it is in the early days – the 'honeymoon period' – that Governments can and should do most must be set the all too common experience that it is precisely then that many mistakes are made that it is very difficult to retrieve later. The Budget of June 1979 is, to my mind, an outstanding recent example.

I am left with some reflections of a general nature – additional to what I have already said about the relation between the DEA and the Treasury – on the machinery of government and the relationship between politicians and Civil Servants. I had occasion, some two years later, to concern myself with these matters during an 'exercise' on this subject but it is perhaps more appropriate to say something more about it here, at the point at which my official connection with government ceased.

In 1968 and 1969 a small group of former Permanent Secretaries met to discuss certain aspects of the machinery of government in the light of their own experience, particularly in view of the many changes that had taken place in the most recent past: the creation of new departments, the changes in the priorities between departments, the merging and demerging of departments and agencies and so forth. The idea was that anything that emerged from these deliberations might form useful briefing for the Leader of the Opposition with whom the group was in touch, should he in due course be called upon to form a Government.

The subject has always, but particularly so in recent decades, held an extraordinary fascination for Ministers and particularly for actual or putative Prime Ministers, and not surprisingly the most senior Civil Servants, though in general less starry-eyed about what can be achieved by means of organizational and structural change, have also shown an inclination to share in this game of governmental 'engineering'. The latest example is to be found in the Reith Lectures on 'Government and Governed' delivered at the end of 1983 by Douglas Wass who had just retired from the posts of Permanent Secretary of the Treasury and Joint Permanent Head of the Home Civil Service.

In more specific terms, the 1968 group to which I have referred tried to answer questions on four subjects: the central machinery for co-ordinating decision-making; the grouping of functions of the economic departments; the place and organization of a 'Prime Minister's Department' and, somewhat incongruously and probably influenced by some of the preoccupations and predilections of the Government then in power, the application to certain governmental tasks of the 'project' approach. Leaving aside the last as being, at best, of a lesser order of generality, the three questions are reasonably comprehensive and useful pegs on which to hang a discussion of the main issues of governmental machinery. Douglas Wass, in the lectures to which I have referred, goes wider than these, dealing for example also with the very important question of the 'openness' of government, but this is outside my present purpose.

I have mentioned the group in which I participated not because it was itself of special importance (nor can I trace many subsequent developments as being directly due to its conclusions) but because, from a personal point of view, it enabled me to collect my own conclusions into a sort of summing-up of a quarter of a century in the public service. I should, however, add one caveat: although I had served as a 'regular' Civil Servant, temporary for over four years, 'established' for over twenty, my career, as the reader will have seen, was by no means typical of the average administrator. The war period was in any case *sui generis*; the spell in the immediate post-war Ministry of Food was still in rather abnormal circumstances and also short. After that, with the exception of four years in the Ministries of Food and Agriculture (again by no means wholly devoted to regular administrative duties) and the two turbulent years in the DEA, my activities had been very largely in international negotiations and special assignments. It may be that this half-player, half-onlooker experience has enabled me to see more of the game without the disadvantage of being wholly detached from the action.

I strongly share the view that many of my former colleagues hold – and that is also expressed by Douglas Wass – that the machinery for co-ordinating central decisions, that is to say by which the collective responsibility of the Cabinet is exercised, is not adequate to its present tasks. I will not go over the arguments, which have been rehearsed by many commentators over many years, and most recently expressed again by Douglas Wass, except to say that essentially each Minister 'fights his own corner' and that Cabinet collective responsibility – if it is understood to imply some conscious direction of the Government's policy as a whole – emerges most of the time as an *ad hoc* settlement of differences of interest and opinion on specific issues. Of course, Governments, especially in their early phases, may start with a strong ideological thrust. This was true of the 1945 Labour Government and of Harold Wilson's first few years; it was true of the first two years of

Ted Heath's Administration and it is true of the present Government. But this, even where it provides a commitment to broad policy objectives, is not enough. More social security and equality of opportunity, economic growth and technological innovation, no support for 'lame ducks', or ensuring greater freedom for markets and heavy reliance on monetary policy, are all very well as slogans, but the daily problems and tasks that crowd in on a Government not only make it difficult to test individual actions against these proclaimed broad objectives, but leave very little time and energy for the formulation of an appropriate long-term strategy.

The establishment of a Cabinet of non-departmental Ministers has rightly been ruled out as unrealistic because it would create a group of disembodied supervisors out of touch with reality. However, smaller Cabinets, achieved by a greater grouping of departments and the devolution of certain executive functions to quasi-independent agencies could help, as could the further extension of the system of parliamentary committees on American lines – a welcome development of recent years – because it provides a machinery for testing departmental activities and policies that could produce more attention to overall strategic objectives.

But more important than anything else that could improve matters would be the existence of a central official staff without departmental duties and serving the Cabinet collectively. This suggestion has been looked at from time to time and usually rejected (as it is by Douglas Wass). In part this is due to a – I believe false – analogy with the case against a Cabinet consisting of non-departmental Ministers; in greater part to a fear that the creation of a 'Prime Minister's Department' would unduly foster already existing tendencies towards a Prime-Ministerial, i.e. presidential, type of Government, and, therefore, be destructive of the foundation of our Cabinet system. I believe this argument to be ill-founded if one thinks of a 'Prime Minister *and Cabinet* Department', which, while it would naturally be closely in touch with the Prime Minister as Chairman of the Cabinet, would be available and responsible to the Cabinet as a whole, as is the present Cabinet Office.

The difference would be that the new department would be larger and would, in addition to the administrative and procedural duties of the Cabinet Office as a Secretariat, also have a division concerned with personnel, machinery of government, and related matters. This was the function of the Civil Service Department and is now in part allocated to the Cabinet Secretary as joint Head of the Home Civil Service. There would also be another division concerned with what one might call the planning of priorities, i.e. something on the lines of what the 'think tank' was supposed to be, but never quite was. While the presidential tendencies that have been discernible in a number of recent Governments and that make many apprehensive can, in the last resort, be contained only by the strength and ability of the Prime Minister's Cabinet colleagues (and by the watchfulness of Parliament), such a central department properly organized and staffed as part of the permanent machinery of government could make collective decision-making and responsibility more, rather than less, effective.

It might be objected that Prime Ministers have in any event tended in recent times to surround themselves with special advisers; these, however, are nearly all recruited from the outside and are temporary. Apart from some general limitations to which I refer below, their effectiveness is dependent not only on their ability but also on the goodwill of other Ministers and departmental officials. Even if that is present, as it usually is, the result can certainly not be guaranteed to be as effective as if they were a fully-fledged and permanent part of the machine. It may also be argued that the Secretary of the Cabinet has, in any event, tended to become the Prime Minister's principal adviser, acting for example as the Prime Minister's emissary in the preparation of summit meetings. But this relationship is first of all dependent on the personalities of the Prime Minister and Cabinet Secretary; it is also apt to create some strains in the exercise of the Secretary's neutrality *vis-à-vis* all members of the Cabinet, and, above all, his position and function is not buttressed by the existence of an effective department.

A more serious argument and one that may in the event be decisive (though it is hard to be certain until the experiment has been tried) is that it may create too powerful an element inside the bureaucracy, not only *vis-à-vis* individual departments of state, but also in respect of the basic democratic control of government. For the life of Governments is short. Even when they succeed in securing a second, or, more rarely, a third term, they can never be sure of that in advance. (This is indeed one of the major, but inescapable, causes of the difficulty of having and maintaining a long-term strategy.) A powerful central department could become a focus of more than continuity, namely of entrenched positions, such as Ministers have been known to complain of even where individual departments are concerned. I believe, however, that on balance that danger has to be faced in the way in which all evil tendencies have to be, by constant vigilance and by suitable checks and balances.

As far as the economic departments are concerned, I believe that there is some case, not for having two central departments as in the Wilson Government, but of having one that combines the functions of the Treasury with those originally intended for the DEA, though I hasten to add that what these are to be in precise detail would depend very much on the general economic philosophy of the Government. It is at least arguable that even a very 'non-interventionist' Government might find it useful to have within its central economic department wider concerns than those that are traditionally special to the Treasury, if only to guide and co-ordinate the basic policies with which other economic departments are concerned.

As I say, I do not believe that this concept is compatible only with an interventionist policy. There are, however, two other arguments that are more telling. In the first place it can be said that since the demise of the DEA, the Treasury has in fact concerned itself increasingly with these wider – non-exclusively financial – questions. It is, however, not certain that to tack these on to the central financial concerns of the Treasury, rather than have both of them integrated into a single economic policy department can ever be wholly effective.

A second, in practice very important, argument is whether an economic and financial 'overlord' would not have so powerful a position as to rival that of the Prime Minister. I do not think that, personalities apart, this needs to be the case. In a system of collective Cabinet responsibility, neither the Prime Minister's nor the Economic Minister's power can be exclusive. Moreover, though economic matters have tended to get the headlines in recent years, they are by no means the only vital issues on which a suitable balance between the power of the Prime Minister and that of the departmental Ministers has to be achieved. This is certainly so in foreign affairs and defence and quite often too in home affairs.

Different Prime Ministers will be under different temptations (and
have the effective opportunity to succumb to them) of being 'their
own' Chancellors, Foreign Secretaries or Defence Ministers!

There remains a final, and connected, question – the broader
one of the relation between the permanent Civil Service and the
elected Government. This, in my experience, is more often a
question for debate, as well as of substantive tension, in our
country than in most other highly developed ones, with the
possible exception of Canada where the system is fairly close to
our own. I can only suppose that the reason why it is not so in the
United States, France or Germany is because the dividing line
between the Minister and the 'privileged adviser' as Douglas Wass
calls him, is different and at critical levels not so sharp as it is
here.

The modern British Civil Service, in its fundamentals as created
over a century and a quarter ago after the Northcote–Trevelyan
Report, has often been praised as one of the greatest achievements
of the British genius for ordering human affairs and has been said
to be the envy of other countries. From time to time, however,
there have been periods when Ministers, particularly of a new
Administration, have been highly suspicious of their permanent
advisers, and have not concealed this fact, often with the result
that the institution itself has become suspect in the eyes of public
opinion. This was so when the 1964 Labour Government came in,
as it was in 1979 when the present Administration first came into
power. The result has been not only a suspicion that those who
had served an Administration of a different political persuasion
could not possibly be loyal to the new one, but a general belief
that the Service was overmanned, overpaid, either underworked
(though the pre-war jibe that the 'fountains in Trafalgar Square,
like the Civil Servants, play from ten to four' has not, I think, been
heard recently) or, alternatively, consumed by a desire for power,
which leads them to usurp the functions of the elected representatives of the people. Anyone with even only a modest acquaintance
with the Civil Service will know that this is a travesty of the facts;
in particular any idea that Civil Servants, whatever their own
political inclinations may be (and they are certainly not political
eunuchs), have difficulty in loyally serving different political
masters is totally misconceived.

Nevertheless, there is something in the relation between the permanent official and the elected (and, therefore, inevitably transient) Minister that creates a problem. Edward Bridges, perhaps the last of the old race of 'mandarins', in a lecture many years ago on the Civil Service – 'Portrait of a Profession' – pointed to some features of this relationship that he clearly took to be praiseworthy, but that could illustrate the existence of a problem. He spoke of the existence of a 'departmental view', a complex of opinions and attitudes formed of long experience, separate from the ideas of inexperienced and perhaps over-eager Ministers, a point of view he also expressed to me on a number of occasions when he spoke – affectionately – of the power of the 'machine'. He also emphasized that the experienced administrator will have learned that 'the walls of Jericho do not fall even after seven circumambulations to the sound of a trumpet.' It is easy to see that these sentiments could well evoke doubts not only in the minds of Ministers but of any serious outside observer and account for the impression of arrogance that the higher Civil Service has sometimes created. In fact, they do no more than point to an inherent difference in position and, therefore, approach to the problems of government. It is fair to say that this difference has in practice usually resulted in a pragmatic reconciliation, since, in the end, the Minister's view must prevail.

This is, however, not readily recognized and accepted: in any event some more definite and systematic solution has been suggested from time to time. In the United States the problem does not arise. In the first place, Cabinet members themselves are essentially technical advisers to the Chief Executive, the President, from whom they have delegated powers, and they are executants of the Administration's policy. (It is perhaps significant that they are always referred to as 'officials'.) In the second place, the permanent Civil Service reaches only into the middle-high levels of the machine. Appointments to sub-Cabinet-level posts, which include many grades that would in England be filled by senior administrative Civil Servants, are occupied by political appointees. This does result in a vast series of changes, with sometimes a period of chaos, when a new Administration takes over, but it avoids, in principle at least, any apparent or real divergence between department and Cabinet officer.

In France and Germany, though not to quite the same extent, the problem is also avoided: in Germany somewhat on the lines of the United States, where at least the *Staatssekretär* who changes with the Minister is something between a Permanent Secretary and a Junior Minister, and there is a tendency for other senior appointments to be more changeable to reflect a Minister's preferences. In France, where the permanent Civil Service, largely composed of members of the *corps d'élite* who have emerged from the *grandes écoles* and usually also from the Ecole Nationale d'Administration, is more firmly entrenched and plays a similar role to that of the British Civil Service, a different solution has been found. French Ministers' Cabinets, something more elaborate and much more potent than British Ministers' private offices, nearly always change with a change of Minister and, while often still composed of members of the higher ranks of the bureaucracy, are chosen because of their closeness, political or otherwise, to the Minister. In France, too, it must be remembered the 'freemasonry' of the *corps*, like the Inspection des Finances, and of the schools, like the Polytechnique, embraces politicians (including Presidents and Prime Ministers), bureaucrats, heads of nationalized industries and many heads of private enterprises as well – something far more cohesive than the public-school or Oxbridge link, which is in any event becoming less powerful in Britain.

While the practices of the United States, France or Germany could not very easily be adopted in our country, steps in a similar direction have been taken in recent years, through the appointment of outside advisers – not an entirely new feature, but one much extended and formalized by post-war Administrations, particularly since the sixties. When I first left the Service and was able to speak and write about this subject freely, I expressed considerable doubt about the value of a major extension of, and reliance on, this method of bridging the gap between politics and administration.

Although I was primarily addressing myself to the question of outside economists recruited as advisers, some of my doubts had a more general application. It is true that in some areas the outside, temporary, adviser has played a very useful part, but I suspect that this has been the case mainly where his function has not been germane to the question of the political commitment of the adviser, but rather in specific areas where scientific, technological or managerial expertness, not readily found in the Service, could be applied.

In the more general area, particularly in that shadowland where economic analysis, economic policy and politics jostle each other, my doubts remain, not so much because of any difficulty of running the permanent and the temporary adviser in double harness, and of preserving the position of Junior Ministers – rarely a wholly satisfying one anyway – but more because of the still remaining, relatively narrow, limits of economics as a tool of policy. While some, though very few, Civil Servants may hanker after a political role, it is not unreasonable to suppose that the outside adviser is apt to be more tempted in that direction. But if such ambition exists, it should in my view be submitted to the test of the hustings. As I said in 1968, in the 'no-man's-land of politics' it is 'not possible to get one's way on the cheap, that is by fighting in that treacherous terrain by proxy'. Perhaps I should have said, 'It *should* not be possible'!

There seems to me to be another problem that it is perhaps worth referring to. It is one that arises – or is an aggravated form of an already existing danger – on the one hand from the tendency I have already noted for the Prime Minister's power *vis-à-vis* the rest of the Cabinet to increase, and on the other the related one of a more extended use of outside, politically sympathetic advisers. That problem lies in the possible emergence of a class of courtiers round the Prime Minister. Although I have been away from it for nearly twenty years, I believe that the tradition of the higher Civil Service is still extremely powerful. It is one that makes the popular suggestion that its members are either yes-men or, at the other extreme, the holders of real power as against the Ministers' illusory one, a complete myth. Certainly, by long tradition, Civil Servants are not given to sycophancy; cases to the contrary are extremely rare. It is not, however, unreasonable to warn against the danger of contagion if the twin tendencies of almost presidential Prime-Ministerial power and the abundance of outside advisers were to become even stronger than they already are.

14

The City

SIEGMUND WARBURG AND HIS FIRM

My departure from the Civil Service was not accompanied, contrary to what I and many friends had expected, by withdrawal symptoms. I remember reading an article by Patrick Gordon Walker, written after the defeat of the Labour Government in 1951, with something like 'On ceasing to be a Cabinet Minister' as the title. While I had no pretentions to compare myself to so exalted a position, I nevertheless wondered whether, as he described, the disappearance of the latest telegrams, the boxes with Cabinet papers, the telephone calls at all hours of the day – and night – would not call forth a powerful sensation of let-down. Fortunately, this was not the case. The obvious decline of the department after the departure of George Brown, though it held the promise of a quieter, but on the other hand less interesting life, no doubt helped to give me a sense of relief rather than regret when I left Whitehall. Moreover, I had by then learned something that I have subsequently come to believe is one of the most striking differences between government and business, that is, that in the former many things, and these often the most important, are never finished. I remember about a year after I had left asking William Armstrong what things were like in Whitehall, to which he replied that if I came back I would hardly know the difference!

There was also something attractive in starting a new career before one actually *had* to retire from the old one. When I left, I had decided, and had so told Harold Wilson and George Brown, to choose merchant banking as the core of my new activities and that of the three possibilities in this area open to me, I had resolved to accept the offer of Siegmund Warburg to join his firm. George Brown spoke – half jocularly – of my folly in wanting to go into the 'jungle', as he called the City, but he and Wilson both knew

Siegmund Warburg and had great respect for him and for the firm he had built up.

As I have already said, before I could take up this, or any other, post, I had to undergo a period of 'decontamination'. I believe that in my case the insistence on this quarantine was not due to the normal avoidance of any appearance of impropriety – the DEA not being an executive department had had no possibility of conferring material favours – but rather as Laurence Helsby put it, somewhat enigmatically, that for some little time after I left I 'would be able to read the signs' of any impending major development of government policy. The only thing I can think of that he might have meant was devaluation – though I doubt whether anyone could have 'read the signs' of what occurred very much later. At any rate, whatever the reasons, I was not sorry to have an interval and the prospect of returning to an academic environment, and so attractive a one as Harvard, would have removed any lingering regrets I might have had about leaving the public service.

So we went to Cambridge (Massachusetts) where twenty-seven years earlier we had had our first experience of the American academic community. We were received with the same friendliness: Don Price, the Dean of the School, and Dick Neustadt, the Head of the Kennedy Center, did all they could to make our stay interesting, agreeable and comfortable, and there were not only new friends to be made, but also most of our old friends from pre-war and wartime days, with whom we had maintained contact throughout the intervening years. I took part in a number of seminars, which were a special feature of the Center, a major development of the 'in-and-outer' culture of the USA with, in addition to the regular fellows, a constant stream of visiting officials and politicians of central, state and local government. But I also had time – this also was a feature of the Center – for my own work. I had undertaken to participate in a series being prepared by the *Encyclopaedia Britannica* on 'perspectives' in different disciplines, and during my period at the Center I was able to complete the first draft of a book later published as *The World after Keynes*. This was much influenced by my experience in the DEA and discussed the use of the various new or refurbished economic policy instruments that Governments were increasingly led to use in modern conditions.

I think in retrospect that I took too optimistic a view of the efficacy of these instruments despite my own rather chastening experience: perhaps the intellectual activism of an academic environment had something to do with my attitude, as had the origin of that book. The project was largely conceived in the Center for the Study of Democratic Institutions at Santa Barbara, which had a number of personal and business associations with the *Encyclopaedia Britannica*. Headed by Robert Hutchins, a former President of the University of Chicago, it brought together a number of resident and visiting scholars and writers with, I think it is fair to say, a somewhat Utopian bent. During my visits to the Center I may well have been influenced by this, though I should add that the man with whom I had most to do, Harry Ashmore, a distinguished former newspaper editor and Pulitzer prize-winner, could not have been more down to earth.

I was also able during this period to maintain through occasional visits contacts with officials in Washington and the financial community in New York. The fact that I would be moving into the private sector was already generally known, although my precise plans were not. As a result, I received a number of approaches both from business firms and from universities, but much as I (and my wife) had come to love America, we had decided, as we had at the end of the war, that we wanted to live in England, and to some of my closer friends I had indicated that I would be working in the City.

Before that, my renewed participation in the life at Harvard gave me the chance not only to recharge my intellectual batteries but also to admire once again some features of American life that are slowly penetrating our own society – much to its advantage. I refer here particularly to the mobility of Americans both personally and in terms of occupation and relationships. Already during my earlier experience as a Rockefeller Fellow I had been struck by the fact that when I mentioned that I wanted to meet X at such and such a university, I would be told that he was spending a year at another university or with a Senate committee or as an adviser in the Department of Justice, or with the US Steel Corporation, and so it went with many others. Washington, particularly, in peacetime as in wartime, was apt to attract a substantial, if temporary, influx of advisers. Although it is generally thought that the Kennedy and Johnson Administrations, in their different ways, were especially prone to it, I believe it to have been a feature of American government almost from the days of the Founding Fathers – encouraged, no doubt, by the American constitution and, as I have described earlier, the presence in its governmental machine of a top echelon of political public servants.

We returned to England in the spring of 1967 and on 31 March (among his many superstitions, Siegmund Warburg counted an allergy to April Fool's day) I was due to take up my new job as an Executive Director of his firm at 30 Gresham Street. Almost at the same time I took up a number of other part-time, non-executive appointments. Lord Shawcross had recently become Chairman of a newly established subsidiary of an important American insurance company and he invited me to join his Board. Some months earlier I had met a very remarkable industrialist, G. G. Bunzl, of Austrian origin, whose family had for some generations run a very old and highly respected pulp and paper business in Austria and whose father had created a new and flourishing business in England when they had to leave Austria. I had met 'GG', as he was always known, through a comparatively new and extraordinary American friend, Hal Korda, a confidant of Presidents and their advisers, one of the liveliest, though completely untrained, minds that I had ever met. He was alas to die in his forties, a great loss to me and to his many friends.

When I returned to England, 'GG' invited me to join his Board. I remained on the Bunzl Board until I felt that I had to reduce my outside commitments. George Bolton, who was also a close friend of Siegmund Warburg, was at that time Chairman of the Bank of London and South America and he, too, invited me to become a Director, which I did. But the Dominion–Lincoln insurance post came to an end after a few years when the company was restructured, and when BOLSA became a wholly owned subsidiary of Lloyds Bank it appeared both to me and to Eric Faulkner, the Chairman, appropriate that I should resign. I also joined, representing the Bank of England of which I had become a Director, the Board of the Commonwealth Development Finance Corporation, of which George Bolton had then become Chairman, and I continued in this capacity even after I left the Court of the Bank in 1977 until the former Deputy Governor of the Bank, Sir Jasper Hollom, became Chairman.

I should mention two other outside appointments that were connected with my association with Warburg's. One was a directorship of Chrysler UK, Warburg's being the financial advisers of Chrysler. The other was a 'national directorship' of Times Newspapers. Warburg's had been advisers to Roy Thomson for some time and had acted for him when he acquired *The Times*. Part of the terms offered by Roy Thomson when his proposed acquisition was examined by the Monopolies Commission was that there would be four independent, so-called 'national' directors, two nominated by Thomson and two by Lord Astor, who would act in some sense as trustees for the paper, ensuring the maintenance of its character and of the independence of its editorial policy. Lord Robens and I were the two Thomson nominees and we both stayed on as directors until 1983. In 1968, when Roy Jenkins was Chancellor, I was also appointed to the Court of the Bank of England, first for the unexpired term of Cecil King who had resigned, then to two full terms, until I had to leave in 1977 under the Bank's age rule. I will say more of these last two posts and of some of my other 'extracurricular' activities, in business and otherwise, later.

Although none of these posts was executive, or involved any heavy call on my time, they had the great virtue from my point of view of being very varied in character and giving me very quickly an insight into a number of business activities, thus forming a kind of 'crash course' of introduction into business life.

My main job was, however, Warburg's. If in the following pages I dwell at some length on the personality of Siegmund Warburg and describe much of my new career in relation to it, this is so for a number of reasons. He had impressed his personality on the firm he founded and with which I have now been associated for nearly eighteen years to such an extent that – happily – it continues to characterize it to this day. For fifteen years, until his death in 1982, I was closely associated with him and spent a large part of my waking hours in his company – more than with anyone else I had worked with either in the academic or in the governmental world. What is more important, Siegmund Warburg had a major influence on the shape of the City as it has evolved in the last quarter of a century. A description of the way in which he moulded and guided his own merchant bank may be useful as a background to some of

the reflections I shall present subsequently on the structure of the
City and its evolution.

My decision to go into the City in the 'merchant banking' sector
may have had something to do with some residual youthful
memories of my father's profession and also a feeling that this area
of business had more affinity both with the academic and with the
public-affairs experiences that I had had. But the decision to join
this particular firm was entirely due to the impression that its
founder – and some of his closest associates – had made on me. As I
have already mentioned, I had known Siegmund Warburg for
several years, particularly when I was in the Ministry of Agriculture, and later in the DEA, where he (and his closest partner Henry
Grunfeld) were sometimes drawn by George Brown, usually over
dinner, into informal groups of business advisers.

Siegmund Warburg was an exceptional man. He managed,
despite an unusually large circle of friends and acquaintances in
many parts of the world, particularly Europe and North America,
with whom he maintained a substantial and regular correspondence, to remain a very reserved person. This created a certain aura
of mystery round him and led to his becoming a near-legend in his
lifetime. Siegmund Warburg had his share of human frailties, but
what distinguished him from most other people was that he was
more conscious of them than anyone else and that he put self-
criticism very high on his list of virtues, both for himself and for
other people.

In the years that have passed since I first entered business life, I
have had even more opportunity than before to meet business
people of many types. I have met those who were shrewd, quite a
few who were not (and whose material success was, therefore, hard
to explain); some who cultivated other interests over and above
making money, and many more who cultivated nothing but that
one. I have, however, not met anyone like Siegmund in whom the
business instinct was so highly developed, yet who at the same time
could not only subordinate it to other interests and not treat these
other interests as entirely separate hobbies, but to combine it and
them into an organically integrated view and method of living. He
knew the importance of money in human affairs and was by no
means indifferent, even personally, to its power. His refusal to
concern himself with his own investments – leaving their manage-

ment to experts—was only in part an affectation (he was not
entirely free from a number of them): he was ready to advise
others on many business aspects and felt that in this as in many
other matters requiring special knowledge, one should not advise
oneself.

He was at heart a humanist, but having chosen a business
career, he eschewed any high-falutin notions about the 'higher'
objectives of business and refrained from philosophizing about
business generally as a 'service' to the community, always moti-
vated by this conception of itself and bringing rewards commensurate with its realization. He was much too realistic for that. But he
was quite clear that his own type of business, that of merchant
banker, or 'private banker' as he preferred to have it called, involved the sort of service that is common to the liberal professions.
The relation between the private banker and his customer was not
that of the manufacturer of a product and its consumer; it was
best compared with that of doctor, preferably family doctor, and
patient in health and sickness.

This view had a number of particular consequences. First of all
it led to the belief that however important technical competence in
the various areas of the business—banking in the strict sense, corporate finance, investment management and so on—might be, no
one could really be a good merchant banker who was only techni-
cally competent: he had to have, and to cultivate, many wider
interests. The second was that relationships were all-important.
Specific individual transactions had to be dealt with, even if they
were non-recurrent, but the bank's business had to rest on a
foundation of close, long-term relationships with customers,
maintained and nurtured when they did, and when they did not,
need the bank's advice on particular problems. These two things
went together: a steady relationship could be maintained only by
those who took a wide interest in men and affairs, and these wider
interests, in turn, were nourished by continuous contact with a
large variety of businesses and their problems. I have often heard
Siegmund Warburg say that he neither knew, nor could hope to
know, about making sausages, or motor cars, or about publishing
newspapers or running hotels, but that there were certain features
of running a business in a modern society—not only specific financial ones, which one had, of course, to master—that were reason-

ably uniform and that experience and judgement enabled one to advise on.

Psychology thus played a large part in his make-up and in his view of his own profession. Like most of us, he was by no means infallible in his judgement of people: his errors tended to be in over-rather than underestimating the abilities and character of individuals (he was prone to love at first sight) and then suffering pangs of disappointment. But he was very skilled in assessing the reaction of different personalities to one another and this enabled him to offer valuable advice in the many business situations – mergers and acquisitions, for example – in which these considerations were often of greater importance than the technical financial aspects.

This emphasis on human personality led him to employ graphology, a feature of the living legend of Warburg's. He relied very heavily on the services of a very distinguished Swiss graphologist, Mrs Theodora Dreifuss, in forming a judgement on somebody with whom he had, or wished to have, a relationship, and no one was engaged by the firm in a position of any consequence without a graphological test. It also led him to seek and maintain wider contacts, including those with prominent politicians. He did not himself hold very marked political views, though he was basically convinced of the advantages of a broadly capitalist system and criticized many of its modern perversions originating on the Left and the Right. He had sympathy with the Bow Group and with the moderate elements in the Labour Party, and, while he was not an undiscriminating admirer of all leading politicians, his wisdom, always displayed very modestly, and his wide knowledge of financial matters, particularly international ones, made him welcome and appreciated by Prime Ministers and other leading politicians of very different political persuasions. The knowledge of the personalities in the political arena that he gained enriched his judgement and his ability to assess business trends and prospects.

My description of him so far would suggest that he was essentially a conservative thinker and actor. In a sense this is true and he certainly imposed a strongly prudent outlook on his firm and on all those who worked with him. But this was by no means his sole characteristic nor was it what he wanted his firm to be. He was very much of an innovator and in some respect had a rebellious streak in him – though always controlled by concentration on a particular 'cause'. His very emergence and progress on the London scene could not have been accomplished without these qualities, which together created a fighting disposition. Of all the parts of the London financial community, the merchant banks, particularly the leading ones grouped in the Accepting Houses Committee, have always been regarded as the inner core of the financial establishment, one particularly difficult for a newcomer to penetrate. This is a somewhat odd view to take of a group of institutions, most of which were founded – admittedly over a long period, going back 200 years – by immigrants, many of whom, like Siegmund Warburg, had to leave an inhospitable climate in their own country. However, the spectacle of those who have arrived guarding the doors against newcomers is not altogether uncommon in many walks of life. In fact, the City of London has generally been guided (in recent years more so than ever) by an 'open-door' policy, even if at any one moment there might have been some resistance to change, and the prejudices that Siegmund Warburg had to overcome not only did not last long, but were matched, as he always was anxious to point out, by help and support, material and moral, from many members of the Establishment.

Nevertheless, the early years were an uphill struggle in which new ideas were the new firm's most effective instruments. It was characteristic of Warburg that in the early years the firm he had founded was called the New Trading Company and that it was not until 1946 that he felt confident enough to give it his own name. Some of the early battles for an important position in the financial community, such as the contest for the control of British Aluminium, have become part of the business history of the last few decades. The firm was much helped by its international connections, particularly at a time when there was still a disparity between the domestic orientation of many of the City's financial institutions and the altered relative economic position of post-war Britain. Close contacts with New York and re-established contacts with Germany, then emerging as a major economic power, gave the firm advantages that could be usefully applied particularly to transnational transactions.

The progress the firm was making was consolidated when, after the merger in 1957 with the old-established firm of Seligman Brothers, S. G. Warburg & Co. became a member of the Accepting Houses Committee. Siegmund Warburg himself also became associated with the eminent Wall Street house of Kuhn, Loeb & Co., and, though his connection lasted only into the early sixties, he did bring to the New York house many interesting transactions, which his own London firm was at that stage not able to carry out. Among these were some early fund-raising transactions in the New York capital market for foreign borrowers, such as the first loans for the Republic of Austria and for the European Coal and Steel Community.

When I joined Warburg's, it was already recognized as one of the leading merchant banks in the City with a number of new developments to its credit, notably the inauguration of the Eurobond market by the issue in 1963 of a Eurodollar loan for the Italian *Autostrade*. I had some, though largely theoretical, knowledge of the financial system (my early study, and subsequent teaching, of 'Money and Banking' helped a little; and my general economic training and experience in governmental economic affairs was relevant) but I still needed a period of intensive apprenticeship. The firm has always had a system of providing tutors to new entrants and I was lucky enough to have Siegmund Warburg himself as mine, assisted particularly by Henry Grunfeld (another brilliant teacher who is rightly regarded by many as the best merchant banker in London) and also by Frank Smith, a highly accomplished corporate finance expert. There was also Eric Korner, well known throughout the City and in many countries of the Continent and in the USA. He was of Austrian origin and a man of extraordinary charm. Right up to his death, at the age of 86, he was still active in the firm and carried himself like the officer in the army of the old monarchy he had once been.

I have already set down above some of the guiding principles that animated Siegmund Warburg in business, which he taught me and which I had no difficulty in absorbing as they were congenial to my own cast of mind. But there was much of a more specific and detailed nature to be learned. I was, through my other non-executive appointments, learning something about insurance and investment and the manufacturing and marketing problems of such diverse industries as pulp and paper (including cigarette filters) and automobiles. Siegmund Warburg used a number of methods with me. There were weekend walks round Belgravia and talks in his flat, not so much about the theory of this or that type of business, but more about individual banks, other companies and, above all, people: here was this German bank preoccupied with some particular industrial shareholding, there some American industrialist, convinced that to survive he had to acquire manufacturing bases in Europe, here again some subsidiary of a British company that would do much better if it became part of a certain American group and so on.

Many of these ideas were highly fanciful and I am sure that he had few illusions about their practicability. Many, I could not follow – the names at first were a total jumble. But in the end much of it stuck in my mind and formed a better basis, I believe, than the reading of any number of textbooks on business would have done. Another method was to bring me into meetings, lunches or dinners with customers and friends, whether specific transactions (in which I had as yet no part to play) were under discussion or not. Yet another most important aspect of this training period was travel to foreign countries. Siegmund Warburg must, I think, have decided at an early stage that while I had to become an all-round merchant banker, my past experience pointed to some degree of specialization in international matters. He had always taken the far-sighted view (not as common in any kind of business as it ought to be) that he should pass on his knowledge, experience and, above all, relationships to others, and this had always been a principle he followed with the younger people in the firm. He applied it to me too, and from the earliest days of my being in the firm, we travelled a great deal together either in connection with some particular – actual or potential – business proposition or, as often as not, to maintain a general relationship (something he greatly believed in) and to meet business friends. Some of these, e.g. bankers in the United States or Germany, I already knew from previous contacts, and this was particularly true of officials in Finance Ministries and central banks, some of whom also reappeared in the private sector. Many others, however, I got to know only through him.

Our journeys in those days took us particularly to New York, Frankfurt, Rome, Paris, Brussels, Luxembourg and (though mainly with Eric Korner) Vienna. The firm had always regarded the United States as of prime importance and when Warburg ceased his association with Kuhn Loeb, a small subsidiary, mainly in the nature of an embassy, was set up in New York. This formed at least a convenient *pied-à-terre* for our visits and those of other members of the firm. Through these visits, the circle of banks and large corporations and their leading figures that I knew grew very considerably, as it did in Germany, where the firm also had a major holding in a small Frankfurt subsidiary. Brussels and Luxembourg were important because they were the seats of the Community institutions for whom the firm had acted. Italy, too, had been cultivated from an early stage (I have already mentioned the first Eurobond issue) and I had also got to know Italy well, partly through my governmental activities, partly through extra-curricular ones (for example, I had frequently lectured at the Bologna Center of the Johns Hopkins University School of Adv-anced International Studies where I chaired for a time the Advis-ory Council). The joint visits to Rome and Milan accompanied by the firm's representative in Milan became particularly agreeable and fruitful.

Siegmund Warburg had had a number of long-standing friend-ships in Paris, particularly with the Banque de Paris et des Pays-Bas and its then head, Jean Reyre, which was to lead to a specially close relation later on, and here, too, I was introduced in a specially warm way. Although I had visited Vienna in other connections since the war, my membership of Warburg's gave me a better opportunity both to revisit childhood haunts and to establish new contacts. These visits to Austria and Germany, as well as the association with a number of colleagues whose native language was German, revived my knowledge and interest in that language and literature. During the Nazi period and the war, I had neither the opportunity nor, indeed, any desire, to cultivate Ger-man, and while my contacts with the country, its people and its language began again during the Marshall Plan, I was then living in France and more concerned to develop my knowledge of French. The opportunity to exchange experiences in German literature with Siegmund Warburg and Henry Grunfeld or to revive some classic Viennese jokes with Eric Korner was an added bonus.

I still had occasion to maintain some outside contacts, national and international, created largely through extracurricular activities in the latter days of my Civil Service career, such as the occasional lecture to academic or similar audiences like the Royal College of Defence Studies or attendance at various international gatherings, like the Bilderberg meetings. I was able to continue to travel, for example, to Japan, to Canada, and to the Scandinavian countries for these purposes, but I also was able to develop the firm's contacts in these countries. Siegmund Warburg had been to Tokyo in 1962 as a member of a mission from the City and had formed immediately a strong interest in Japan (and a close friendship with a distinguished Japanese public figure, Jiro Shirasu); I had known Japan somewhat since 1958, so when I joined the firm I was very glad to be able to develop our contacts and business with that fascinating country.

Scandinavia, more particularly Sweden, he had known of old. He had in 1926 married, in Stockholm, a Swedish lady, Eva Philipson, and had many close contacts in Swedish industry and finance, and he had also developed important business contacts in Oslo. Partly during the war, more so afterwards, I had had many contacts with statesmen and officials in all these countries and also some academic relationships, and the combination of our interests proved to be particularly interesting. Our joint interest in public affairs, particularly in the economic field, was never far from the surface and we often tried to make some interesting new business idea subserve some longer purpose. One such instance was the invention of a new currency unit which we christened the 'Euro-Moneta' – an early forerunner of the European Currency Unit (ECU) – and we thought that a bond issue for a sovereign Scandinavian borrower would be an excellent way to launch it. This particular idea came to nothing, but is worth recalling at a time when there is in many quarters pressure for the greater use of the ECU in private markets.

I had also much to learn about the internal management of a firm like Warburg's, at that time having barely one-third of the numbers it has today. The style of management is extremely difficult to describe in the conventional terms of a handbook of organization. In many ways, and true to the founder's predilection for the private banker as a model, it operated like a partnership, though as the physical possibility was not present, it substituted an 'open-door' policy for the partners' room or rooms—i.e. in principle anyone could go into anyone else's room at any time. There was a formal hierarchy of Board members, executive and otherwise, general managers, etc., but this was supplemented and sometimes even supplanted by a sort of natural hierarchy of knowledge and experience in specific areas. Great stress was laid on two features: internal communication and the bringing up of the younger members of the firm. Various devices were used to achieve these objectives and these were frequently changed or added to as experience dictated. The spirit was a very special blend of democracy and speed of decision based on authority! 'Chains of command' were anathema as leading to blurring of responsibility rather than making it more precise, as well as to a loss of 'rhythm'—a favourite word in the firm. Self-reliance was encouraged, but only in the sense that everyone was supposed to develop his own perception of when to consult and whom, thus leading to an almost natural hierarchy of importance of different decisions and to appropriate methods of reaching them. An especially heavy emphasis was placed on accuracy of a most meticulous kind to the point, sometimes wrongly characterized as pedantry. Big errors of judgement—if they were recognized by those responsible—were more readily forgiven than small mistakes due to carelessness.

The regime was severe, certainly more so than in the Civil Service in which the decision-making process is more complex and responsibilities are more widely shared. But it would be quite wrong to equate this tight style of management with an atmosphere lacking in cheer. Siegmund Warburg himself believed strongly that the firm could not prosper unless people working in it had 'fun', a word he was fond of. As a result, the 'sporting element' in the pursuit of a particular business transaction was always recognized and encouraged.

To me the new activities and the environment in which they were carried on were very congenial. I have often been asked, particularly by young men choosing a career or by men at or after retirement seeking new activities, to describe my new life in the terms of my previous experience. My answer has usually been on the following lines. Business is different from public administration as well as from teaching and research. The material rewards —

though rarely as high or as widely available as popularly imagined – are different, the motives tend to be different, and the criteria by which achievement is assessed quite different. While neither individual financial reward nor the financial results of the enterprise are the sole (and unambiguous) measures of success, 'the bottom line', to use one of the telling imports from the United States, is, in the last resort, all-important in business. Certainly a bottom line consistently in the red must lead to extinction. This is not so in academic work nor is it in public administration except in those selected parts that are akin to the industrial or commercial activities of private business. As far as administration in the broadest sense is concerned, the activity, for example, of the top echelon of the administrative class, it is not susceptible to the monetary calculus any more (perhaps even less) than is that of their political masters.

This distinction applies, I believe, to all business activity. Within it, one's views will naturally vary according to individual temperament. For my part, I would always say that the one I had chosen seemed to have more affinity to what I had done before than anything else I could imagine. The intellectual input required in my sector of the financial system has always seemed to me to be high. Adequate capital resources, good organization, technical competence are essential, but it has been said with considerable aptness that merchant bankers 'live on their wits', that judgement and wisdom are more important than any of the other considerations. And the methods employed to arrive at correct judgements and the business decisions that flow from them are not fundamentally different from the type of analysis required in academic work or those that go – or should go – to the formulation of advice to Ministers.

I do not mean to overstress these similarities – to see them as I do is very much a personal matter. In particular, I would not wish it to be thought that such analogies as there are can be reversed, and that, for example, the principles operating in business, or even the techniques, can be transferred to the purposes of government, given the constraints under which a Government must operate. The idea sometimes put forward of 'Great Britain Ltd' is, I think, misconceived, even if there are areas of state activity in which business principles and methods can and should be employed. This, as I have said, is undoubtedly so in the industrial and commercial operations of government – defence contracts, the mint, or the printing of banknotes are obvious examples – which – *pace* the extreme flights of Hayekian or Friedmanite fancy – even free-market Governments cannot escape.

I could observe Siegmund Warburg's qualities as a teacher (something that I believe he would have dearly liked to be) not only as practised on me, but particularly on the brilliant young men (and now, and I hope increasingly, women) the firm was able to recruit. It is true that a few – a very few – either did not live up to expectations or left because they could not stand the short but tough early period of training. But those who did, and who did not disappoint early promise, were promoted very rapidly both in status and responsibility. The search for good new recruits was and is one of the main preoccupations of the senior members of the firm: the personnel is always regarded as its principal asset.

Two other guiding principles are worth mentioning because they are not, I believe, universally respected. One, which Siegmund Warburg always impressed on both colleagues and customers, was that the modern craze for better results each year was misguided and dangerous. The solidity of a business's success was much better assessed by looking at its evolution over a period of years and also by looking at its ability to cope with both favourable and unfavourable tendencies in the future. This may sound trite, but was and is worth emphasizing, especially given the excessive emphasis that the vastly increased media coverage of business results is now placing on playing up short-term considerations. The experience that some of the leading members of the firm had had in previous decades and on the Continent had led them to a strong realization that 'things may go down as well as up', that there was 'no natural law that stipulated that every year had to be better than the previous one' and, perhaps especially apt for a business in the financial sector, that political developments – always unpredictable – may have a heavy and totally unexpected impact on business fortunes.

There was one further attitude, particularly significant for a service business like merchant banking, which has always had – and despite certain new tendencies, always will have – a strongly personal character, that is the attitude to customers' reaction to the advice they are offered. That 'the customer is always right' as a principle on which business generally rests, must, in its broadest sense, be accepted, but in merchant banking probably more than in any other business it requires qualification. Siegmund Warburg believed that there are limits, perhaps wide ones, but limits none the less, to which this doctrine can be taken. If a customer, either consistently or on a very major issue, ignores the advice he is given and takes a course of action that the adviser regards as wrong, one should part company with him. Since the relationship is one of utmost mutual trust, and the adviser's reputation is inevitably involved, the decision to take on any particular client must also be carefully weighed. In obedience to these principles the firm has occasionally found itself obliged to separate from a customer, or not to establish a relation in the first place if it had serious doubts about the potential customer.

This chapter in no way pretends to be even a partial history of the firm and I do not propose to expatiate on the many types of business transactions that I have been associated with since I joined it. From my point of view these years have meant an extraordinary enlargement of my knowledge of people, circumstances and countries. To have worked with Siegmund Warburg on such classic transactions as the setting up of the firm's alliance and cross-shareholding with Banque de Paris et de Pays-Bas (brought to an end in consequence of French banking nationalization), the merger of Leyland and the British Motor Corporation and on numerous international capital market transactions, or to have been intimately involved in the negotiations between Chrysler and the British Government, which led to the 'rescue' of the British company, or in the subsequent sale of Chrysler UK to Peugeot, provided invaluable lessons in an area of human affairs of which up to then I had had only theoretical knowledge. It also provided the raw material out of which to fashion some conclusions on the economy, business and finance, or to modify many previously held on inadequate evidence, about which I shall have something to say presently.

EXTRACURRICULAR ACTIVITIES

I have already mentioned that although 30 Gresham Street was by far my most important daily port of call, I was engaged in a number of other areas, and I have referred particularly to those in what might broadly be called the business world. As far as the Bank of England is concerned, of which I was a Director for nearly ten years, what I have to say is best said in connection with my reflections on the structure of our financial system. As for the other strictly business appointments that I held, the only thing I would say is that they added to the knowledge I was acquiring an element of concreteness that I found particularly helpful in counteracting what, if one is dealing with and in money, can become a somewhat one-sided and even distorted view of how the economy behaves.

In this context I have also found it particularly useful to be associated with institutions, which have become fairly widely used in recent years, namely the international advisory councils or boards. In my case, this included for many years an important New York bank, now a large Continental bank, as well as two important American industrial companies. These bodies bring together people with different experiences and backgrounds from a number of countries, and the wide-ranging discussions, including, but by no means confined to, the affairs of the particular companies, are stimulating and instructive.

Much more distant from business life were some other occupations, which I either took on afresh or continued from previous involvement. Of these, the one most akin to my previous work in the public service was membership of the National Economic Development Council. I have already mentioned at an earlier stage and should add now that, in the days of the DEA, the Council was meant to play an important role in supplementing the Government's direct effort to establish and maintain a continuous dialogue with both sides of industry. Under its constitution it consisted of equal numbers representing Government, employers (through the Confederation of British Industry (CBI)) and workers (through the TUC). There were also two independent members and in 1971, under the then Conservative Government, I was appointed as one of these and served until 1980.

The Council was supported by an office, under a distinguished Director General, sometimes an ex-Civil Servant, and its work was largely carried out by a series of national development committees, the so-called 'Little Neddies', usually chaired by a representative of one side or the other of industry, often the head of an important company. The Council itself was (and is) presided over by the Chancellor of the Exchequer (during the DEA days, by the First Secretary of State), though on occasions, often at the first meeting after the budget, by the Prime Minister. During the second Wilson Administration the Council, following an elaborate meeting at Chequers, was given a further impetus and a series of working parties – so-called 'sector working-parties' – were added to the existing Little Neddies with more specific terms of reference on such topics as increased productivity, export promotion, import-saving and technological innovation.

The Bank of England and the Treasury had generally been opposed, or at least lukewarm, to the setting up of a Little Neddy or anything similar on the City, on the not unreasonable ground that the specific rationale for a tripartite organization did not apply and that the consideration jointly by Government, CBI and TUC of the broader financial issues would take place in the Council itself. However, under the new impetus, though at a slightly later stage, a committee was established to enquire into the problems of finance for industry, of which I was made, and continued to be, Chairman until I retired from the Council itself. I believe that this committee still continues in being and has produced a number of useful reports, including comparisons of British institutions and practices with those of a number of other countries.

Almost simultaneously and as a result of considerable political interest at the time in financial questions – including such far-reaching issues as the nationalization of banks and other financial institutions – the Government set up a more elaborate enquiry under the Chairmanship of Harold Wilson, who had by then ceased to be Prime Minister and Leader of the Labour Party. This Committee, which carried on for about four years (1976–80), reached broadly conservative conclusions as far as any possible major changes in the structure of the City were concerned, but, in the process, produced a series of valuable reports, which at the very least form an excellent reference library for students of the subject.

The place and function of the National Economic Development Council are controversial matters. All theory apart, their practical expression will depend on what the parties that constitute it want to make of it, and more particularly to what extent and in what manner the Government wishes to use it as a piece of the machinery of economic management. At one extreme, if the view is taken that the role of government in the economy is a very limited one and that in playing it the Government does not need to have any formal recourse to the advice of organized labour or of the organization of employers, and if the broad field of industrial relations (including the level of incomes) is to be left to the free bargaining of the two parties, then the rationale for the Council disappears. Such educational or research activities or the dissemination of information that its staff engage in can be left to universities and research institutes. At the other extreme, given the planning proclivities of the 1964 Labour Government, the Council enjoyed considerable influence, and even in the Heath Government it played an important role. It could in my view have been, and very nearly was, used to good effect in the industrial dispute that finally brought down that Government.

In 1979 when Margaret Thatcher's first Government came in – I was still on the Council, but had long since left the public service – I had a long conversation with the Chancellor, Geoffrey Howe, about Neddy. My advice to him was to carry on with an organization that, whatever critics may say about 'talking shops', provided a ready and established opportunity for maintaining contact and discussion with important and representative elements of the economy. I am glad to see that the Council, whatever practical influence it may have had on the course of events, continued to function for a number of years. Its future existence was for a time in doubt as a result of a boycott by the TUC, but it is now operating again.

Another activity close to the public domain came my way in 1975, though its origin was in 1974. Helmut Schmidt, who had recently become the German Federal Chancellor, took the initiative in 1974 to suggest a private study of ways of dealing with the oil problem, the first and second 'oil shocks' having recently taken place. At that time Wilson was Prime Minister again with Denis Healey as Chancellor, Valéry Giscard d'Estaing had become President of France and Gerald Ford President of the United States. Schmidt suggested to them as well as to Prime Minister Fukuda of Japan that each should nominate one person to a group of five for the purpose of such a study. They should be people with experience of government, access to the existing administrations and enjoying their confidence, but not actively involved in government. After some correspondence, the group was constituted and consisted of George Schultz, recently Secretary of the US Treasury, Raymond Barre, who had been Vice-President of the Commission of the European Community, Wilfried Guth, a distinguished banker with governmental experience as German Executive Director of the IMF, Hideo Suzuki, who had recently left an important post in the Japanese Finance Ministry, and me.

The idea was that after the group had been working for some time it would be joined by a similarly constituted group representing producer countries, Algeria and Iran having apparently already been sounded out and responded favourably to the suggestion. It was, of course, realized that the producers' group was unlikely to be quite so unofficial and private as ours was, but this would have been a small price to pay for a procedure that seemed to offer some hope of breaking through the deadlock that threatened to be the fate of more official negotiations between producing and consuming countries. In any event, such negotiations seemed to be impossible to get off the ground despite occasional demands for them by statesmen, at least from the Western countries, partly because of the apparent impossibility of creating a common view among these (our group was meant to help achieve this), partly for fear that the creation of such a common view could be regarded as 'ganging up' and would, therefore, be counter-productive.

I should mention here that from an early stage of the revolution caused by the quadrupling – later quintupling – of the price of oil in a very short time, I had formed the view that the measures taken or contemplated would prove inadequate. I felt that even after policies of conservation and substitution to reduce demand, and after the recycling of the suddenly created financial surpluses through greater imports and foreign investment by producing countries and the operations of the international banking system, a major problem would remain. I expressed this view at one of the Bilderberg meetings, since I felt that there was a danger of complacency engendered by the undoubted technical virtuosity of international finance – a danger that even the widely recognized current problem of the great debt 'overhang' has not entirely dissipated – and also at a dinner party given by the Governor of the Bank in November 1974.

I subsequently set them out at some length in a letter to the Permanent Under-Secretary at the Foreign Office at his request. I felt that a conference was needed – one had been suggested by President Giscard, though of a somewhat different kind. Drawing, with due reserve, on the analogy of the Marshall Plan, at least in its techniques, I suggested that a programme over at least five years had to be drawn up in terms of 'real resources and needs' that could be translated into financial terms and then juxtaposed to estimated financial surpluses and deficits. I recognized in my letter that this 'seemed rather starry-eyed', but I felt that even if it could not be completely accomplished, the mere suggestion of such a conference and such a procedure would at least provide a starting point for a more fruitful dialogue between producers and consumers.

The objection to these ideas, apart from the obvious practical difficulties of getting such a conference going, was that by talking about real resources it would crystallize the views of the producers on indexation of the price of oil, something of which officials of the Governments of consuming countries were very afraid. In the event, as I argued at the time, indexation of a kind did in fact take place and the world, whether one is thinking of industrial oil-producing, or non-oil-producing developing countries, was reduced to 'muddling through', leaving the major consequences of these massive changes still unresolved.

The 'Group of Five' met a few times, usually with some pretence of secrecy, in places like the Schlosshotel in Kronberg near Frankfurt or the Links Club in New York. We approached our task without any preconceived ideas and with some appreciation of the difficulty of any coherent, comprehensive plan of action, and we quickly concluded that we would have to confine ourselves to laying down some broad guidelines for policy in different areas. The resulting conclusions were not exactly earth-shaking, and it was left to each one of us to report them in our own way. We did think that the build-up of surplus OPEC (Organization of Petroleum Exporting Countries) funds would level off and then decline; in this we were proved right, and we were not far out on the timing of the change (which we put at 1980), but we greatly underestimated the level the surpluses would reach and the consequences of the multiple effect that they would produce in Euro-currency markets. Our expectation of an eventual softening of the oil price was correct, although, again, not as far as its timing was concerned. Otherwise we had some reasonable but not particularly original things to say about investment in and by surplus countries, and the creation and use of special funds to deal with emergency liquidity and balance of payments situations, as well as about conservation and substitution measures.

It is not easy to say what effect our work might have had had it been possible to carry it forward into a joint study by producing and consuming countries. As it was, our reports were received and accepted with expressions of appreciation by those who had commissioned them, but no further sign of any sequel to them ever appeared. The 'regulars' in the departments concerned in the five countries, though helpful, had never really liked these interventions by 'outsiders' – the fact that we had all been 'in government' in one way or another made it, if anything, rather worse, and I do not think they shed any tears over the fact that our work was sunk without trace. In fact, much later Schmidt said to me: 'The bureaucrats sabotaged it.' (I was reminded of a splendid line in a play by Marcel Aymé: 'L'Eglise se méfie des franc-tireurs.')

Another activity on the fringes of officialdom related to the summit meetings of the seven highly industrialized countries. On three occasions, first on Bob Roosa's initiative, then on that of Helmut Schmidt, and finally on mine, a group of people drawn from these countries (usually two or three from each), who were not in government or the public service, but had been in or close to it and having the necessary economic and finance knowledge and experience, met before the summit meetings themselves to discuss the problems likely to be before the heads of government. Given the composition of the groups, the documents that resulted from their deliberations (and which were sent to the heads of government) clearly reflected compromises on national positions. Nevertheless, they were much more outspoken and specific than the usually very bland communiques issued after the summit meetings themselves.

I have on a number of occasions mentioned the Bilderberg meetings. These take their name from the first meeting held at a hotel of that name in Holland, and they have been going on for some twenty-five years. They were started very much with the Atlantic Alliance as the central concern and they bring together once a year a group of politicians, officials, representatives of industry, trade and finance, academics and other public figures for a weekend of intensive discussion in one or other of the countries represented. I first attended in the early sixties and have been associated with the group ever since. The discussions fall naturally into economic, foreign affairs and defence problems and, being totally private and confidential, provide an exceptional opportunity for those who have to take decisions in matters of great importance to discuss the broader aspects of their responsibilities with those holding other responsibilities, but who are vitally concerned in the actions of statesmen.

Like others, I am sure, who have taken an active part in these international gatherings, I have sometimes wondered about their value, particularly after reading Arthur Koestler's *The Callgirls*, a hilarious description of those addicted to conferences. I have concluded that, carefully chosen and limited so that they do not loom too large in one's total activity – let alone impinge on one's main one – they do perform a useful function. But one must take good care not to get on to the international 'conveyor-belt' or one might never get off!

Some of the other activities that, like the Bilderberg meetings, have helped to keep me, both during my official and now my business careers, from developing too narrow an interest and outlook, had some academic character, such as the Policy Studies Institute – resulting from a merger of which Political and Economic Planning was one constituent. For many years I had been associated with PEP (becoming Chairman of its Executive Committee, and later President), one of the relatively few outside organizations considered compatible with the position of a senior Civil Servant, and in its new guise the deep concern that it has had with a wide variety of social issues has found an even better means of being exercised.

I have also been President of the National Institute of Economic and Social Research for a number of years, the premier organization in this field in Britain. The Institute was started in the thirties, largely as the result of the efforts of Noel Hall who became its first Director. Its research publications and its *Review* enjoy a world-wide reputation and apart from the research grants it receives from public funds and various foundations, it is strongly supported by donations from business. As a result of the rise in fashion in recent years of monetarist doctrines (of which more presently), the Institute has sometimes been criticized for being a stronghold of 'Keynesian' views. Leaving aside the question of what exactly is meant by that phrase – or, for that matter, why it should be regarded as a proper object for criticism – the truth is simply that the Institute has continued to employ, cultivate and further develop all proper tools of economic analysis and of applied economics research and has refused to become addicted to one narrow doctrine. Its reputation is, thus, protected from the winds of fashion as distinct from genuine advances in the disciplines with which it is concerned.

I entered into a more specifically academic association when I was invited to become Chancellor of the University of Southampton. University Chancellorships are essentially ceremonial posts, but during the ten years that I occupied this particular one, it certainly gave me not only much pleasure, but also a further link with an aspect of life in our society of which I had particularly happy memories. The close contact with two outstanding Vice-Chancellors, first Jim Gower (now further renowned for his report on investor protection), then John Roberts, as well as with many eminent academics in a University with the highest standards in so many different subjects, humanistic, scientific and technological, has been a source of great inspiration.

Rather more directly related to business was an association (which still exists tenuously) with the publishing industry. From early childhood I had an almost romantic attachment to books – in the most generalized way – and had often thought of bookselling or publishing as a particularly desirable occupation if one had to be in business. I was, therefore, delighted when an opportunity occurred to become closely associated with the book industry. The Publishers Association had set up a Book Development Council as its export arm, backed in the first instance by a grant from the Foreign Office and, in part at least, in response to similar American efforts. Patrick Gordon Walker was its first Chairman, but soon after the formation of the Council he became a Cabinet Minister and had to resign. I was then invited to take his place. My closer acquaintance with the industry and the many friendships I was able to form with many outstanding publishers, proved to me that my youthful ideas were not illusions. Of course, like any other business, publishing and selling books requires hard-headed business acumen, prudence, a money sense, and so on. But there is still room for demonstrating talents, the value of which is more difficult to quantify, such as taste and a regard for standards, which are not always easily reconciled with the most remunerative activities. Among those I met in this environment there seemed to me to be a rather larger proportion of people with these talents than is normally found in other businesses.

Apart from participating in the efforts at export promotion, I was also drawn into attempts to improve the physical aspects of book distribution in the country and chaired a working party in which the Booksellers Association participated. We produced a number of recommendations, some of which were adopted by the trade, with, I think, beneficial results. Later, I was also concerned, while Chairman for a few years of the National Book Committee (which groups together all the bodies concerned with books from authors to libraries) with other matters such as postal charges or public expenditure on school books and libraries, an area in which business, government and wider considerations meet and often clash.

A rather different contact with publishing, to which I have already referred, was my directorship of *The Times*, an association that lasted for sixteen years. Not surprisingly in view of its exceptional and long-standing position in British society and in the world press, and being itself part of the 'media' industry, the recent history of this paper (and, in less degree) of its stablemate, the *Sunday Times*, has attracted a good deal of public attention. This has been further stimulated by the last editor of *The Times*, Harold Evans, in a book devoted to his own association with the two papers. I do not have any secrets to reveal and do not propose to deal with the gossip to which changes in the papers' ownership and editorship have given rise. But the subject is important in itself, and my own connection with it long and close enough to merit some account.

When I first joined the Board as a national director following the merger of the *Sunday Times* and *The Times* under Roy Thomson's ownership, a number of people, including friendly journalists, expressed surprise and criticism. The approval of the merger under the terms of the Monopolies legislation was not universally accepted, and the safeguards, Roy Thomson's own undertakings, including financial ones, and the creation of national directors were not regarded as adequate. One letter written by an old friend from a rival paper, more in sorrow than in anger, spoke with surprise of my agreeing to act as a 'fig leaf'.

The idea of independent national directors was inspired by an arrangement that already existed in *The Times*. This made it impossible to transfer controlling ordinary shares from the existing owners except to a person (it had to be a natural person and not a corporation or other body) approved by a special committee. This consisted of the Lord Chief Justice, the Warden of All Souls College, Oxford, the President of the Royal Society and the Governor of the Bank of England. The four national directors to be appointed under the new dispensation were a more modest version of these personalities, but their function was meant to be much the same, for the then existing Articles of Association of *The Times* provided that while the Committee should have absolute discretion and were not obliged to give any reason for their decisions, they were instructed to have regard to certain considerations. These were: the importance of maintaining the best traditions and political independence of *The Times*, as well as national rather than personal interests, and of eliminating 'as far as reasonably possible questions of personal ambition and commercial profit'. Leaving aside the latter, the duties of the national directors could be said to reflect similar concerns. In the light of subsequent experiences, it is, however, worth noting that the Monopolies Commission accepted the 'opinion of many witnesses that the inclusion of national figures could only be window-dressing'; and, at best, a declaration of good intent by the Thomson Organisation. The Commission also doubted whether conferring on the national directors the power to veto the dismissal of an editor would be realistic: 'Newspapers remain the property of their proprietors . . . who cannot be prevented from dismissing an editor if they do not like the way he is running their newspapers.'

I knew Roy Thomson, though at that time not well; I knew and greatly respected William John Haley, the editor of *The Times*, who was to be Chairman of the new company in the first phase. I also knew well and had formed a close personal friendship with Denis Hamilton, editor of the *Sunday Times* – who was to become editor-in-chief of both papers and, later, Chairman of the company—not only an outstanding newspaperman, but a man of the highest principle and the most rigorous standards as far as the public interest was concerned. I, therefore, had no qualms in accepting my share of responsibility for the new enterprise. Nor were my expectations disappointed. It is true that some of the early experiments for improving the financial position of *The Times*, though they succeeded in producing a substantial, but, as it turned out, only temporary, increase in circulation, had to be revised or abandoned. But such errors as there were lay in the commercial field and in no way caused any concern to me or to my fellow national directors in regard to what were meant to be our special responsibilities. For many years it proved entirely possible to combine our position as directors of the company, having the same legal and moral obligations as any other company director, with the trustee-like responsibilities incumbent on us as 'national' directors.

Two things in particular made this possible. The editorial leadership of the group was in strong and capable hands and even if there had been any inclination towards proprietorial interference it could not have succeeded, quite apart from any assistance the national directors could have provided in resisting it. In any event, there was no trace of any such interventionist inclination. I doubt whether any serious editor could ever have had or hope to have a proprietor less inclined to make any attempt to influence editorial policy in matters large or small than Roy Thomson.

A further factor was that the discussions at the Board were full and detailed, touching commercial and financial as well as editorial policy matters. These meetings were moreover supplemented by regular dinners at which the editor-in-chief, sometimes accompanied by the editors of the two papers, would discuss with the national directors in the frankest possible way matters of editorial concern. We, the national directors, were thus able to be fully familiar with the thinking of those responsible for editorial policy and to make any contribution we could from our knowledge of the outside world without in any way diminishing the authority of the editors for running the papers.

This is not to say that we were individually or collectively always in agreement with the line the papers took on this or that issue. Like any other reader we each had our own tastes and opinions, which we expressed as vigorously as those who write letters to the editor. But we did not in practice experience any difficulty in keeping separate our views about whether *The Times* 'was not what it was' or whether this or that section was better or worse than it had been, or whether this or that feature writer was given more space than he deserved, from, on the one hand, the need to maintain the fundamental character of the papers and, on the other, from the factors that would make the company financially viable.

The difficulties of Times Newspapers certainly did not arise in connection with any of the fears that existed here and there at the time of the merger. They stemmed from the broader commercial difficulties of the British newspaper industry, and especially from the state of industrial relations in Fleet Street. This is not the place to recount the history of the crises to which the latter problem gave rise and which at one point led to the disappearance of the papers for little short of a year. Suffice it to say that a worsening financial situation, which was largely the consequence of these industrial troubles, reached a point at which the Thomson Organisation felt that it could no longer continue to finance the unending series of deficits out of the other interests of the group and, therefore, decided to sell the papers. Warburg's, for many years financial advisers to the Thomson Organisation, were closely concerned in the preparation for and the negotiation of the sale. I did not become personally involved and left this transaction entirely to some of my colleagues in the firm. I wanted to avoid even the slightest possibility of interference with my duties as a national director although, in fact, no real cause for a conflict existed. The ultimate commercial decision on whether to sell, on what terms, and to whom, was that of the owner. My duty, jointly with the other national directors, was to satisfy myself that the safeguards that Thomson had given would be at least maintained by any new owner, whoever he might be. Accordingly, a so-called 'vetting' procedure was agreed at an early stage, through which not only the national directors but also the editor-in-chief and the two editors would be able to satisfy themselves on this point.

Harold Evans in his recent book has described in considerable detail the various stages through which the sale of the papers went, the ebb and flow of potential buyers and the ultimate emergence of Rupert Murdoch as the successful candidate. There is no point in

going over these minutiae here, nor am I in a position to do so for
the reason I have already given: I took no part in these negotiations.
I was, however, satisfied at the time, and I believe the other national
directors were also, to accept the conclusion reached by the
Thomson Organisation that Murdoch's was the only serious offer
remaining on the table for the purchase of both newspapers
together, an objective that Thomson had laid down from the
beginning. It is far from certain whether even had this not been so, a
successful sale of each paper independently – advocated (indeed
attempted) by each of the editors at the time – could have been
secured.

I took a very active part in the 'vetting'. I had, in a private
conversation before the formal meeting, done my best to impress on
Rupert Murdoch the importance of satisfying all of us that he
appreciated the reasons that had led to the creation of independent
national directors and the very special character of the newspapers
he wished to acquire, particularly *The Times*, which were very
different from the papers he then owned. I emphasized to him then,
as I did later at the formal meeting, that satisfying us personally
would not be enough. As far as possible – and we all recognized the
difficulty of formal 'legislation' in these matters – his undertakings
would have to be embodied in a suitable form of words for all the
world to see.

At the meeting Murdoch showed himself fully aware of the
importance of the 'cross-examination' to which he was subjected
and not only gave satisfactory answers but agreed to formulae that
were at least as strong as those that had gone before. Harold Evans
has many critical things to say about the manner in which these
subsequently worked out in practice, particularly in view of his
departure in 1982 from the editorial chair of *The Times*. I had
myself had doubts about his appointment to that post, although I
liked Evans and greatly admired his journalistic talents, which he
had developed enormously under Denis Hamilton's guidance, first
as an assistant to Hamilton when he was editor of the *Sunday
Times*, and later, after the merger, when, on Hamilton's recommendation, he was made editor of the Sunday paper. I felt, and so told
Murdoch – who later reminded me of this – that in moving Evans
from the *Sunday Times* to *The Times* he was making a double
casting error. In my view, while Evans was a brilliant editor of the

Sunday Times, *The Times* was not quite 'his cup of tea' – Murdoch or no Murdoch.

I have no means of telling whether, as Evans claims, a supposed anti-Government bias during his editorship of *The Times*, as compared with a pro-Government (i.e. Conservative Government) bias before or since was the real cause of his disagreement with the proprietor. It certainly never came before the national directors in this form when there might have been a case for them to intervene. What I believe is more important, is that the dispute between Evans and Murdoch brought out very clearly the difficult, indeed ambiguous position in which the independent national directors found themselves. The two main objectives for which their special responsibilities were designed were, in practice, not easy to define. To preserve the 'character' of the paper is a criterion that is only in some respects easily applied: adequate coverage of parliamentary proceedings, law reports and the other items that make of the paper one 'of record'. For the rest, to be sure for example that the paper is an authoritative organ of opinion (though by no means necessarily eschewing a strong view on controversial matters) with a full and unbiased news coverage is perhaps more difficult to assess but was made possible in the Thomson days by the close and frequent contact at the editorial level that the national directors enjoyed. The task was relatively easy since Roy Thomson, his son and the other chief people in the organization, while owners of newspapers, were not themselves newspapermen.

As far as editorial independence is concerned, there could obviously be cases of gross interference by the proprietor, but in the nature of things those charged with maintaining safeguards in this respect could act only when appealed to by the editor and having specific grounds for complaint before them. It is easy to see that the relation of trust and loyalty that must exist between owner and editor could be eroded in a way that makes it difficult, if not impossible, for the watchdogs to operate while at the same time it makes continued partnership between the two principal parties impossible.

In both these respects the situation becomes more difficult to handle when the owner is himself a newspaperman. Murdoch is very much one, and it must clearly be difficult, if not impossible, for him simply to suppress any views he himself may have on what the paper he owns and its editorial policy should be. The conclusion I, therefore, reached and it had something to do with my resignation in 1983 (though after sixteen years this was in any event not inappropriate) and that I believe also played a part in the same decision, which Alf Robens took, is that the limits within which the concept of 'national' directors has validity in present circumstances are very narrow indeed, perhaps so much so as to make the whole idea not worthwhile.

PAST, PRESENT AND FUTURE

I have already referred to my appointment in 1968 to the Court of the Bank of England and it seems appropriate to say something about that venerable and important institution not so much as part of my extracurricular activities but more in the context of the wider issues of our financial structure. I was naturally delighted, as were my senior colleagues in Warburg's, when I was appointed and I was made very welcome by the Governor, Leslie O'Brien. (Not long after I retired from the Court, my colleague David Scholey was, to the pleasure of all of us, made a Director.) Like so many ancient British institutions, and like so many connected with the operations of money and credit, the Bank of England is enveloped in an aura of mystery that adds greatly to the prestige that being a Director of it confers (and which is considered to much more than make up for the modest fee of £500 per annum, unchanged since nationalization in 1946.) It also evokes a certain reverence in those on the outside. This persists at least for a time when one becomes an insider. The newcomer will after a time discover that there is a good deal of hustle and bustle throughout much of the Bank and that it does not in fact give an appearance different from that of any other active place of business. But the atmosphere with which Directors are particularly familiar – the parlours, the Court Room and the Committee rooms with their liveried 'waiters', the absence of haste, the hushed tones, all contribute to creating a certain awe, which, fortunately, does not last long.

The formal proceedings, when I first joined, also contained many quaint survivals of an earlier day, but under Leslie O'Brien, later under Gordon Richardson, many of these were abandoned and I am sure that under the present Governor this process of modernization continues. I am sure, however, that they will not go so far as to deprive the Bank's proceedings of all ceremonial aspects. These, however much they may be lacking in rational justification, lend a certain form to its activities, which, like other institutions that display the dignified parts of the British constitution (as Bagehot called them), has its uses. I remember Walter Stewart the American economist and banker who, as I mentioned earlier, had had experience of the Bank of England, saying to me in the early New Deal days: 'Things in Washington would go more smoothly if it was "Mr Secretary" and "Mr Chairman" and not "Henry" (Morgenthau) and "Mariner" (Eccles) – the Chairman of the Governors of the Fed.' While outside formal meetings the style of address in the Bank has become as relaxed and informal as elsewhere – with first names almost as quickly adopted as in the United States – Walter Stewart's preference still holds sway where appropriate. Having mixed with Ministers, I had no difficulty with this dual practice.

Being a Director certainly makes a substantial call on one's time. The Court meets every week. To this must be added meetings of committees – both standing and *ad hoc* – as well as visits to provincial branches in which the twelve outside Directors are expected to take an active part. I was fortunate enough well before my nearly ten years in the Bank were up to 'graduate' to the Committee of Treasury, the small central policy committee, as old as the Bank itself, which sees all committee reports before they go to Court, but this added a further weekly meeting. Depending on the *modus operandi* of each Governor, outside Directors may also get involved in many informal consultations inside the Bank, though very rarely in those involving outside parties, unless they themselves appear in their non-Bank-of-England capacity. In the all-important contacts between the Bank and the Treasury, between Governor and Chancellor (and Prime Minister) the outside Directors have, as far as I am aware, no direct part to play. At the departmental level, these are left to the executive Directors of the Bank and the staff; at the ministerial level, mainly to the Governor and Deputy Governor.

The Bank of England is at the centre of the country's financial solar system, the constituents of which – and their precise path round the sun – have undergone many changes in the 290 years that the Bank has been in existence. These changes are still going on, and more – perhaps more radical ones than ever – are in prospect. The Bank's central role and power has, however, in recent times not changed as much as the functions performed by the different parts of the rest of the financial system. Its power is in part real, and no doubt ultimately deriving from that reality it rests also on the traditional acceptance of its guidance in many matters not directly related to its central functions, namely to be the bankers' bank, the lender of last resort and the controller of the country's money and credit structure. It is, of course, also the Government's banker responsible for issuing and managing government debt and also for the issue of banknotes.

The Bank of England has traditionally also been a bank in the ordinary commercial banking sense, and Directors and staff may, and usually do, have current accounts with it. I do not know how far the practice – which to my surprise still existed when I was a Director – of welcoming (perhaps seeking?) accounts from commercial and industrial companies continues. It does, of course, create a degree of competition with the clearing banks. This may be considered as being *de minimis*, though it may in part account for the fact that no one actively engaged in one of the major clearing banks was (and perhaps still is) likely to become a Director.

This is not the place to dilate on the manner in which these functions are exercised. What is important to note is that in the 1946 Act that nationalized the Bank it was specifically given the power, if authorized by the Treasury, to give directions to bankers. More generally important is the fact that within the constraints imposed by government policy (of which more presently) the Bank has substantive power that consists of its ability to vary the volume of credit and the terms on which it is available and on which the whole of the rest of the City's financial operations depend, whatever the particular and specialized form in which different institutions carry them out.

As I have said, over the years the Bank has added to these considerable powers of guidance and suasion, which can be made effective quite apart from its more direct influence on financial affairs. The result is that the leaders of the City institutions directly engaged in money and credit activities – clearing banks, merchant banks, discount and finance houses and so forth – would not only seek to avoid any action that they could expect to cause displeasure to the 'Old Lady' but would more often than not seek guidance from the Governor before embarking on any new action not hallowed by precedent.

These practices may give the impression of a generally conservative bias both in the controller and the controlled, but actual experience does not necessarily point in that direction. Certainly, the changes that are in prospect in the City do not appear to suffer from a lack of the innovative spirit nor does the attitude of the Bank appear to be a brake on these new developments. Moreover, since nationalization, but I do not think directly flowing from it, the Bank's actions and its relation with those parts of the financial business that it regulates must be viewed within the context of government policy as a whole and particularly the relation between the Bank and the Treasury. The relations between a central bank and government – more specifically Finance Ministry or Treasury – vary from country to country and have been the subject of much learned discussion. As so often in these matters the reality of the independence or otherwise of the central bank is not always as laid down in its statutory position. At one extreme, in the United States the Federal Reserve Board is independent of the Executive, while at the other the Banque de France is to a considerable degree under the authority of the Finance Ministry; the Bundesbank in Germany and our own Bank of England occupy a middle position. The Act of 1946 explicitly lays down that the Treasury may, after consultation with the Governor, give directions to the Bank, and it is in practice inconceivable that the Bank should act contrary to the general direction of government policy. Nevertheless, the precise balance of views taken in particular issues and in particular circumstances must vary in accordance both with the general direction of central policy as it relates to what the Bank conceives to be its traditional function as well as with the personalities involved.

As a very broad generalization I have observed that central banks tend to consider a Government's economic policy and, more particularly, fiscal policy as carrying the major responsibility in determining the course of the economy, while Treasuries will tend to regard monetary policy as being responsible for either furthering or frustrating the direction of the economic policy they wish to pursue. This is perhaps not surprising, since one has the major responsibility for the execution of monetary policy, while the other acts directly on fiscal policy – leaving aside other and generally newer and more experimental instruments. The differences of opinion that were so patent in the first years of the 1964 Labour Government were clearly of this kind.

I do not believe – surprisingly perhaps – that the possibility of such differences arising is altogether removed either by broad agreement between central bank and Treasury on the priority objectives of economic policy, e.g. the scotching of inflationary tendencies, or even on, say, the outstanding role of monetary policy (what is nowadays described as 'monetarism'). I shall have more to say about this in discussing any lessons that recent economic history may have to offer on the relation between economic ideas and economic policy. But it is clear that, however 'monetarist' a Government may be (and our own present one and the American Administration have probably come closest to full reliance on what that doctrine appears to prescribe) they cannot, on the one hand, totally divest themselves of the exercise of many other policy instruments, nor will they readily accept all the consequences that a strict application of monetarist dogma would bring about. The frequent disagreements between the US Treasury and the Federal Reserve Board in recent years on the relative influences of fiscal and monetary phenomena and on the policy requirements to be derived from them are an outstanding example of this inherent tendency towards a degree of schizophrenia in these regards.

I have mentioned personalities and these are obviously important, though there is not much of a general character to be said about the part they play. Governors are not high Civil Servants: the fact that the Chancellor's power of direction – something that is inherent in the Civil Servant–Minister relationship – is specifically enshrined in an Act of Parliament and that it explicitly must include consultation with the Governor makes the 'ultimate resort' nature of this clause clear. I have no means of telling whether it has ever been formally exercised even in the stormy days of the first two years of Harold Wilson's Administration, but I doubt whether it could be so exercised except on extremely rare occasions. The Radcliffe Committee (Committee on the Working of the Monetary System) went into this question. What is clear from its deliberations, and from later inquiries by parliamentary committees, is that in the event of a serious clash of views over policy, the Governor would wish to arm himself with the support of the Court or, at any rate, the Committee of Treasury, and resignations might then become the inevitable outcome. This has not happened. In practice, Governors, Permanent Secretaries of the Treasury, Chancellors and Prime Ministers will tend to establish a relationship that, even if it is not consistently harmonious, will provide an adequate framework for carrying on. The knowledge of and access to financial markets provides the Bank and its Governor with a powerful source of arguments, as the knowledge of political and administrative realities and of the economy as a whole does for Ministers and officials.

In this context the role of the outside Directors is of interest. They are in a majority on the Court (twelve out of eighteen) and on the Committee of Treasury, a situation that is, on the whole, rare on the boards of commercial and industrial companies. As a rule, they include a number of leading merchant bankers and there may be representatives of overseas banks or retired leading figures of major clearing banks or of smaller ones. The majority are drawn from commerce and industry and often include one or two trade unionists. Sometimes, a distinguished economist is included, although he may be one of the four executive Directors. All Directors, including outside ones, have to make a declaration pledging their best advice and assistance to the Bank and faithful and honest conduct. This naturally includes preservation of confidentiality in all matters relating to the affairs of the Bank.

In describing the role of outside Directors, for example, to the Radcliffe Committee, the Bank has stressed the intimacy that grows up over a number of years between them and the Governors and executive Directors and senior staff. In consequence, the outside Directors, apart from their formal attendance, can be, and are, effectively called on by the Bank's management to advise on a great variety of business affairs and personalities, and they for their part, by virtue of their position in the Bank, are made aware by their fellow Directors – not only the full-time ones – of many matters that make them more effective in their own businesses and in others with which they may be associated. This aspect of their relationship has, especially after the famous Bank Rate Tribunal, led to the question as to whether they are in a privileged position in regard to

certain policies, actions or prospective actions by the Bank that
could, if they were to yield to such temptation, give them an
improper advantage in their outside business affairs.

Those who gave evidence to the Radcliffe Committee denied that
such situations would arise. In fact, whether it is as a result of the
Bank Rate Tribunal (as has sometimes been claimed) or not, the
outside Directors are not, to my knowledge, privy to those affairs of
the Bank, including the most sensitive ones such as the considerations leading up to decisions on Bank Rate – or, now, Minimum
Lending Rate – that could lead to improper use, even if one were to
allow for the possibility of a lapse from the high standards expected
of the Directors and to which they are pledged. Outside Directors
do participate in one way or another in discussions on broad issues
of public policy in the economic and financial field and will become
aware (but so do very many other people, including newspapermen!) of varying and conflicting currents of opinion in Westminster, Whitehall and the City, including the Bank itself. Their
position would be completely useless if they did not. But the idea,
so often encountered outside, that to be a member of the Court
gives one special knowledge of and a direct say in the important
policy decisions of the Bank is way off the mark. Indeed, outside
Directors have been known on occasion to question this state of
affairs, and in recent years Governors have increasingly tried
various devices for organizing more wide-ranging discussions on
economic and financial matters. It is, however, safe to assume that
the most sensitive matters, those for example in the fields of credit,
interest-rate and foreign-exchange-rate policy, will continue to be
dealt with between the Governor, the Chancellor and their closest
advisers and, more often than not, the Prime Minister.

There is much in these arrangements that may not appeal to the
tidy mind. Moreover, in the critical moments of our recent
economic history – some of which I have described – the question
has been raised, usually though not only from the left of the
political spectrum as to whether the existence of a West End
Treasury with an 'East End Branch' is best calculated to provide the
machinery necessary for handling the often tempestuous situations
particularly in the international financial field. This question is
separate from that of the adequacy of our financial system for a
growing and prosperous economy, on which I will have something

to say. The extreme suggestion that somehow the Bank should become 'part of the Treasury' has rarely been taken very far even by radical reformers. It is difficult to see how this could be done in practice once it is accepted – as I think it must be – that there is need for a central financial institution, in and of the City with practical day-to-day responsibilities that it would be extremely difficult to entrust to a section of the Treasury as now constituted. A different line of thinking has been to suggest that the Court should be much smaller, that there should be no outside Directors (though there might be an advisory council) and that senior officials of the Treasury – and perhaps Junior Treasury Ministers – should be on the Court. Less is heard of ideas of this kind now than in the sixties and seventies.

Whatever may be considered the lack of logic of the present arrangements, it is difficult to see what improvement the alternatives would produce. If there were thought to be a danger that the Bank might frustrate government policy then, even though explicit directions may never have been given by the Treasury, that possibility is always there. A more direct involvement of outside Directors in the formulation of policy in those matters on which the Bank is the major source of advice to Government as well as its executant, is theoretically possible and seems to have been the case at an earlier period in the Bank's modern history. This might perhaps involve reducing the size of the Court, with the attendant disadvantage of a narrower range of experience and knowledge for the Governor to draw on. This might not be decisive in relation to the Bank's function as an arm of public policy in the monetary field. It would, however, be a weighty one in relation to the Bank's wider functions, particularly in view of the changes in the structure of financial markets and institutions that are in the making.

The City is widely regarded as being well set in its ways and in a sense this may be true. It has, however, undergone many changes even in its recent history. A reading of such different books as Bagehot's classic *Lombard Street*, written over 110 years ago and the comparatively straightforward description by a well-informed Frenchman, R. J. Truptil, *British Banks and the London Money Market*, published in 1936, shows clearly both the features that have remained constant and those that have changed out of all recognition. In recent times the City has been characterized by a high degree of specialization, moreover one that is different from examples of specialization that can be found in other financial centres. Since the war, the distinction between the functions of the different parts of the City, particularly clearing banks, merchant banks, stockbrokers, has tended to become somewhat blurred.

Clearing banks have, through acquired or specially created subsidiaries gone into merchant banking (corporate finance, underwriting, investment management) and merchant banks, which have always engaged in general banking business, though usually only wholesale rather than retail, have expanded that side of their business. Stockbrokers, for their part, have expanded their investment-management functions, often for institutional clients, such as pension funds, and have also tried to develop underwriting and issuing business. This process has been much influenced by the increasing presence in London of branches or subsidiaries of foreign banks (now numbering several hundred), often engaging in merchant banking (or investment banking as it would be called in America), something from which the American commercial banks are statute-barred in their own country.

Up to now these changes have not altered the fundamental features of the financial landscape, one which is different from that in New York and Tokyo where a different pattern of specialization (though also showing a tendency to become blurred) or from Germany where the so-called 'universal' bank tends to combine a wide range of London's specialist activities within one institution. More drastic changes may, however, now be seen to be in the offing. Two lines of development have set in motion forces that may eventually produce a different structure from that which has persisted for so long. (I leave out of account here, as going too far afield and well beyond my own experience, such matters as the increasing activity of clearing banks in mortgage finance and, conversely, the ability of building societies to engage in 'straight' banking.) These two developments relate, in the first place, to the organization of the market in securities – the Stock Exchange – and, in the second, to the growing concern over the protection of the investor, responsible now, particularly through institutions such as insurance companies and pension funds, for a vast majority of the country's capital.

The history of the development of different financial instruments is an important part of economic history, including that of the last few decades since the end of the Second World War, but it is not my purpose to give even a summary account of it here. I must, however, point to some aspects of it in so far as they have had an influence on the structure of the country's financial system and fall within my own experience during these seventeen years that I have been active in the City and also as they seem likely to affect its shape in the near future. Fundamentally, that is to say as a theoretical economist might analyse it, nothing much has changed in the last hundred years or so. There is a demand for financial assets of various kinds, distinguished primarily by their degree of liquidity (or maturity), and the financial institutions have developed different instruments to meet this demand, ranging all the way from non-interest-bearing current-account balances with commercial banks to fixed-interest debentures of industrial companies. Markets have developed that enable most of these instruments to be dealt in, i.e. enabling those holding them to realize them for cash, regardless of their original maturity. Thus, these instruments and the markets they are dealt in are communicating vessels, and the more perfectly the markets operate, the more perfect the analogy, that is the continuous flow of funds from one to another so as to create an equilibrium position, i.e. one in which further movement would not produce any advantage. Like all 'equilibria' in economic theory, this one is never attained in practice, and the most one can say is that if markets work as they should there will always be a tendency towards such a position. Meanwhile, as the markets 'overshoot' and 'undershoot' and are constantly 'correcting' the position, those operating in them can make a living and those using these markets can add or subtract from the value of their financial assets!

Indeed, these fundamentals in the process have not changed, but the variety of forms in which it appears has been vastly increased in recent decades, with greater opportunities – and risks – for those involved in it in one way or another. It is probably fair to say that the market that has changed less than others is the most formally organized of all, the Stock Exchange. The two principal features of the Stock Exchange (apart from the rules concerning membership) that also distinguish it from other exchanges are the maintenance of fixed commissions – a condition that was abandoned in New York some years ago – and the division of members into jobbers, dealing

on their own account, and brokers, who act as agents. Both these
are to disappear in the course of 1986, and from then on the
operations of the Stock Exchange, and its membership rules, will be
much more akin to, for example, those of its New York
counterpart. These changes, above all negotiated commissions and
'dual capacity', i.e. the ability to act as agent and dealer on one's
own account, are radical enough. They are, however, only the pre-
conditions for further very considerable changes in the structure of
the British financial system and the survival of the specializations
that have hitherto been characteristic of it. A considerable
movement towards the combination of merchant banks and
jobbers and/or brokers, as well as one involving commercial banks,
British and foreign, has already begun against the day when the
Stock Exchange rules are in fact changed, and this movement will
almost certainly gather further momentum. It is a fairly safe
assumption that, say, within five years of the day when these
changes become possible, the City will present a very different
picture from that of today, even when one allows for the blurring of
demarcation lines that has already taken place and to which I have
already referred. As so often happens with deep-rooted British
institutions, they take a long time to change, but when they do, they
do it with a vengeance!

I have so far spoken mainly of certain domestic trends, which
have brought the City to the threshold of these changes. Internatio-
nally, the developments in the last few decades have been even more
far-reaching and I have already referred briefly to the very great
number of foreign banks that have set up branches or subsidiaries
in London. This is just one consequence of the internationalization
of financial markets. Without going into the details of the history of
this development, it should be noted that today those in need of
funds, whether they are governments, state agencies or corporate
entities, can have access not only to their own capital and money
markets but also to those of other major centres (New York,
London, Tokyo, Zurich, Frankfurt and so on) as well as to an
international market in which funds denominated in different
currencies (dollars, sterling, Deutschmarks, Swiss francs, yen and
European Currency Units) are available and are characterized by
the fact that they are not held under the direct control of their own
national financial authorities. These Euro-currency markets have

grown to very large figures indeed – on a net basis (i.e. avoiding possible double counting of interbank balances) to the equivalent of over $1,000 billion, and the credits arranged, or the bonds issued in them, are counted in terms of many billions per annum.

As might be expected, in the fact of these changes, the firms carrying on this business, their personnel and their *modus operandi* have also undergone considerable changes. Naturally, they have each, sometimes with and sometimes without the help of their authorities, tried to maintain some special hold over their sectors of the market. London has maintained more of an 'open-door' policy than any other centre and while this has on the whole not been to the disadvantage of indigenous firms, an important factor that has made for their ability to maintain their competitive position has been the enormous growth of the market as a whole. The changes that are in prospect will tend to make competition more acute, both by removing the traditional practices that have had a protective, or even monopolistic, effect, by still further eroding those specialisms that have rested on skills, access to which had been restricted in the past, and by still further widening the international accessibility of all types of financial business. The policy of the authorities that is leading to these changes in the London scene is based on the proposition that since the financial requirements of the world's economy are inevitably creating a more competitive environment, our domestic structure must be given the opportunity – indeed the impulse – to adapt quickly to these changes, even if in the resulting climate individual firms may find it difficult to survive.

The other line of change to which I have referred goes – paradoxically – in the opposite direction, even if much the same forces have generated it. The growth in size, in multiplicity of instruments and in the international dimension of financial markets has tended to make investors much more aware of and alert to opportunities as regards the management of their financial assets. It has, however, also made it a more difficult task to keep track of all the fluctuations, their causes and consequences, and it has created some disquiet on the score of the possibility that the active participants in the market (particularly intermediaries and managers and advisers of investors with their much more detailed and sophisticated knowledge of markets) may, even if they do not indulge in downright fraudulent practices, be tempted into actions to the disadvantage of the ultimate investor. Investor protection has, therefore, become an important concern of government and of the financial authorities. Hitherto the protection has been provided in the main, apart from the criminal law, by the rules and traditional practices of the Stock Exchange, combined with the organization of institutional investors themselves and such new self-regulatory agencies as the Council for the Securities Industry and its Panel on Takeovers and Mergers. In expectation of the impending great structural changes with the possible combination of brokers, dealers, merchant banks with their corporate finance activities and investment management and advisory services, the feeling has grown up that the existing provision for protecting the investor may not be adequate. Professor Gower (whom I have already mentioned as a distinguished Vice-Chancellor of Southampton University) was asked to produce a report on this question, and this, together with the comments of the various associations of different sectors of the City are now under study by the Government as well as by a committee set up by the Governor of the Bank of England.

As always in these matters, particularly in Britain, the argument lies between the degree of imposed regulation and the degree of self-regulation to be adopted. The British prejudice is in favour of self-regulation – there is probably no other country in which so much of the policing of their activities is left to the 'guild'-like organizations of practitioners in different businesses and professions. The record of self-regulation is by no means such that it would of itself lead to a very strong case for replacing it by something based on statute. Nevertheless, with the developments to come, it is unlikely that public opinion will be content with a system relying solely on self-regulation, even though the example of the total statutory control by the United States Securities and Exchange Commission is unlikely to be followed. In the opinion of many unbiased observers, this has neither entirely eliminated malpractice nor has it proved as expeditious in its proceedings as one would wish – particularly in the financial field where delay can be very costly indeed. The outcome is almost bound to be a typical British compromise.

Whichever form that takes, one has to recognize that investor protection must involve some measure of restraint on competition or at least on the practices of financial institutions over and beyond those imposed by the law of the land in its widest sense. It may well also impose constraints on the future structure of financial firms, which will result in a different pattern of ownership, grouping, and range of activities from that which would be produced by the forces of competition and the criteria of greatest efficiency and profitability. What this will mean for the continued international competitiveness of the City cannot be determined until more is known about what will be possible and what will be ruled out. Nor can one ignore the simultaneous changes that may take place in other countries; nor yet the effect of the harmonizing proclivities of the European Community as they may evolve in relation to financial institutions.

On the whole, I would judge that the City will absorb the coming changes on all fronts well and that its chances of maintaining a strong competitive position against the institutions of other countries—the Americans with the great advantages of being backed by a very large, strong and resilient economy, the Germans with an already existing 'universal' and highly concentrated banking system, and the Japanese with a unique, and largely socially and culturally rooted, interpenetration of industry, trade and finance and government. But the going will be rough.

Another question, though obviously related to that of international competitiveness, is that of the efficacy of the City's role in the economy. On one measurement, the financial institutions have served the national economy well, namely in their contribution to our external balance. The 'invisible' earnings, of which the financial services of the City form an important source, have for many years been in substantial surplus and have helped to offset deficits on trading account. If we can maintain our position, we shall be better able to use continued earnings on this account as a cushion for the inevitably precarious future in other of our international economic operations.

Rather more difficult to answer (because the question itself is somewhat obscure) is whether the City of today and even more that of tomorrow is best organized to aid and support the 'real' economy. This question is nearly always on the agenda of discussion of British public affairs. It was so before, and even more so after, the First World War, and it has been so now, though under the present Administration, with its greater *laissez-faire*, market-oriented attitude, it is perhaps less than it was some ten years or so ago. Usually the problem is put in the form of 'Is the City sufficiently geared to providing finance to industry rather than for purposes (including overseas investment) that may yield favourable returns quickly but may not be in the longer term interests of investment in our industry?' Or, 'Are funds available in adequate measure and speed for new enterprises that may be hazardous to start with, but on the overall success of which our economic future depends?' These and similar questions lead from time to time – and at different points in the political spectrum – to specific policy proposals, ranging from such relatively limited experiments as the Industrial Reconstruction Corporation of the 1964 Labour Government, of which I have already spoken, or the essentially private-sector Industrial and Commercial Finance Corporation or Equity for Industry, to the more extreme proposals for the nationalization of the clearing banks and some other parts of the City's institutions.

The classical economic point of view, or at any rate that which would be espoused by extreme free marketeers would be that financial intermediaries are in no different position in the economic process from traders or transporters, i.e. from those who adapt the commodity or service of its original producer in time, or space, or financial availability to the needs of the consumer (who may himself be a producer of a commodity or service) and that the rules of the market must apply to him as they do to anyone else. There are certain practical examples to be adduced in support of this rather abstract and arid thesis of the theorist, and defenders of the existing state of affairs have usually argued, for example, that no worthwhile new project need be frustrated by lack of finance. The evidence, I believe is mixed: in any event negatives cannot be proved, and nobody will ever know what interesting ventures withered on the vine for lack of financial support. I believe, however, that whatever negative aspects our financial system may have in relation to economic progress are due to institutional factors in the widest sense, i.e. cultural and social ones, rather than to the technical characteristics of the financial system itself.

Perhaps as – or even more – speculative are the changes that all these as yet uncertain developments may have on the style and conduct of the people working in these areas of business, although what has already emerged in the last decade or two may provide a guide. When observing some of today's practices in the City in the sector with which I am more familiar and forming a picture of what it will be like under the conditions that seem to be emerging, I have wondered what Siegmund Warburg would make of them, how his conception of the private banker – the family doctor in the financial sphere – would stand up to the rough, tough climate that has developed. When doing so I have had to say to myself in the first place that while his views were congenial to me and were by any standard humane and civilized in a larger sense (and, indeed, by no means quixotic even from a narrow business point of view), they never, and certainly not in recent times, corresponded wholly to the most common practice – the ethos – of the financial community. That, despite its gentility, its good manners – indeed its usual genuine kindliness and co-operative spirit – has always, in the end, been devoted to financial success in the narrowest sense and can even be said on occasion to have been quite ruthless in pursuit of it. Perhaps one should not expect it to be otherwise; nevertheless, whatever it was fundamentally was certainly until the present not only overlaid, but truly moderated, by a certain code of conduct that helped greatly to make the more selfish motives tolerable.

Will even an adequate element of this survive in the new world? The question is legitimate, because even now the forms that competition has taken would make many departed bankers of the old school turn in their graves. When I was an undergraduate, and was taught the elements of, for example, advertising standards, 'knocking' your competitor was strictly taboo. This has long since ceased to be the case in commercial and industrial advertising. Since in the financial community advertising is not so widely practised (Warburg's have never done any), it is not easy to compare present and past practice. However, in the competitive rush for business, knocking the competitor has become quite a common feature even in the genteel circles of the inner financial establishment. The consequences of such attitudes for the type of person recruited and the training he receives can easily be imagined.

Furthermore, the developments I have described and those still to come have inevitably led to certain forms of the search for business that would certainly have given the bankers of the old stamp some heartache. Of course, the mere fact that much of the cosiness, the clublike atmosphere created by a largely monopolistic framework, has gone should not cause one to shed tears, and if efficiency in a new climate requires tougher attitudes and an abandonment of some of the frills of an earlier day, so be it. But there must still be a question mark over the ultimate value of the sort of 'product '-oriented business with its emphasis on trading, which is now prevalent, rather than the 'client'-oriented type of old, which emphasized service. The disappearance of the 'London Banker' described by Bagehot over a hundred years ago in these terms—

> The name 'London Banker' had especially a charmed value. He was supposed to represent, and often did represent, a certain union of pecuniary sagacity and educated refinement which was scarcely to be found in any other part of society. In a time when the trading classes were much ruder than they now are, many private bankers possessed a variety of knowledge and a delicacy of attainment which would even now be very rare.

—would certainly deserve a passing tear.

15

Scholarship, Government and Business

The experience of the three careers that I have had is by no means unique, but until recent years it was not very common and certainly not as common in Britain as it has always been in the United States. Leaving aside my undergraduate years and some brief later episodes, I have spent more than twelve years in an academic environment, twenty-five in the public service at home and abroad, and seventeen in business. Some reflections, additional to those relating to particular events which I have already given, may be in order.*

I begin with remarks on economics, which, despite my relatively brief concern with it in an academic sense, has constituted in one form or another a thread that has run through all my subsequent activities. Since it is concerned with man in the ordinary business of life, it is not a bad starting point for considering many other aspects and problems of our times. I should, however, say at once that I do not regard myself as primarily an economist, and certainly not as one who has made any significant contribution to the corpus of economic analysis. I was in my early thirties when I stopped any systematic cultivation of the subject as an academic discipline. I do not know whether I would have achieved more in it had I gone on with my academic work. If it were true of economics what is often said of mathematics – that no one does any creative work after the age of 25 – the answer must be no. I believe, however, that my early training and continued interest in the evolution of economic ideas and my subsequent experience of public and private business have given me some insight into the place of economics in these two areas of practical activity, which determine to such a large extent the course of our lives.

---

*I have dealt in greater detail and in a more analytical way with some of the points that follow in two lectures, the Sidney Ball Lecture in 1968 and the Stamp Memorial Lecture in 1976, both republished in my *The Uses and Abuses of Economics* (1978).

The dominant thought with which I am left is that the limits within which economics can be relied on for precise guidance are very narrow indeed. I must, however, guard against giving any support to obscurantist views and I would, therefore, not wish to underrate the recent advances in many aspects of economics, econometrics and statistics, particularly in the – perhaps peripheral – areas where they have a direct bearing on specific industrial matters or questions of business management. Even at the central core of economic theory, the last thirty or forty years have seen progress in our understanding of economic processes and in the analytical follow-through of different assumptions regarding the responses of human behaviour to different economic stimuli. Furthermore, there are some basic propositions of even the most elementary economic theory that it would be very imprudent for the politician or business man to forget even if some of them, such as the principle of opportunity cost, are more like the prose that M. Jourdain had been speaking all the time without knowing it.

Nevertheless, it remains sadly true, as the German writer Ludwig Börne remarked over 150 years ago, 'The trouble with economics is that its frontiers are too narrow, for they exclude politics, which they should not.' Perhaps this is not the best formulation of the problem for it tends to lead into sterile semantic argument. A simpler way of putting it is to recognize that even the most refined proposition in economic theory can do no more than assume certain responses to certain stimuli, whereas the possibilities in reality of what these responses might be are much more numerous than can be grasped by theory, stemming as they do from a whole mass of ideas and beliefs in the minds of those making the responses. This is, I believe, one of the reasons why heavy reliance on one simple set of economic propositions for the purpose of determining economic policy as is fashionable from time to time can rarely be effective and can sometimes be very dangerous indeed. There are some, though happily only few, economists who take an exaggerated view of the practical applicability of their theories; those that do belong to the more extreme doctrinaire schools, distinguished not only by the narrowness of their beliefs but also by the arrogance with which they hold them. Sometimes they make disciples among politicians, and when the political climate happens to be propitious, we may get an unholy alliance that can produce results that may take a long time to undo. The present fashion to extol the free-market forces (though it is used essentially as a slogan with very considerable compromises in practice that belie the fervour with which the dogma is preached) that has excessive reliance on monetary policy as its main, if not sole, practical expression, seems to me to fall into this category.

I hasten to say that while the broad spectrum of economic analysis that dominated not only professional thinking, but also economic policy, for more than a quarter of a century after the Second World War was both more reasonable and more useful, it was given in the end to some excesses of self-assurance – a hubris that must in a measure be held responsible for the nemesis of the present, monetarist tendencies. I have already mentioned earlier this exaggeration of 'fine tuning' of economic policy, as it came to be called, one that I criticized sixteen years ago, as soon as I had left the public service. It is easy to see that after the strains of an activist policy that this involved – and after its perfectly understandable failures in some particular instances – the opposite view should have its intellectual attractions, and its political appeal. It is undoubtedly a seductive thought for politicians that non-intervention, a kind of automatic pilot provided by the free play of markets – though with that quite major derogation, monetary policy – would relieve them of many painful decisions. Non-intervention, i.e. 'keeping government out of business' is always popular with the business community (although not a few of its members are ready to fall for the temptation of particular intervention to their own real or imagined advantage) and from time to time the political climate turns in this direction. Moreover, any failures of monetary policy, or an excessively non-intervention-ist policy, can always be blamed on the fact that the policy had not been sufficiently non-interventionist or monetarist. So, proof is impossible. I am reminded in this connection that a friend of mine asked a German social-democratic *émigré* in the thirties whether he still thought that his Party's 'toleration' policy (*vis-à-vis* Hitler) had been correct, to which he replied, 'We did not tolerate enough.'

Current debates on the question of wages and unemployment seem to me a case in point. I have already stated my belief that, in an open economy at least, an ability to adjust the level of incomes to major changes is extremely important for stability and growth prospects. (I have also argued that in advanced industrial economies this points to the need for an incomes policy.) It is undeniable that a persistently high wage level (in relation to other relevant economic categories), e.g. as the result of strong trade-union pressure, may produce unemployment, although it must be remembered that volumes have been written in the last 200 years about what is true and what is fallacious in the doctrine of the 'wages fund'. But to argue as some do that it is trade-union pressure in pushing wages up that is alone responsible and that such factors as interest-rate and exchange-rate policy have nothing to do with it is not only incorrect reasoning (these factors can radically alter competitiveness, profitability and employment opportunities – and very quickly at that – making previous, economically rational, decisions suddenly uneconomic) but it is plainly contrary to the experience of the last few years.

My own experience in the fields of public policy has led me to the view that a fairly eclectic policy – within such broad principles as the democratic process may impose – is inevitable, and my observation of the course of economic events in more recent years has not only strengthened that view, but has convinced me that, however extreme the rhetoric, stubborn facts will force even the most doctrinaire Government into a series of compromises. Thus, difficult, indeed painful, decisions in government cannot be avoided by constant reiteration of this or that doctrine. The alternation of extremes of political rhetoric may correspond well to the deep-rooted traditions of our electoral system and party-political landscape; indeed it may for these reasons be inevitable. But it is perhaps my academic background combined with service under Governments of various colours that makes me hanker sometimes after what I suspect is probably unattainable.

It may in this connection be permissible to revert to Keynes. As I have already indicated, he also possessed a certain arrogance and could be disdainful and dismissive of those he disagreed with. But the self-assurance from which this attitude sprang was not primarily due to his own particular beliefs – which changed from time to time. It was based in the main on his attachment to rigorous argument, and there is plenty of evidence in his writings of his readiness to change his position in response to arguments that he could respect. Nobody can read even a fraction of his voluminous works without being impressed by the essentially utilitarian direction of his thought, i.e. for the purpose of discovering more and better means for improving the human condition (science in the widest sense had for him to answer Bacon's 'tendency to use') and the practical applications that he was always examining. Not for him the constant taking of refuge in some eternal verities, reminiscent of the attitude of Mrs Mary Baker Eddy, which is much to be found in his present-day opponents. To me, their attitude – as at the other extreme, that of Marxists – produces an essentially arid body of views, incapable of further development.

More than strictly economic argument goes into the making of public policy, even when it forms an important ingredient of it, while extreme economic views – nationalization and its opposite, protectionism, including the extremes of 'planning' with all the paraphernalia of control of exchanges and capital movements or extreme reliance on free markets, and many other examples – have certainly caused many of our post-war troubles. The list of major 'errors' in British policy contains examples where wrong decisions were taken not only for strictly economic reasons. Our policy *vis-à-vis* Europe, of which I have said much, is an outstanding example of a complex of issues in which the economic may not always have been the decisive one. Our continued refusal to join the European Monetary System – which is certainly capable of being debated on strictly economic grounds – is, I suspect, also based on other considerations that are probably quite inchoate even in the minds of the most stubborn opponents. But perhaps this is one problem that will be resolved rationally by the time these lines are read!

I have already said that the direct application of economic analysis to the problems that arise in the daily practice of business is limited. Public policy affects business very much. The general economic and financial environment in which business is carried on is influenced not only by specific developments within it, but also by forces operating on it from outside, both domestic and foreign. These, in turn, depend to a large extent on the thrust of policy both domestic and foreign, the former often in response to the latter. Thus the path from a particular business situation that has to be dealt with to the circumstances that have created it and, even more, the intellectual or ideological impulses behind them (or, if one wishes, the economic reasoning behind them) is a long and uncertain one.

Even in the financial field where a more direct relationship might be expected, this is not always so. Take the changes in interest rates and exchange rates on which directly the success or failure of those operating in financial markets depend and that influences in such a major degree the vast bulk of the world's business. For example, the earnings of multinational companies, when they are repatriated, will depend on the changes in the value of their domestic currency (the recent rise in the dollar rate has produced considerable difficulties), and in the current discussion on the debts of many sovereign borrowers, particularly among the developing countries, it is well recognized that changes in interest rates and changes in the rate of the currency in which their debts are contracted can aggravate or alleviate that problem considerably. Since treasuries and central banks, the decisions of which have the major influence on these matters (even when they decide to do nothing!), have many learned economists to assist, advise and sometimes even direct them, and since most financial institutions in these markets are not short of expert economic advice either, one would imagine that a fairly straight line would lead from economic analysis of money and credit and other relevant conditions to appropriate decisions. At the same time, those who will be primarily affected may be expected to be capable of reasonably correct anticipations of these decisions. The history of monetary phenomena of the last few years would, in my view, be difficult to interpret in this rational way, and the hazards of forecasting these movements and the risks attendant on wrong forecasts are as great as ever.

To look at the economic element within the social sciences, in government policy, or in business decisions is to ignore many other elements that make up the academic environment or that in the public service or in business. I have often been asked what life is like in these three areas in which I have myself lived. This may not be a very sensible question to ask; it is certainly not an easy one to answer. I suppose that 'life' in the sense of this question is really made up of a large number of activities and episodes, some connected as a series, some quite disparate. With many of my own that seem to me to have any lasting significance I have already dealt. But there is perhaps something more to be said about the environment as a whole that they create and about the people who share it.

University life, in England at least, was as far as I can tell very different forty years ago from what it is today. Even in a small provincial university life was very much patterned in the tradition of Oxford and Cambridge. In the humanities, including the social sciences, the work comprised practically nothing but lecturing and tutoring in term time, and the load was generally not heavy. There were relatively few official extra-curricular activities: most of them were closely related to one's own research, including occasional outside lecturing (as well as evening classes in adult education courses), articles, mainly in learned journals, and book reviews. The vacations were long, and unless one was either very enthusiastically attached to specific other activities or very hard up one could devote them entirely to the pursuit of one's own inclinations, with a certain time occupied in the preparation of next year's lectures. My own life, during the nine years that I taught at Hull, conformed more or less to this pattern. (I read, travelled and wrote a number of books.) It was primarily in engineering and medicine that the outside activities of at least the more renowned academics were as important as their internal ones, or even more so.

In the United States, as I have already indicated in speaking of the great mobility of American society, the situation has always been very different. Today in Britain too, partly as a result of the great extension of tertiary education that followed the Robbins Report and other reforms, partly through the greater use of academics (particularly economists) in various consulting capacities and in the media, the picture is a very different one. The opportunities for outside activities and additional remuneration are enormously increased. Despite the limits that I believe exist and should be recognized in regard to what economics can effectively do for government and business, I naturally welcome the fact that economics has become a 'growth' industry, with several hundred employed directly by government and a very large number indeed in banks and other financial institutions and in industrial and commercial companies. One of the gratifying results has been that the spread and level of understanding of broad macro-economic factors is greater than it has ever been and that the quality of the economic memoranda, notes, newsletters and so on issued by banks, stockbrokers and others is considerably higher than at any time in the past.

I am not sure what it has done to the practitioners themselves. In this discipline they have rarely been of the ivory-tower variety, and very few are so today. Indeed, the tendency to be guarded against is the opposite one: that propinquity to, even intermingling with, the governmental or business machine may make them too much disposed to see the problems from the narrow point of view of a specific objective and perhaps create a class separated from those devoted to pure speculation. Maybe this is inevitable. I was for a long time convinced – though I am less certain of it now – of the truth of Kant's rejection of the theory of the philosopher-king: 'That kings should philosophize or philosophers become kings is hardly to be expected; nor is it to be desired. For the possession of power ineluctably corrupts the pure judgement of reason.' In governmental affairs, in which the economic element nowadays looms so large, the danger is particularly clear and is allied to what I have said about the pitfalls that Civil Servants will continue to need to avoid.

There is no uniformity about life in the public service. The variety of activities and duties of the public servant at home, and in a measure even abroad, is such that no general rule can be laid down. It is still possible to lead a relatively quiet life in some departments of state, particularly the regulatory ones or in some minor foreign mission. But if that is what one is after, one should realize that there are hazards. Unexpected coups, kidnappings, or, less violently, sudden discovery of important natural resources, may project one into the limelight and turn what seemed a quiet, idyllic post into something quite feverish. As for the home Civil Service, much depends on the level one wishes to reach; at the top, I doubt whether nowadays there is anywhere in Whitehall where a quiet life can be expected, let alone guaranteed. Moreover, even lower down the scale, Civil Servants may not be immune, for the politicization of so many of the issues with which government departments have to deal, means that one can never know when something will crop up that will engender the most acute anxiety for the Minister and, perhaps, the Cabinet.

There is nothing to add to what I have said already about business except to emphasize that with its still largely clublike atmosphere the City resembles more than any area of business the rather close societies of the academy and Whitehall, and personal contact between their members – particularly the City and Whitehall – is usually easy and smooth, particularly as their educational background (if no longer their social and economic backgrounds) are often the same. It is a moot question whether the *homines novi* whom one can expect in the financial institutions of the future will fit together in this way, with whatever the future denizens of Whitehall may be like.

Many have discovered long before me and have said so that good, indifferent and bad human qualities are distributed randomly. It is, therefore, useless to enquire whether any one of these is present in greater or less degree in the three areas in which I have worked. I have met some of all kinds in each of them. Nevertheless, each activity – as many others – will tend to put the emphasis on one or other trait of character. Perhaps one aspect in which the three might be distinguished is the way in which the competitive spirit – present, of course, in them all – appears and what it is addressed to. Renown in one's own field of study and corresponding position, in so far as it is relevant, is the dominant impulse in the academy; the material rewards would be expected to be commensurate, but only within the established institutional framework. Only rarely – an occasional bestseller for example – can it be substantially modified. Status is, therefore, more important than money, because more open to competition. Intrigue in the struggle for position is not unknown; I have myself witnessed directly and indirectly instances worthy of C. P. Snow's novels.

In business, the situation is almost the reverse. Since achievement is primarily measured (because measurable) in money terms, making money, both for one's firm and oneself, is the major form in which the competitive spirit appears. Here, intrigue, as distinct from shrewd judgement and skilful negotiation, is hardly possible. But status as an objective is not absent, and material achievement and status in the community do, thanks to the activity of the media, often go together. For the purpose of position and status some degree of politicking may be used. Boardroom intrigues are no more unknown than those in senior common rooms, though they are perhaps rarer.

In the public service material rewards are almost entirely linked with professional advancement and are strictly predetermined. It is, therefore, not possible to pursue them as an objective in themselves.

As for position and status, the system is so hedged round with institutional constraints that it is difficult to visualize circumstances in which individual pressure for advancement could of itself be successful, and intrigue to that end – as distinct from discreet alliances for and against particular policies – is practically unknown in the public service, even though rare cases of promotion of 'Ministers' pets' have occurred. In fact, the opposite charge that advancement is by 'Buggin's turn' is also quite unfounded, at least for important administrative appointments.

Thus, if absence of acute competition, including even intrigue, for personal advancement is to be taken as a particularly desirable feature of one's working environment, then the public service would have to have pride of place. Lionel Robbins may have had this feature in mind when he once called the Civil Service 'a priesthood'. But there are countervailing disadvantages that will have become clear to the reader. Serving Ministers – and it is in the end only through them that one can serve the common weal – can be frustrating.

I had myself long thought that academic work would offer the best prospect for a satisfying career, in its freedom from the competitive pressures for money and relatively so as far as position is concerned. But, having chosen a subject so intimately linked with reality, I do not think that even if the wartime call for a change had not occurred, I would have continued in it very long. There are aspects of business life that are not among the most attractive one would choose. One can rarely choose those with whom one would wish to do business and has to accept congenial and uncongenial ones. On the other hand, there is a certain clarity (even if not always simplicity) about business propositions which can be very refreshing when compared with the complexities of public policy, the mixture of motives and objectives often difficult to disentangle.

Both business and the public domain are characterized by the great importance of negotiation. I wish that I could distil from my own quite extensive and varied experience certain general principles beyond those that I have already mentioned in connection with some of the particular negotiations in which I have been involved. I have only one thought when looking back on these and that is how almost invariably in any prolonged negotiation the sporting instinct begins at some point to take over and how easy it is then to forget the original objective. Perhaps that is why, in common with some of my friends who have been similarly engaged, when I think of some of the battles fought long ago, I wonder what they were all about, and whether this or that point—won or lost—was really worth fighting for.

I have spoken of competition in the three lives I have led and the different weight attached in each to material as against non-material rewards. There is also, finally, the more difficult question, that is the relation between reward and merit. In its most general form, this has preoccupied wiser men from time immemorial and I would not dare to add anything to what they have said, except that in my own experience there is not much difference, in this regard, between the three spheres in which I have moved. In each I have met some of all kinds: inevitably, now and again, the feet of clay, but also well-rewarded ones as well as unsung heroes.

Index

Figures in italic refer to illustration numbers